A Cold Cold Heart

by

John Nicholl

First published in 2018 by Bloodhound Books

www.bloodhoundbooks.com

Print ISBN: 978-1-912175-89-5

For Dianne, Laura, Ben, Edward and Ava

Chapter 1

Charles Turner made an unnecessary adjustment to his old school tie, looked across at his client, and frowned. 'So, here you are again, Peter. It seems to be becoming something of a habit.'

Peter Spencer shifted in his seat and focused on the wall, rather than meet his solicitor's gaze. 'I thought the bitch would've withdrawn her statement long before now.'

Turner raised an eyebrow. 'Maybe she's had enough of being a punchbag. Have you considered that possibility? It wouldn't be surprising, if you think about it. There's only so much most people can put up with before they snap.'

'I tell her I'm sorry, buy her some flowers, and promise I'll never do it again. That's usually enough to shut her up.'

'But then, it happens again, despite your assurances, despite your well-intentioned words of remorse and regret. You do the exact same thing, or worse: alcohol, violence, remorse, and repeat. That's it, isn't it? It was only a matter of time before you were here back at my door. And here you are, Peter, here you are.'

Spencer swallowed hard, not wanting to sound squeezed, or desperate, and lose face more than he already had. 'It's not like I plan to do it. I'm not a violent man by nature. It's the drink. I've never touched her when I'm sober, not even once.'

'Then why drink? That's the obvious question. I'm sure she must have asked you much the same thing more times than you care to remember. You drink, you become intoxicated, you lose control, and then, you hit her. It's always the same. Has been for years. So why not go teetotal and resolve matters once and for all? Just stay off the booze. That's all you've got to do. It doesn't take a genius to work it out. I'd be willing to bet she's begged you to stop drinking. Am I right?'

Spencer sat in brooding silence, swallowing his resentment and searching for a response he couldn't find.

'Have you tried apologising on bended knee? Have you thrown yourself on her mercy? "Sorry I broke your nose, Tina; sorry I punched you in the face time and time again; sorry I've been such a total arsehole; it's not my fault; I was drunk; I won't do it again." That sort of thing.'

Spencer was breathing more heavily now, hot and sweating, despite the winter chill. 'Of course, I fucking well have. I'm not a complete idiot. What do you take me for?'

'But your words of regret fell on deaf ears. Is that what you're telling me? Is that what you're trying to convey?'

He parted his lips in a momentary sneer. 'She's even had the fucking locks changed. A bastard social worker arranged it for her. A right mouthy bitch I hadn't met before. I can't even see my own kids without supervision since she stuck her nose in. I'm their father, not some stranger. It's a fucking disgrace.'

The solicitor opened the blue cardboard file on the desk in front of him and perused the contents for a full two minutes before looking up with his reading glasses perched on the tip of his nose. 'The police have been called to your home six times in a little over ten months. Am I correct?'

His nostrils flared. 'If you say so.'

'I do, Peter, it's all here in black and white as clear as day. That's four times by the good lady herself, in need of urgent assistance, and twice by a concerned neighbour who dialled 999 and requested the police. Social services tend to frown on such things.'

Spencer lowered his head and snarled, 'They're a bunch of interfering bastards.'

'Who are you referring to exactly?'

'Social fucking Services.'

The solicitor stalled for a second or two as images of his own troubled childhood flashed in his mind. 'They've got a job to do.'

'They can go fuck themselves.'

'If you hit your wife, why not your children? That's what they're asking themselves. They aren't going away anytime soon. I can promise you that much. You're on their radar now. They'll see it through to the end, however long it takes. And it looks as if Tina's going to do likewise. She's changed, maybe forever.'

'So, what the fuck do I do now? There's only a few days before my court date.'

The solicitor took out some cigarettes, removed the cellophane wrapper, and pushed the box across the desk. 'Keep the packet. You look as if you could do with them.'

Spencer snatched them greedily. 'Is it okay if I smoke in here?'

'Yes, no problem. Do you need a light?'

He took a cigarette from the packet, placed it between the first two fingers of his right hand, and fumbled in his trouser pocket with his left. 'No, you're all right. I've got a box of matches here somewhere.'

'You can use the saucer as an ashtray. I don't want any ash on the carpet.'

Spencer lit the tip and sucked the toxic fumes deep into his lungs. 'I was banged up for a few months as a teenager after a bit of burglary. It was a fucking nightmare. I don't fancy prison one little bit. I'm not ashamed to admit it.'

The solicitor rose, crossed the room, and opened the window a little wider before returning to his seat. 'You're right to be concerned. Your court appearance is fast approaching, as you so rightly say. I suggest we focus on the criminal aspects of your case for now, and worry about the civil matters once that's well out of the way. Are we in agreement?'

Spencer looked at him with a puzzled expression. 'What the fuck's that supposed to mean?'

'I thought I'd made myself perfectly clear. Police first, social services second. Let's try to keep you out of prison, and worry about your access to the children, if and when that's achieved. It's a matter of priorities. Are you with me?'

He nodded twice as reality dawned. 'Yeah, makes sense.'

'It seems you're faced with something of a predicament. You've tried pleading with your good lady. You've grovelled, so to speak, and, despite your best efforts, you've got nowhere. Am I correct?'

Spencer took a long drag, savouring the nicotine hit as clouds of grey smoke swirled around his head. 'Well, yeah, I've told you that. It's like she's a different woman or something. She's easily led, that's her problem. Always has been. I blame the social worker. She's a pussy-licking lesbian with a big mouth. I'd like to punch her in the fucking throat.'

'I think it's rather more complex than that, if you don't mind me saying so.'

'What are you talking about?'

'Your wife has turned against you, Peter, that's the unfortunate reality. After all you've done for her and the children. She's let you down.'

He flicked a length of glowing orange ash into the saucer and growled, 'Yeah, that's right. I've worked my balls off to put a roof over their fucking heads, and now, I'm back at my old mum's place, like a stupid kid again. What the fuck's that about?'

'Tina's not prepared to be reasonable, despite your promises of a better future, is that what you're telling me?'

Spencer took one last drag before grinding the butt into the saucer with his thumb. 'The bitch won't even speak to me. Not a fucking word. I don't deserve that. Nobody deserves that. She's treating me like shit. Who the fuck does she think she is?'

'So, your usual methods of reconciliation haven't worked, no?'

'No, they fucking well haven't.'

'And you don't want to be locked up again. You're an adult now. Not some snotty kid with too much to say for themselves. Prison would be a great deal more onerous than any secure unit you experienced as a young man.'

'Of course I fucking well don't. Who would? Goes without saying.'

The solicitor nodded his acknowledgement and ran a manicured hand through his short blond hair before speaking again. 'Of course you don't. Why would you? Most prison residents tend to look down on men of your ilk. Men who abuse women or children are considered a prison underclass; the lowest of the low. The other inmates can't be at home to protect their own from your kind. I think that's the origin of their resentment. It wouldn't go well for you. You'd be eaten alive.'

'I'm not a fucking paedo!'

The solicitor shook his head and frowned. 'No, no, of course not, I wasn't suggesting that for a moment. But you'd be treated much the same, that's the regrettable reality. There's no denying it.'

Spencer was shaking now. Fearing what the future may bring. 'Really?'

'Oh, yes, I've seen it before. Two of my previous clients killed themselves in very similar circumstances; they tied bed sheets around their necks and hanged themselves from the bars. Not a pleasant way to die, but it seems even that was better than living in the circumstances in which they'd found themselves. They just couldn't stand the degree of ill-treatment they were receiving. It was relentless, brutal, far too much to bear.'

Spencer raised a trembling hand to his face. 'It looks like I'm well and truly fucked.'

'Maybe you are, maybe you're not. Things are rarely as simple as they first appear.'

Spencer's eyes widened as a barely perceivable light shone at the end of a very dark tunnel. 'Okay, I'm listening.'

'Your options are limited, as we've already established, but that doesn't mean they're non-existent. It seems to me that you've got two potentially viable courses of action left open.'

'So, what are they?'

'Tina's got a rather obvious nasal fracture and severe facial bruising. I've reviewed the photos. Not a pretty sight. You really went to town this time. And she's made a written statement which is strongly supported by the available medical evidence. Corroboration – that's the technical term. The prosecution has a virtually watertight case. A trained chimp could convict you.'

Spencer began clawing at his head with a broken fingernail, as the colour drained from his face. 'But you said I've still got options. That's what you said, yeah?'

The solicitor moved the saucer to one side, and spoke quietly, clearly pronouncing each word in hushed tones that he thought impossible for his young secretary to overhear despite her excellent hearing. 'Oh, you have, Peter. You can either plead guilty – say you're sorry and hope the court doesn't send you to prison for too long – or you can threaten Tina into silence. I don't think there's much more than a ten per cent chance of the first option succeeding, so you may wish to seriously consider the latter. Needs must and all that. All's fair in love and war, to quote the cliché. Do you get my meaning?'

'You're telling me to threaten my wife? Really? Is that the best you've got?'

The solicitor nodded twice. 'That's what I'd do in your place. Extreme circumstances demand an exceptional response. Make no mistake – grievous bodily harm is an extremely serious charge. You'd likely be looking at an eighteen-month period of imprisonment, at least, if convicted; probably longer. Anything up to five years is a distinct possibility.'

'Five years for a few miserable slaps. That's fucking ridiculous.'

He took a ten-by-six-inch colour photo from the file and held it up. 'Oh, yes, make no mistake. Take a good look at your handiwork, because that's what the court will see: her battered face, the misaligned nose, the missing teeth, the swelling and the congealed blood. Look at it all. Look what you did. You need to shut her up before the big day if you're to have any real chance of remaining a free man. It really is as simple as that.'

Spencer put his hand to his throat. 'You want me to shut the bitch up? But you're a solicitor. You're…'

'It's your best hope, that's all I'm saying. Your only real hope if you want me to spell it out for you. But can you do it? That's the big question. Can you do it?

Spencer appeared very close to panic as his blood pressure soared and his head began to ache. 'Going to the house would be a lost cause. The pigs fitted one of those panic alarms. They told me that themselves. It's linked directly to the police station. I'd be arrested again. It's fucking obvious.'

'I can't argue with your logic, but surely there have to be other possibilities. You just need to be creative. Think outside the box. There's always a way, if you want to find it badly enough.'

'She does the food shopping every Tuesday. In that new discount place in the high street. You know, the one with all the freezers. I could follow her and pick my time when no one's about. Perhaps when she's walking back towards the estate, all weighed down with the bags. There's no cameras to worry about once she's out of the town centre.'

Turner smiled broadly, revealing flawless white teeth that gleamed. 'That's it, Peter, good man. Now you're thinking along the right lines. And do it when you're sober. When she knows you mean it. That matters; I can't stress that sufficiently.'

Spencer nodded his understanding as the solicitor looked on and carefully considered his choice of words. 'And I'm not talking about some minor threat she can choose to ignore. You need to utterly terrify the woman this time. Shock her. Make her scared for her life if she doesn't withdraw her statement.'

Spencer sat in silence, lost in thought.

'Or better still, threaten your children. Make her scared for *their* lives. That would do it. That would work. She's a caring mother – you've told me that yourself. Why not play on her vulnerabilities? Her worst fears. There's no room for sentimentality where your future freedoms concerned.'

'It all seems fucking risky to me. Do you really think I should do it?'

Turner nodded assuredly. 'Oh, yes, there's no doubt in my mind. That's my best advice, off the record, man to man, so to speak.'

'Okay, if there's no other choice. She's got it coming anyway. If that's what I've got to do; she's driven me to it. It's down to her. If she wasn't such an irritating bitch, I wouldn't have touched her in the first place.'

The solicitor fixed his client with unblinking eyes. 'I like you, Peter. I want to help you. But there are limits. We never had this conversation. If you ever tell anyone what I've said, I'll cut you adrift. I'll deny it. I'll say you're lying. It would be the word of a respected lawyer against…well, you know what I'm saying. The authorities would believe me and not you. It's how the system works. The cards are stacked in my favour. I'm a member of the club, and you're not. Do you understand? I need to hear you say it.'

'I'm no fucking grass.'

Turner approached the only door in the room. 'Then get it done. Get it done before it's too late. You're running out of time, and prison's best avoided if possible; I think we've established that much well enough.'

Spencer pushed his chair aside. 'Thank you, I'm grateful. I don't know what I'd do without you.'

The solicitor led his client into the reception, which also served as his young secretary's office. 'Can you check to see if Mr Spencer's pending court appearance is marked in the diary for a week today, please, Helen?'

She opened the diary, flicked through the pages, stopped, continued, and stopped again. 'Ah, yes, here it is, ten a.m. in Caerystwyth Magistrates Court. Do you want me to make another appointment while I've got the book open?'

The solicitor shook his head and smiled warmly. 'No, no, I don't think that'll be necessary. I'll see you in court on the twelfth, Mr Spencer, all being well. And remember what I've told you. Heed my advice. Don't go anywhere near your wife. Stay away. I need you to take your bail conditions and the injunction seriously; it's absolutely essential in the circumstances. The court would not look on it favourably were you to transgress again.'

'Okay, I've got the message. Enough said.'

Turner reached out and shook Spencer's hand. 'I'm glad to hear it. And put on a shirt and tie for the magistrates. They appreciate a bit of effort on the defendant's part. Play the game as I've advised, and you'll have a much better chance of winning. Is that clear enough for you?'

Spencer looked back and winked as he approached the exit, with the hint of a smile playing on his lips. 'You can rely on me, I'll do exactly what you've told me to do. I'm feeling more confident about things already.'

The solicitor's irritation was palpable as he glared at his client. The man was an utter pleb; a moron. 'Say no more for now, Mr Spencer. It's time to be on your way.'

Chapter 2

Detective Inspector Gareth Gravel, or Grav as he was known to all in the force, stuffed half a stale sausage roll in his mouth, washed it down with a slurp of excessively sweet coffee, and picked up the phone on the fourth ring. 'CID.'

'Hello, sir, it's Sandra on the front desk.'

'Yes, I do know, love. We've been working together for about fifteen years. You say the same thing every single time.'

'Really, only fifteen? It feels like longer.'

He chuckled to himself. 'What can I do for you, love?'

'I've got your daughter here with me. Such a lovely, pleasant girl, unlike some I could mention. She must take after her mother.'

Grav silently observed that Sandra had never said a truer word in her life. Emily was so like her mum, with her brown eyes, dark, Celtic good looks, and friendly persona, and he still missed her every second of every single day. 'Does she seem in a good mood?'

Sandra looked up, trying not to be too obvious and failing miserably. 'I'd say so.'

'Glad to hear it. It must be good news. Tell her to wait for me in the canteen. I could do with a bite to eat. I'll be with her in two minutes max.'

Grav approached his daughter as she stood in the queue behind three uniformed officers at the canteen's cluttered counter. He lifted her off her feet and engulfed her in a powerful bear hug, which caused her to gasp for breath, before setting her down again. 'Good to see you, love. Any news?'

She took a single sheet of embossed paper from the back pocket of her blue jeans, unfolded it theatrically, and broke into a smile that lit up her face. 'I got the job. What do you think of that, Mr Policeman? Your daughter's going to be a kick-ass lawyer.'

He beamed. 'Oh, that's brilliant, love. I never doubted you for a moment. Mum would be so very proud of you.'

Emily looked away as the past closed in and surrounded her mercilessly. 'I wish she was still with us.'

'Me too, love... Oh, here we go. What are you going to have? My treat. I know how skint you student types are.'

She smiled thinly. 'What do you recommend?'

'Well, most of it's terrible, but Gloria here does a passable egg and chips on a good day.'

He turned to face the long-suffering cook-cum-chief-bottle-washer, who was swaying from one foot to the other with her arms folded in front of her. 'What'll it be, Grav? Come on, I haven't got all day. You're not the only one who needs feeding.'

'I'll have two of your gourmet egg and chips, please, love. Nice and greasy, mind. Just like you usually make it. And some baked beans too. You should be able to manage that without too much trouble.'

Gloria stifled a smile, not wanting to encourage him more than she already had. 'Yeah, hilarious as usual, Inspector. You always manage to eat it all from what I've seen. It can't be that bad.'

He patted his overhanging beer belly. 'I'm a growing boy, love. A man's got to eat. I can't afford to be fussy.'

'Anything to drink?'

'A cup of tea for me, and what about you, love, any preferences?'

Emily suspected the answer would be an emphatic no, but she met Gloria's tired eyes and asked anyway. 'Do you have herbal tea of any description? Camomile or peppermint would be lovely.'

Gloria glanced around the room and shook her head. 'Not a chance. It would be wasted on this lot.'

'Just a coffee, then, please.'

'Milk and sugar?'

She briefly considered asking for cream but decided against it. 'Just a splash of milk, please. Semi-skimmed, if you've got it.'

Gloria walked away and returned a few minutes later with two unappetising looking meals, followed by their hot drinks in steaming white porcelain mugs that were long past their best. 'Anything else?'

Grav took a crumpled ten-pound note from the inside pocket of his tweed jacket. 'Nah, that'll do it thanks. And keep the change. You deserve it, with all your hard work.'

'What, all twenty pence of it? I'll try not to get too excited. Maybe I'll book a holiday somewhere nice for a bit of sun.'

'You do that, love. I hear Barbados is nice at this time of year.'

Grav led his daughter towards his usual table, tray in hand, and winced on sitting down as his overburdened knees stiffened and complained. 'Right, tell me all about this new job of yours. I could do with a bit of cheering up.'

Emily took a gulp of gradually cooling coffee and grinned. 'Two years of on-the-job training, and I'll be a fully qualified solicitor.'

'I'm pleased for you, love. Honestly, I am, that goes without saying, but why here in town? Why Harrison and Turner?'

Her mouth fell open. 'You told me they had a good reputation when I asked you a couple of months back. You're not going to tell me something different now, are you?'

'No, no, it's nothing like that. They're a decent firm, from what I've seen. But I thought you loved Cardiff. You've told me that yourself more than once – the nightlife, the theatres, the galleries, and music venues. Don't get me wrong, I'm delighted to have you back in this part of the world, of course I am; it'll be good to see more of you. I'm surprised, that's all.'

She shifted her food around her plate before responding. 'I had a brilliant three years at university. Some of the best times of my life. But I've decided it's time to come home. Time to move on.'

His eyes narrowed. 'Are you certain there's not more to it? I felt sure you and Richard were settled in the city for the foreseeable future. What about his job? Is he going to commute? It's a fair old drive from Caerystwyth to Cardiff five days a week. I wouldn't fancy it myself. Particularly at rush hour, and when it's throwing it down. It's going to add a good three to four hours to his day. There's only so long anyone can do that sort of thing.'

'We've split up. It's over.'

'Oh, for fuck's sake, when did this happen?'

Emily put down her knife and fork and exhaled slowly through pursed lips. 'At the beginning of October; the sixth, to be exact. It's engrained in my psyche. Carved in tablets of frigging stone never to be forgotten. I've been sleeping on a girlfriend's settee ever since. I couldn't keep up the rent on the flat once he'd gone.'

'Why the hell didn't you say something before now? I could have helped you out. You only had to ask.'

She focused on the table top. 'Don't take this the wrong way, Dad, but it's the sort of thing I used to talk to Mum about. We haven't spoken that often while I've been at university, if you think about it. And when we do, it's usually small talk, not relationship stuff. When was the last time we had a real heart-to-heart?'

His face reddened. 'I do my best, love. It's difficult, what with the pressure of work and all that. And your mother was good at this kind of thing. Well, you know what I'm saying. We played to our strengths. Worked as a team.'

'Fucking cancer.'

He reached across the table and squeezed her hand for a moment before releasing it and slumping back in his seat. 'You've got that right. It's become something of a mantra.'

'Yeah, it has.'

'So, what happened? I thought you and Richard were going the distance.'

'So, did I, until he screwed some tart he works with.'

Grav shook his head. 'What an idiot, throwing everything away because he couldn't keep his dick in his pants. Some people don't seem to value what they've got until they've lost it.'

'I got suspicious when he started coming home late from work a little too often; he's hardly the dedicated sort. Then, I discovered bright-red lipstick on his shirt, and it stank of cheap perfume I didn't recognise – something I'd never wear. I knew something was up. I was certain of it.'

'Did you challenge him?'

'Oh yeah, but he denied it, said I was being stupid, and stormed out of the flat full of feigned righteous indignation. He even slammed the door on his way out. He almost had me convinced for a while. He's a good liar, I'll give him that much.'

Grav glowered. 'The evidence spoke for itself.'

'I did a bit of detective work of my own after that and found some photos he'd taken of her. Let's just say, they didn't leave anything to the imagination; you know what I'm saying. She was all high heels, black stockings, sex toys, and no knickers. The dirty bastard! I really trusted him. I'd never felt so betrayed in my life.'

'What a tosser.'

She laughed despite herself. 'Yeah, that's one word for him. I can think of a few more. I called him most of them.'

'What did he say when you told him what you'd seen?'

'Oh, some total crap about it not being what it looked like. She meant nothing to him, it was just sex, he still loved me, he'd never do it again. The usual shit men come up with when they're caught out and faced with the undeniable.'

'Not all of us, love. I want you to remember that. We don't all screw around.'

'I wanted to forgive him – I was desperate to forgive him and convince myself it was a one-off aberration, but a girl on my course told me he'd done it before. He'd had sex with one of her drunken mates after a party, when I was tucked up in bed with the flu. The girl was legless, apparently. It all happened in a pub car park, really classy. It seems everyone knew all about it, except me.'

Grav clenched his hands into tight fists before consciously relaxing them and focusing on his daughter. 'You're well rid of him, love. I know men like him; some with wives and kids. Blokes who take off their wedding rings when they go out for a few pints on a Saturday night. Most of them never change. It's pathetic, really. Why the hell they get married in the first place is a mystery to me.'

'I never want to see his ugly face again.'

He reached across the table for a second time and patted her hand. 'That's the spirit, love. Forget the cheating bastard. He doesn't deserve you. You'll find the right man. Mark my words. It's just a matter of time.'

'Thanks, Dad. You're getting better at this relationship stuff.'

'So, come on, let's stay positive. Why not focus on the future? Life goes on, whether we laugh or cry. You're back in God's own country, things could be a lot worse. When are you starting this new job of yours?'

'This coming Monday.'

He jerked his head back. 'What, as soon as that?'

'Yeah, it surprised me as well. Mr Turner seems really keen for me to start as soon as possible. I was hoping to move into your place until I find somewhere of my own, if that's okay with you? It shouldn't take too long, maybe a month or two.'

He nodded less than enthusiastically. 'You'll be very welcome, love; it'll be nice to have a bit of company again. Do you need a hand with the move?'

'Have you got the time?'

He paused before responding. 'I could probably manage a couple of hours over the weekend, if that's any good to you?'

'How's the murder investigation going?'

'Don't ask.'

'What, that bad?'

'Worse.'

'You don't want to talk about it?'

'Not really, there's nothing positive to say; the investigation's going nowhere.'

'Okay, message received loud and clear. Can I borrow your car on Sunday afternoon?'

Grav relaxed. 'Yeah, no problem. I'll add you to the insurance.'

'You're sure you won't need it? I can always ask a friend, if it's an issue.'

'No, I'll borrow one from work. Keep the Golf for as long as you need it. It's the least I can do. I'll even fill it with diesel for you.'

'Thanks, Dad, that'll do nicely. I haven't got that much to pack anyway. I've already taken a load of stuff to the charity shop. A lot of it his. Too many memories. I want a new start.'

'If you're sure.'

Emily nodded her reluctant acceptance. 'It's going to be a lot of change all at once. Leaving my friends in Cardiff, starting work for the first time, and finding a place of my own. I just hope I can handle it all.'

He smiled warmly, picturing the little girl who'd become a woman. 'You'll be fine, love. You've got a first-class degree, a good head on your shoulders, and your old dad's good looks, wit, and sparkling personality. What could possibly go wrong?'

She laughed as the tension lifted. 'I'll be a legal eagle before you know it. Watch out world. The Old Bailey, here I come.'

'Of course, you will, love, and that Charles Turner's not a bad looking bloke, according to one of our PCs. She only met him the once and was banging on about it for ages. He looks a bit like a young Paul Newman, apparently. I can't see it myself.'

'Men aren't very high on my priority list at the moment.'

'No, I guess not. But you'll have to get back on the horse sometime.'

'Like you have, you mean?'

His facial muscles tightened. 'Oh, come on, that's different. Me and your mum were childhood sweethearts. We were together for a very long time.'

'Turner's a bit too much of a charmer for my tastes. He's a ladies' man – that's obvious from the second you meet him. I'll be looking for someone a bit more reliable when the time feels right.'

'Oh, you mean someone like your old dad.'

She laughed again and started eating with gusto.

'There you go, love. Things are looking up. You're forgetting about Richard already.'

'Richard who?'

'I've got no idea who you're talking about.'

Emily swallowed her last two eggy chips and drained her mug. 'Right, I'd better make a move. Things to do, people to see. There's no rest for us busy professional high-flyers.'

Grav rose stiffly to his feet with the aid of the table. 'Are you okay for cash?'

'I could do with a few quid until the end of the month, if that's okay with you? Just something to tide me over until my first pay packet.'

'Of course, it is. Who else am I going to give it to? Is five-hundred quid all right to be getting on with?'

She extended her neck and kissed him on his stubbled chin. 'Thank you. If you're sure it's okay?'

'I said so, didn't I?'

'Thanks, Dad. You're a lifesaver.'

'So I'm told. Maybe they'll give me a medal.'

She took his hand in hers. 'Come on, you can walk me out.'

He turned towards her, on reaching reception, with a sudden sullen expression that seemed to age him. 'Look after yourself, Emily. And remember, there's a killer on the loose. Don't go out alone after dark, and be wary of any men, whoever they are. It could be anyone. Remember that. These people don't come with psycho stamped on their foreheads, more's the pity. They can be the last person you'd expect, the seemingly ordinary and unthreatening. That's how they avoid detection for as long as they do. The bastard's likely hidden in plain sight, only his victims see the monster behind the mask.'

She smiled reassuringly. 'I'm a copper's daughter. I know how to look after myself.'

'Just be careful, love. That's all I'm saying. Three girls are already dead. That's almost one a month, and all on this patch. It doesn't get more dangerous than that.'

She clutched her left arm with her right hand. 'Yeah, I've been watching the Welsh news. It's awful.'

'Yeah, it is.'

'You've got to catch him, Dad. Catch him before he kills again.'

He nodded. 'I'm trying, love, but some things are easier said than done.'

Chapter 3

Charles Turner pulled up his pants and trousers, looked down at the broken body of the young woman at his feet, and silently acknowledged that his work for the night was done. An itch had been scratched. A fantasy brought to life. And, for a time, like it or not, the memory would have to sustain him. You could only kill them once. That's what he told himself. The glorious high would gradually fade, to be replaced by the insatiable longing to do it all over again. The overwhelming and all-consuming desire to strangle and rape that he found so utterly impossible to ignore. It made his life worth living. It gave purpose to his very existence. It was a case of survival of the fittest; evolution at its rawest and most intense. Such things defined him, and there was nothing wrong with that.

He took a deep breath and sucked the cold, early morning air deep into his lungs, as his erection slowly subsided, to be replaced by the nagging fear of arrest that plagued him after each killing.

He looked to left and right, searching the riverbank with quick, darting eyes for non-existent potential witnesses, and clutched his midriff as his gut spasmed and twisted. Come on, Charles, hold it together, man. Deep breaths. That's it. Count to ten. Calm yourself. No need to panic.

He looked down at the lifeless body just a few feet away, smiled as he recalled the terror in her eyes, and felt a little better almost immediately. What the hell was wrong with him? Now wasn't the time to fall apart like some inadequate client in times of adversity. He had the intelligence, the attention to detail, the superior intellect. He just had to make use of those gifts and take full advantage. He had to outwit his potential captors and continue his journey with all that entailed. It really was as simple as that. He was back in control. An alpha male on top of his game.

Turner took a brown paper bag from his jacket pocket, removed a cigarette butt, and placed it on the semi-frozen ground precisely two inches to the right of the young woman's head. Wasn't it odd how she appeared to be staring into the far-off distance but seeing nothing at all. Like a life-size doll or mannequin, oblivious to his very existence, as if she'd forgotten him already. The circle of life, survival of the fittest, she'd served a useful purpose, and now, she was gone, lost to him, nothing but a memory. But in a strange way they'd be linked forever: Bonnie and Clyde, Anthony and Cleopatra, Ian and Myra. Maybe one day, they'd be famous too. Celebrated in the annals of history.

He checked his surroundings, in the light of a half-moon partly shrouded in cloud, and felt a further pang of regret as he strolled in the direction of his car, a twenty minute or so walk away. It was all over so very quickly in the end. Weeks of planning, invention, and anticipation had led to just a few brief minutes of ecstasy that had pleased him like nothing else could. One moment, her eyes were alive with the light of life, and then, they paled and dulled as he'd placed his hands around her slender neck and squeezed until she'd drifted off into inevitable oblivion. He'd held the power of life and death in his hands and, at that moment, had been a god. A creature at the very pinnacle of the evolutionary tree. An all-powerful predator at the peak of his almost limitless powers. If only he could go back in time and stay there forever.

He pushed up his sleeve, checked the high-end Swiss watch – bought to celebrate his second killing – and increased his pace. Maybe next time he should take his victim close to death and revive her before signing her death warrant. Yes, yes, why not? Why the hell hadn't he considered it before? It seemed so obvious now he thought about it. Why not draw out the experience for as long as possible? Maximise his pleasure to the nth degree. Give the bitch hope, and snatch it away again just when she thinks she may survive to live another day. It was brilliant, inspired.

And maybe repeat the process time and time again until he could barely stand the anticipation.

Turner broke into a smile that dominated his boyish features. He was getting hard again. Stimulated. It would be so good, so fucking good. The best yet. It was just a matter of finding the right girl and putting his newfound plans into action.

Turner looked up and began trotting along the river path as night threatened to turn to day. It was time to head home to get an hour or two's shut eye before getting up for work. It was such a regrettable inconvenience, but he had to keep up appearances. He had to work to an acceptable standard and keep up the misleading persona of middle-class respectability that he'd so carefully crafted. It was all done for a purpose, for good reasons, that's what he had to remember. It helped facilitate his true self; the moments that mattered. And he was good at it – he had to acknowledge that. It was just a matter of keeping control and wearing the metaphorical mask, and the fools didn't suspect a damned thing.

He began to run at full pace as the sun slowly rose above the distant horizon, and the sky softened. Shit. How the hell had that happened? Time had passed by so very quickly, relativity in action. It seemed minutes had become hours in the blink of an eye. Be careful, Charles, avoid the mud, step on the grass, don't leave footprints. Quickly, man. Even the slightest mistake could be costly. Maybe buy different sized shoes? Size ten, or even eleven. Yes, that made sense. Drive to Swansea or Cardiff, buy them for cash, and wear them next time. Another stroke of genius. He could pad them out with extra socks. Two pairs, or maybe three. Warm feet and misdirection. Smoke and mirrors; it was a win-win.

Turner was back on a high as he unlocked his red Italian sports car and climbed into the driver's seat. Fifteen minutes and he'd be home. Back at the house, fed, showered, and rested, as if nothing of any significance had happened. As if he were an ordinary man with all the limitations that entailed.

He took one hand from the black leather steering wheel, delved into the inside pocket of his suit jacket, and took out a gold, sapphire, and diamond pendant, taken from his victim's slender neck soon after her death. It was good to have a physical reminder to feed his fantasies. A token, something tangible to add to his growing collection. It made the treasured memories more vivid, more visceral. He could almost taste her on his lips, feel her, and smell her lavender perfume. The gift that kept giving, as if she were still with him, ready to die all over again.

He returned the item of jewellery to his pocket and began to knead his genitals with one hand while steering with the other. That new trainee he'd recently appointed was rather attractive in a somewhat unconventional way. The hair was wrong, the clothes not quite right, the shoes not nearly high or feminine enough, but such things were easily remedied. And there was a beautiful, tight body under the somewhat staid navy business suit she'd worn to her interview. That was blatantly obvious to any man who looked closely enough. "Yes, Mr Turner, I'd love to work for you, Mr Turner. I'd love to join your practice." Of course, she would; moths to a flame.

He switched on the radio and nodded along to Classic FM. What was it she'd said? Yes, yes, that was it. "Thank you for the opportunity, Mr Turner. I won't let you down." Professional? Driven? Keen to succeed? Who was she trying to kid? She was gagging for it. Dripping wet and waiting. Desperate to feel his hands on her, squeezing tighter, tighter, tighter; a bitch in heat.

He laughed until warm tears ran down his handsome face, negotiated the final bend of his journey, and approached his large, detached Victorian house located in an affluent tree-lined residential side street on the outskirts of town. She was definitely worth considering. Emily, Emily, Emily? It had an undoubted ring to it. A rhythmic musical quality he hadn't considered before. Like a wanton slut panting in sexual congress. Yes, what the hell, why not? She was the right height, the right build, and within the required age range. And her neck was willowy and sylphlike, eminently squeezable for a man of his inclination and abilities.

He pulled up in his garage, turned off the engine, unzipped his tailored trousers, and began masturbating frantically as if his life depended on it. Congratulations, Miss Gravel, you've just been selected. You're at the very top of the list. It's just a matter of when and how you die.

He pictured her twisting face as he crushed her windpipe and ejaculated with a loud groan of delight. She was perfect, absolutely fucking perfect. What the hell was wrong with him? Emily, lovely Emily, she was ready and waiting. Ready for plucking. Why hadn't he thought of her before?

Chapter 4

Winter suited Caerystwyth, thought Detective Sergeant Laura Kesey as she hurried along the riverbank in her newly acquired green Wellingtons, head down, collar up, in the direction of a young, uniformed constable who was clapping his hands together in a hopeless attempt to ward off the early January frost.

'Morning, Sarge. You're a welcome sight. I'd nearly given up on you.'

Kesey fastened the top button of her wax jacket with trembling fingers and looked down at the cold and twisted body of a young woman, with shoulder length, dyed copper-blonde hair, lying on her back in the long grass to the side of the path, with her tights and knickers tangled around one blue-white, mottled ankle. 'So, who found her?'

'Some bloke walking his dog about half an hour ago.'

'You don't know his name?'

PC Harris shook his head. 'No, I just got told to come down here and check it out.'

'Where's your sergeant?'

'Back at the station. We're a bit thin on the ground this morning. There's just me, him, and one traffic car for the entire area.'

She pointed at a faint footprint in the dark earth immediately next to the victim's right shoulder. 'Is that yours?'

The constable looked at his feet self-consciously and shook his head. 'No, definitely not, no way; I walked on the grass to the left of the path and then stood in the one place. I haven't been within six feet of her.'

'You're sure? Now's the time to say if you're not. No one's going to hold it against you.'

'No, she's dead, that's blatantly obvious to anyone. I just called it in and waited for someone from CID to arrive. There was nothing I could do for her, however much I wanted to.'

She smiled for a beat without parting her lips. 'Good lad, one way in and one way out. Now, let's make sure everyone else does likewise.'

'Do you think it's the same killer?'

Kesey picked up a cigarette butt with a gloved hand and dropped it into a clear plastic evidence bag, before sealing it, returning the bag to her pocket, and marking the spot with one of several white plastic golf tees she always kept handy. 'Yeah, I'd say so. She's about the same age as the first three, same hair style and colour, very similar clothes and shoes, and it's the same general area. The bodies have all been found within a ten-mile radius of town. It's what the FBI like to refer to as a zone of comfort. Most serial killers tend to kill and dispose of their victims within a defined geographical area that they know well. Or at least that's what the DI tells me. It's the same killer, all right. I'd bet my pension on it.'

He focused on the victim's dead body for a second, before suddenly looking away. 'What a way to end up. She can't be more than, what, twenty-two or three at the most?'

Laura Kesey sighed. 'Yeah, I'm sure she's had better days... Right, let's crack on. That river's getting far too close to the banks for my liking.'

The constable pushed up the sleeve of his navy-blue greatcoat and checked the time. 'We've only got an hour before full tide. This area was under about two feet of water this time yesterday.'

She stared at the swirling, fast-flowing water. 'You're certain?'

'Oh, yeah, one hundred per cent. I drove over the bridge on the way to Pembrey.' He raised a hand and pointed to his right. 'Some of those horses on the higher ground were trapped by the water.'

Kesey took her two-way radio from her jacket pocket, turned her back to the wind, and pressed down the transmission button. 'DS Kesey to control, come in please.'

'Control to DS Kesey, what can I do for you, Sarge?'

'Who's that?'

'PC Lee.'

'Oh, hello, Mike, I didn't recognise your voice. Is DI Gravel about?'

'No, he's not in this morning. He's getting on with a bit of paperwork at home from what I'm told. His back's playing up again. Will anyone else do?'

'No, you're all right thanks, mate. I'll give him a bell at home. This can't wait.'

She dialled and waited until Grav's voice filled her ear. 'Hello, Laura, What's this about, love?'

'Give me a second, boss. We've got a visitor.'

She turned to the young PC, who was repeatedly moving from one foot to the other in a further attempt to ward off the cold. 'Tell whoever that is to piss off back in the direction they came from. The last thing I need is some idiot trampling all over my crime scene.'

He glanced towards the approaching man and frowned. 'I recognise him. He's with the local paper.'

'Oh, that is frigging marvellous. Just get rid of him, Kieran. And threaten him with obstruction if he doesn't sod off immediately. We haven't got time to piss about.'

'Will do, Sarge. It might be an idea to tape off the two sides of the path before anyone else comes along. What do you reckon?'

She delved into her trouser pocket and threw him her car keys. 'There's a roll of tape and a few poles in the boot of my car. Get it done as quickly as you can. Let's say about thirty feet to either side of the body, yeah? That should suffice.'

She returned her attention to her call as the young constable followed orders. 'Sorry about that, boss. The press are sniffing around. Someone must have tipped the bastards off.'

'What's the urgency, love?'

'We've got another body.'

He exhaled loudly before speaking. 'Oh, for fuck's sake, where?'

'I'm on the Caerystwyth bank of the Towy, about halfway between the quay and Johnstown Railway Bridge.'

'Another young woman?'

'Yeah, about the same age and general description as the others. Slim, reddish-blonde hair, average height. It's the same killer, that's bloody obvious.'

'Raped and strangled?'

She nodded in reflexive response. 'It's looking that way. There's bruising to her throat and her knickers are around her ankles.'

'Is she smelling of that same lavender scent as the other three?'

'Yeah, I'm sure I got a hint of it on the wind. We'll know for sure when we get her inside.'

'And the clothes?'

'Much the same. It all looks like stuff that was fashionable years back, maybe in the fifties or sixties. You don't see it much these days.'

He sighed as he pictured the scene. 'Where was she dumped exactly?'

'Just a few feet off the path.'

'On flat ground?'

'Yeah, no more than twenty feet from the water.'

'So we haven't got a lot of time.'

'No, the tide's rising as we speak.'

'Just our fucking luck. Right, let's crack on. I'll get hold of the police surgeon and a couple of scenes of crime officers, and get them down there ASAP. I'll drag them down there myself, if I have to.'

She laughed, realising he meant every word.

'Think of our victim as our most likely source of evidence, Laura. The quicker the body's in the morgue and away from the river, the happier I'll be.'

She smiled thinly, thinking he had a talent for stating the obvious. 'Do you want me to ring the pathologist from here?'

'No, you're all right, love. I'll give Sheila Carter a ring myself and see what time she can do it. We're going to need her experience on this one, that new bloke's next to fucking useless. He falls apart as soon as the defence put a bit of pressure on.'

'You're not coming down here yourself?'

He glanced out of his lounge window as the grey sky darkened and cast its shadows. 'Nah, I'll get myself down to the morgue and catch up with you later in the day. There's no point in inviting allegations of cross contamination. We've got enough problems without making more for ourselves.'

'Okay, boss, makes sense. Is there anything else?'

'Make sure the scenes of crime boys take plenty of photos for me. And get some plastic bags over her hands and feet as soon as. The heavens look ready to open. If there's evidence to find, let's ensure it's not washed away by a sudden downpour.'

'Will do, boss.'

'Anything else you want to ask me before I leave you in peace?'

Kesey glanced up at the leaden sky and winced. 'No, it's just started spotting. I'd better get on with things.'

'Sod's law, love. But we'll catch the bastard, and hopefully sooner rather than later. Men like him don't stop killing until someone stops them. It's just a matter of time until there's another victim.'

Chapter 5

Charles Turner followed Emily up two flights of office stairs, intensely focused on her shapely buttocks as they moved rhythmically under her knee length skirt as if dancing to the beat of an African drum.

He increased his pace, skipping up two steps at a time, to catch up with her and get a closer view. Yes, she'd do very nicely. A few tweaks here, a few adjustments there, and she'd be almost perfect.

Emily turned and faced him on reaching the landing. 'Oh, hello, Mr Turner. I thought it was probably you. Did you have a good weekend?'

He manoeuvred past her and held the door open, relishing the opportunity for one further look. 'Wonderful, thank you. It really couldn't have gone any better. And, please, call me Charles. There's no need for formality. We're colleagues now. Members of the same team.'

She entered the reception area and stood waiting, seconds seemingly becoming minutes as he stood facing her. 'Are you ready for day one?'

'I'm looking forward to it.'

He looked her up and down and lingered; estimating her height and likely dress size: a ten or maybe a twelve, yes, a twelve at most – depending on the make. 'Glad to hear it. You look every inch the young professional. Very smart, very, um...business-like. Yes, that's the word I was looking for. I'm sure you'll fit in perfectly.'

Emily felt her face flush and realised she was blushing. 'I'll certainly do my best.'

So desperate to please, so sycophantic. This was going to be easy. 'I'm sure you will. Now, first things first. Have you met Helen? She's the glue that holds our little practice together. An essential cog in the legal machine. I don't know what we'd do without her.'

Emily acknowledged the young secretary-cum-receptionist with a subtle nod of her head, as she looked up and beamed.

Turner pushed up the sleeve of his bespoke suit jacket and checked the time. 'I need to be in court in a little over an hour. Perhaps Helen would be kind enough to make us both some coffee while I show you your new office.'

'Oh, that would be lovely, thanks. White without sugar for me, please.'

Helen approached the kettle, resigned to her role, as Emily followed Turner down a brightly lit corridor, surprised and pleased to be getting an office of her own.

He pushed open the door and stood aside to allow her to peer in. 'Here we are. This is it. It's a little on the small side, regrettably, and there's no window, but it will have to suffice, I'm afraid. Adequate space is the one thing we're rather short of at Harrison and Turner. The room was used to store various case files prior to your arrival. It's more of a broom cupboard than a place of business, to be frank. I hope it's not too much of a disappointment.'

Emily stood and stared into the claustrophobic box room with a sinking feeling in the pit of her stomach. 'I was expecting to share.'

Turner checked his watch again, more obviously this time, as Helen appeared with a mug of steaming coffee in each hand. 'That's the spirit. Look on the bright side. Now, you settle yourself in, and we'll talk just as soon as I get a free hour. I've left one or two things on your desk for you to be getting on with. It might be an idea to familiarise yourself with the files before we get together.'

She accepted her mug gratefully and sat down behind an aged, dark oak desk that filled almost the entire space. 'Would you have time to talk through your specific requirements? It would be useful to know exactly what's expected of me.'

He stiffened. Was she deaf as well as stupid? 'I'm a little pushed for time. I thought I'd made that perfectly clear.'

'Just a quick run through would suffice. If you can point me in the right direction, I'll get on with things from there.'

He raised his arm, made a show of checking the time yet again, and faced her with a contemplative expression on his very attractive face. What size were her feet, a five, or six maybe? Probably a six and a little on the narrow side. 'There are one or two things I really do have to do before leaving for court.'

'Perhaps later in the day? I really would appreciate it.'

He turned his head and called out, 'The diary please, Helen.'

The young secretary reappeared from reception a few seconds later with the diary open at the appropriate page. 'You've got a child protection case conference at Prince Philip Hospital at two p.m. today. You said you'd be attending. You asked me to remind you.'

'Ah, yes, the Spencer family. I really can't be late for that one. Mr Spencer is rather relying on us to help him see his children again, if he avoids a custodial sentence. We wouldn't want to let a client down now, would we?'

'And you're fully booked for the rest of the day.'

'How's the rest of the week looking?'

Helen flicked through the pages, confirming what he already knew. 'You're booked solid.'

Turner met Emily's hazel eyes as Helen closed the desk diary and walked away. 'Look, I think the best thing we can do is meet up this evening for a bite to eat. It will give us the opportunity for a proper chin wag, so to speak. I can't see me finding time otherwise. How would that suit you?'

Emily wrinkled her nose. 'What, after work?'

Wasn't it fucking obvious? 'Needs must. It's the best I can offer, unless you want to leave it until sometime next week? I've no objections, if that's your preferred option. Just say the word; it's up to you.'

She struggled for an appropriate response, questioning his motives but not wanting to offend. 'What sort of time were you thinking?'

Reel her in, Charles, reel the bitch in. 'How about we say seven-thirty at the Golden Pheasant in Laugharne? They have a reasonably competent chef and an interesting enough wine list. That would work for me. What do you think?'

'Um…I'd like to, but I can't place it. I haven't been to Laugharne for years.'

He smiled broadly and tapped his watch three times with an outstretched finger. 'Not a problem. I'll pick you up at seven o'clock sharp. I'm sure Helen will have your address on file.'

'I'm staying at my dad's place at the moment, in Dyfed Close.'

Jackpot! 'Ah, yes, Detective Inspector Gareth Gravel. It would be good to meet him socially. Perhaps you could introduce us?'

Her brow furrowed as events took an unexpected turn. 'He's very busy with the murder investigation – you must have heard about it. He thinks of little else.'

'All those poor girls. One minute alive and full of life, the next dead and gone. Life can be so horribly unpredictable.'

'It's just awful.'

His eyes lit up as he stifled a smile. 'It's a terrible world…but not to worry. I'm sure your father's more than capable of heading up the investigation. He seems like a very able man, from the little I've seen of him. I'd like to get to know him properly.'

She nodded. 'Oh, I'm sure he won't mind if you say hello.'

Perhaps buy some more lavender oil. A large bottle or two. 'Right, I'd better be on my way. Needs must and all that. I'll see you this evening. Business and pleasure in one helpful package.'

Emily watched as he turned and walked away. 'Thank you, Charles. I look forward to it.'

Chapter 6

Doctor Sheila Carter, an eminent consultant forensic pathologist with thirty years' experience, had already started the post-mortem by the time Grav arrived at Caerystwyth Morgue. She looked up from the stiffening cadaver as he entered the room and acknowledged his arrival with a subtle nod of her head. 'I was wondering how long it would take you to get here.'

Grav smiled, revealing uneven, nicotine-yellowed teeth as he approached the dissection table. 'So, what are we dealing with?'

'You look tired.'

He chose to ignore her observation and focused on the young woman's bruised and swollen neck with a quizzical eye born of experience. 'Let's get on with it, Sheila. I haven't got time for chit-chat.'

She prized the victim's mouth open and peered in. 'Impatient as always, some things never change.'

'Anything of note?'

'Well, her teeth are still in situ, so there's no reason we can't compare dental records, when given the opportunity.'

'How did she die?'

She turned her head, looked up at him, and scowled. 'I've not long started the examination. I should have a full report ready and waiting for you by about four o'clock this afternoon. Do you think you can manage to wait that long?'

'Oh, come on, Sheila. Do we have to go through this every fucking time? Surely the bruising to her neck gives the game away. It doesn't take a medical protege to work that out. I'm just looking for your early assessment, first impressions, that's all. I won't hold you to it. Just tell me what you're thinking.'

She looked down and pushed the young woman's head to one side then the other. 'There's no likelihood of you shutting up unless I tell you, is there?'

'Not a chance.'

'Well, at least you're consistent… I'd say she was strangled, while laying on her back, by someone straddling her – sitting on her abdomen or chest. The attacker would have had to apply considerable force to inflict this degree of damage. Her windpipe is crushed, and there's extensive bruising to the front and sides of her neck. Whoever did this is a powerful individual with relatively large hands. You can quote me on that, if you like.'

'Okay, that's a start.'

She held out her hands in front of her, as if squeezing someone's neck until they breathed their last. 'Like this, see? With the fingers to the sides of the neck and the two thumbs pressing down forcibly on the exposed windpipe. The poor girl never stood a chance. It would have been over in a matter of seconds.'

'Was she raped?'

The pathologist sighed theatrically. 'I was just coming to that. I completed my internal examination shortly before your arrival.'

'And?'

'She'd had both vaginal and anal intercourse either shortly prior to, or soon after death. Rectal and vulval injuries strongly suggest that the sexual activity was both frenzied and violent. I think we can safely assume it was non-consensual.'

'Much like the other victims.'

She nodded twice. 'Absolutely, Grav. It appears to be the same killer, as I'm sure you've already surmised. He dispatched her much as he did the others and inflicted very similar injuries in the process. Although, in this case, there is one very significant difference.'

Grav clasped his hands to his chest. 'What are we talking about exactly?'

'There were traces of seminal fluid in the reproductive tract.'

'You've found semen?'

'That's what I said.'

'Sufficient for DNA profiling?'

Carter paused, knowing Grav was on tenterhooks, and making him wait. 'Oh, yes, there's no problem in that regard. We should have the results within a day or two, if I get the samples off this afternoon. I'm sure they can be rushed through, given the circumstances.'

'I'll make fucking sure they are. You can count on it.'

'I think you've had a notable break, our man's getting careless.'

'This could be it, Sheila. Let's hope the bastard's on the National Database. I want him off the streets and fast.'

She took a scalpel and prepared to make her first incision. 'I was thinking much the same myself.'

'I'm guessing the markings to her wrists and ankles mean she was tied up at some point?'

'You know she was, Grav. Just like the others. I'd say she was restrained for four or five days, given the colour of the bruises.'

'Laura told me she was dressed much the same as the others.'

'I had a very similar dress as a young girl. Have you checked out where you can get hold of that sort of stuff these days? We're not talking designer. But it's nice quality. It will have cost a bob or two when it was new.'

'Yeah, there's any number of charity shops and a few vintage stores in the area. I've got one of the team looking into it for me, but I don't hold out much hope. She's come up with nothing so far. He could be getting them anywhere.'

'I was thinking maybe all the victims could be members of some club or other. You know, where they dress up and recreate times gone by. Some people do that sort of thing.'

Grav shook his head. 'No, I don't think so, Sheila. The two girls we've identified were working as prostitutes to fund a chronic drug habit. There's some suggestion that the first victim had an unusual dress sense, but there's nothing to say the second was anything other than conventional. I'm guessing the killer probably provided the clothes himself.'

'Fetish?'

'Yeah, something like that.'

'Of course. That's why you're the detective and I'm the doctor.'

She returned to her dissection as Grav shook his head slowly and deliberately, pondering humanity's seemingly unlimited capacity for evil. 'Have you got an estimated time of death for me?'

'You don't let up, do you? Can't you wait for my report like everyone else?'

'A best guess based on the available information would be appreciated. Just give me something to work with.'

She remained focused on her dissection and talked as she worked. 'Well, given her rectal temperature on arrival, and the degree of rigor mortis in the muscles, I'd suggest she was killed no more than three to four hours before being found. I'll take a temperature reading from the liver in due course, which will provide a more accurate core body temperature, and that should help me confirm my initial observations, although I doubt my conclusions will change significantly. Is that good enough for you?'

'Thanks, Sheila, it's appreciated. Is there anything to help us identify her, beyond her immediate description?'

'She's had her appendix removed at some point.'

'Anything else?'

'There's a tattoo of a stereotypical red heart on her left buttock. It's about three inches by two inches, with a name: Simon. I'll include the full details in my report. That should suffice.'

'Okay, that's helpful. I'll ask Laura to check the missing persons records. You never know your luck.'

Carter began examining the stomach contents, as Grav took a single step backwards, fighting his gag reflex despite his familiarity with the process. 'Right then, Grav, is there anything else you want to know before you shut up and leave me to get on?'

'Just her natural hair colour?'

'Light brown, from what I can see. There's some recent growth under her arms and in the pubic area.'

'Mousey?'

'A little darker.'

'Okay.'

'There's half a packet of chocolate biscuits in my office, if you fancy one before heading off, the kettle's on the windowsill.'

He turned and walked in the direction of the door. 'Splash of milk and one sugar?'

'Yes, you know how I like it. I'll just give my hands a quick swill, and I'll be with you in two minutes. I can finish this later. I wanted a quick chat with you about sponsoring my niece. She's doing a ten-mile bike ride to raise money for her youth club.'

'Is it all right if I light up a cigar?'

She gave a little wry smile. 'Are you going to put your hand in your pocket?'

Grav sighed. 'Will twenty quid do you?'

'Very generous. She'll be delighted.'

'Can I use the phone to give Laura a quick call? I can never get a signal down here for some reason.'

She approached the sink and began washing her hands thoroughly, right up to her elbows. 'Of course, no problem. The quicker we find out who this young woman is, the better. How is Laura, by the way? I haven't seen her for weeks.'

'She was off work for some time after a miscarriage. It's not something she's made public, so keep it to yourself.'

'Oh, I'm sorry to hear that. How's she coping?'

'She's throwing herself back into the work and trying to get on with her life. Keeping busy, you know what I'm saying. I did the same thing when Heather passed. Less time to think.'

'She's got to grieve, just like you had to, Grav. Burying your head in the sand doesn't help anybody. You should know that better than most.'

'Yeah, I found that out all right. Heather's death hit me right in the gut like a physical blow.'

'This is where you usually swear, loudly and crudely, and kick something.'

'Fucking cancer.'

'There it is. That's the Grav I know and love. Now, put the kettle on, light the cigar you mentioned, and telephone that DS of yours. The quicker you give her the description, the quicker she can get on with her enquiries.'

'You think?'

She switched off the mixer tap and began drying her hands with a paper towel. 'You're becoming somewhat sarcastic in your old age, if you don't mind me saying so. Has anyone ever told you that?'

'They have, Sheila, more times than I care to remember. The detective chief superintendent said much the same thing only last week, God bless her.'

She grinned. 'And with very good reason no doubt. Have you got any good news for me? Something to restore my flagging faith in humanity?'

He took a cigar from a packet of five, held it to his nose to appreciate the rich, aromatic tobacco, but didn't light it. 'Emily's back home from Cardiff. She's joined a local law firm after splitting up with her boyfriend.'

'Oh, that'll be nice for you. My two are still in America. I miss them terribly.'

He held the door open and allowed her to enter her small magnolia office, piled high with medical text books and scientific papers on every conceivable surface. 'I'm going to be crapping myself every time Emily goes out on her own until we catch this bastard, that's the truth of it.'

Carter switched on the kettle and began spooning instant coffee granules into two matching pottery mugs. 'Do you think you're nearer to catching him?'

'We had fuck all, Sheila. I really thought the bastard was on top of his game, but maybe not. Maybe he's blown it. I'm hoping today's the day our luck's changed. Laura found a fag butt and footprint close to our latest victim's head, and now, there's the semen. Any one of those three could be game changers.'

Chapter 7

Grav parked his West Wales Police Mondeo in the busy Caerystwyth Headquarters car park, just as the sun broke through the grey clouds and bathed the world in light. He said a quick hello to Sandra on the front desk and used the lift, rather than ascend the three flights of stairs, to reach the training room that was serving as a serious incident room for as long as required. His arthritic knees were particularly problematic in the winter months, despite regular anti-inflammatory medication, so it seemed sensible. Less effort and less pain.

DS Kesey was entering information pertinent to the investigation on the computerised H.O.L.M.E.S crime intelligence system when Grav pushed the door open and entered the room. She looked up and stifled a laugh as he took off his padded jacket, which his subordinates secretly joked made him look like the Michelin Man on steroids, and slowly approached her.

'What the hell happened to your eye?'

She raised a hand to her right cheek and touched a swollen welt that was gradually turning blue. 'Oh, it's nothing, just kick-boxing.'

'What, again? You look as if you've gone twelve rounds with Mike Tyson.'

'Yeah, I was waiting for that one.'

'What was it, a competition or something?'

'No, just sparring, I took an extra class when the usual instructor couldn't make it. I lost concentration; it sometimes happens when you're teaching. I was trying to focus on too many things at once.'

'The world's gone bleeding mad. Mine's a coffee, if you're making one.'

Kesey nodded. 'Give me a second, boss, nearly done.'

Grav sat himself down, took off his shoes, and massaged his cold feet for about thirty-seconds before pushing some files aside so he could rest them on his desk. 'How's Mike getting on with the CCTV?'

'There's no cameras anywhere near the river, but he's been looking at the surrounding area at the relevant time.'

'Anything of interest?'

'No, nothing so far. No-one with any history of violence or sexual offences.'

'Tell him to keep looking.'

'Will do.'

'Any joy with the missing persons records?'

She nodded, pleased to be able to reply in the affirmative. 'Yeah, I think I may have found our girl.'

'As quickly as that?'

'The tattoo was the clincher. If I'm right, her name's Amanda Williams, a twenty-two-year-old from the Uplands area of Swansea. She was reported missing by her fiancée a few days back.'

'Another sex worker?'

Kesey poured boiling water into his chipped, but much prized, black and white Neath Rugby Club mug, added powdered milk, coffee, and five sugar lumps before stirring. 'No, not this one. She was a paralegal based in Llanelli. She'd left work early for a dental appointment last Wednesday afternoon, and that was the last anyone saw of her until her body was found this morning. The local police deemed it a medium risk case – after the family insisted her disappearance was totally out of character.'

'High risk would have been a more appropriate designation. The bastard's deviated from his usual victim profile.'

'It seems so.'

'Has she got any history of drug use, anything at all?'

'Nothing, and no record; I ran a check.'

'That's not good, it's not good at all. Not that I'm saying one victim's more regrettable than another; a dead girl's a dead girl, whoever they are, whatever their life choices.'

'There you go, boss.'

Grav accepted his mug and cupped his big hands around it to warm them. Thanks, love, it's appreciated.'

'So, where do we go from here?'

'I want you to get yourself down to Swansea and speak to the girl's relatives sometime today. The boyfriend, the parents – poor sods. One of them will have to formally identify her. And let's get hold of a recent photograph for the media. Someone may have seen her with the killer. The family deserve to know the truth, however unpalatable.'

'Okay, boss, will do. I'll have a quick bite to eat before heading off, if that's all right with you? I didn't have time for breakfast.'

Grav lowered his feet to the floor and picked up a scuffed, brown leather shoe that was badly in need of a polish. 'Yeah, of course it is, love, no probs. I'll come down to the canteen with you, if you fancy a bit of company? My treat.'

'Ooh, let's hope they've added caviar to the menu, or lobster maybe, something really expensive.'

He laughed hoarsely as he fastened his laces with broad fingers and spoke with a smoker's rattle that was getting gradually worse with each month that passed. 'What, in this place? You've got no chance. It'll be egg and chips, if you're lucky.'

The two detectives sat together, eating their respective meals and making intermittent small talk for a few minutes before returning their attention to the case. 'So, it looks as if he kept the poor girl tied up somewhere before finally killing her in the early hours of this morning.'

Grav swallowed a well-chewed piece of salty bacon and nodded twice. 'Let's wait to see what final conclusions Sheila comes to in her report, but yeah, it's looking that way, much the same as the others.'

'Will her report be available today?'

'I'll be sending someone to pick it up shortly after four, but you know what she's like. She gave me a summary; I'm not expecting any surprises.'

'Why take the victim all the way down to the river before killing her? Why risk it, unless she was already dead? Maybe it was just a dumping ground. I hadn't considered that.'

He shook his head. 'I don't think it's likely. It's a fair way from any potential parking spot to where the body was found. He'd have to be built like a brick shithouse.'

'It doesn't make any sense. He could have killed her wherever he'd kept her and dumped the body wherever he chose. Why so near town? It's not like we're short of remote locations in the area.'

'Nothing the maniac does is particularly rational, love. Think about it. Fuck knows what goes on in his head. It looks as if he's not as forensically aware as we'd feared. Let's just be grateful for that.'

She opened and closed her mouth before finally speaking. 'Yeah, I get what you're saying, but something's not right, boss. He's left significant clues for the first time. Why do that?'

'It's no mystery, love. Either he's gaining confidence, or he's getting sloppy. I've seen it before. It's not unusual in cases like this. They think they're indestructible and get complacent.'

She shook her head. 'I'm not so sure.'

'What are you saying exactly?'

'I can't put my finger on it. It's just a feeling.'

'Look, just think about it. He's left all the bodies in beauty spots – this time's no different in that respect. He abducts them, he imprisons them, and he kills them where and when it suits him. He wants the attention; he wants the publicity. He wants them to be found, and he wants to shock. He wouldn't be the first serial killer to crave infamy.'

Kesey drained her cup and nodded. 'Yeah, I guess so… The detective chief super was looking for you this morning. Did she manage to get hold of you?'

'Oh, for fuck's sake. Did her majesty say what she wanted?'

'She mentioned something about a press conference.'

Grav relaxed. 'Okay, makes sense. I'll give her a shout sometime this afternoon, if I get the time; doff my cap, curtsey, and all that. If he's on the National Database, we've got the bastard. Hopefully, she'll agree to hold off until we get the results back from the lab. It would be nice to give the press some good news for a change.'

'Fingers crossed.'

'And everything else, love.'

Kesey delved into her black leather handbag in search of her car keys. 'Any final instructions before I head off to the big city?'

'Find out as much as you can about the girl's recent movements and contacts. And let's get hold of her computer and the like for the tech people to have a look at. She may have been in touch with the killer.'

'Will do. Are you about in the morning?'

'Yeah, I'll see you then, love. Just to confirm, you did send the cigarette butt off for testing, yeah?'

'Of *course* I did. Do you really feel the need to check up on me?'

'Just asking.'

'You don't need to do my job for me, Grav. I'm a detective sergeant, not some kid straight out of training college. I know what I'm doing.'

'I know you do, love. It's just my way, that's all. I didn't mean anything by it.'

'I'll be on my way, then.'

He raised a hand in mock salute. 'Keep an eye on the weather. The forecast mentioned the possibility of snow. I wouldn't like to see you stranded somewhere on the motorway for God knows how long. Who'd make the coffee?'

'You are pushing your luck.'

Grav grinned mischievously. 'And make sure you dress up nice and warm. Perhaps put a vest on. It's freezing out there.'

Kesey raised a fist in the air and shook it playfully. 'One of these days, I'll frigging swing for you.'

Chapter 8

DS Kesey parked almost opposite the Williams family's modest, 1950s semi-detached, Swansea council house and stared at the front door for almost five minutes before exiting the vehicle. The lights were on; someone was almost certainly in. She had a job to do, and it was time to get on with it. She was the purveyor of bad news, and the family would know it as soon as she appeared at their door.

Kesey approached the house, knocked, less than enthusiastically and kept knocking until a careworn, middle-aged woman, with tightly permed brown hair, stood facing her. 'What can I do for you? If you're selling something, I'm not interested.'

The DS took her warrant card from her coat pocket and held it up. 'Detective Sergeant Laura Kesey, West Wales Police, and you are?'

The woman swallowed twice as her face paled. 'Is this about Amanda? I'm her mother. Have you found her?'

'Can we speak inside please, Mrs Williams? There are things we need to discuss.'

Mandy Williams grabbed at the doorframe to either side of her as her legs buckled. She hit the floor hard, grazing one knee, and banging her head on the wall to her left.

'Come on, Mrs Williams, up you get. Let's get you in the house.'

The ragged mother looked up at Kesey with hazy eyes, but she didn't attempt to get up. 'What's happened to my Amanda? Just tell me. I need to know.'

'Is there anyone else in the house? Anyone at all?'

Mandy Williams lifted herself into a seated position and shook her head. 'No, there's just me.'

Kesey reached out and helped her to her feet. 'Let's get you into the lounge and sat down properly. Come on, that's it, up you get, one step at a time.'

The woman was weeping as she slumped into the nearest armchair. 'I w-want to know what's h-happened. It can't be any w-worse than m-my imagination. Just tell m-me, please.'

The detective took a deep breath and tried to speak as calmly as possible, fighting her emotions and losing. 'There's no easy way of saying this. The body of a young woman meeting your daughter's description was found early this morning. I'm so very sorry to have to give you the bad news.'

'Is it d-definitely her?'

'We'll need to confirm her identity, but it's likely.'

Mandy Williams looked up, eyes wide. 'So, it m-may not be my Amanda, you could be mistaken? That's a possibility, that's what you're saying, yes?'

Kesey moved to the very edge of her seat, her hands resting on her knees. 'I'm sorry. I think you need to prepare yourself for the worst.'

'Where was she f-found?'

'On the riverbank in Caerystwyth.'

Williams sensed hope and clung to it. 'Why would she be in Caerystwyth? Why by the river? You've got it wrong. I know you've got it wrong. It's not my lovely girl. It's some other mother's child.'

'The dead girl has a red heart, and the name Simon, tattooed on her left buttock. I believe your daughter has a tattoo meeting that description.'

All hope was suddenly lost. 'The two of them had them d-done last summer on holiday in Ibiza after a few drinks too many. But it's not as if anyone else could see it. That's what I told her. They're getting married in April. Everything's booked and paid for. She can't wait.'

'Is there someone I can contact for you, Mrs Williams? Your husband, perhaps?'

Mandy Williams let out a loud, guttural gasp of air from deep in her throat, that Kesey thought was the saddest sound she'd ever heard. 'I want to see her.'

'That's going to be difficult today, but I'll try to arrange something for first thing tomorrow morning. If you could give me a recent photograph, that would be helpful.'

The woman's mouth was wide open, her eyes glaring, and her voice rose to a hysterical whine. 'Are you winding me up? I want to see her now. Do you hear me? Now!'

'I can understand your urgency, but it *really* would be better if you waited.'

'Are you a mother?'

Kesey's eyes reddened as they filled with tears. 'No, no, I'm not.'

'Well, if you were you'd know that tomorrow's just not good enough. Have you got that? Have you got it into your thick head? It's just not fucking well good enough.'

Kesey remained in her seat, looking up as Mandy Williams stood over her. 'Look, there's no easy way to tell you this. There was a post-mortem earlier today. The young woman's body is at Caerystwyth morgue. We haven't received the pathologist's written report yet, but we have very good reason to believe that she was murdered.'

Williams clutched her stomach with both hands and resisted the impulse to vomit. 'I want to see her now. Not tonight, not tomorrow morning, right *now*. I need to know for certain. Surely you can understand that? If it's her, I need to start grieving. And if it's not, if you've got it wrong, as I pray you have, I need you to find my lovely girl before it's too late.'

Kesey nodded. 'Give me two minutes. I'll make a phone call and see what I can do.'

'Thank you.'

'It's the least I can do.'

'There's a framed photograph of Amanda on the dresser, if that's any good to you. You can take it with you, but I want it back when you're finished with it. It's one of my favourites.'

'Thank you, Mrs Williams, that's very helpful.'

Mandy Williams was ready and waiting, with her hat and coat on, when Kesey re-entered the lounge a minute or two later. 'It's all arranged. The pathologist will meet us on arrival.'

'Okay, let's go. I want to get this over with.'

'What about your husband?'

'I've rung him. I've told him what's happening. He's not Amanda's father – he cleared off years ago. This is something I've got to do myself.'

The journey passed slowly; both women struggling to make intermittent small talk, given the gravity of events, right up to when Caerystwyth Morgue came into view about forty-five minutes later. Kesey parked as near to the entrance as possible, as a single grey-black cloud moved slowly across the sky and masked the winter sun as if God were mourning humanity's many failings and frailties.

Kesey turned off the engine and turned to face her passenger. 'Okay, this is it. Are you ready?'

Williams screwed up her eyes and nodded once. 'As ready as I'll ever be. Let's get on with it.'

The detective led the distraught mother of two into the building to be met by Doctor Carter, who smiled thinly, introduced herself, and held out a hand in greeting. 'Come into my office and take a seat, Mrs Williams. I realise this is going to be somewhat traumatic for you, but I want to do everything I can to make the process as easy as it possibly can be under the circumstances.'

Mandy Williams sat, as instructed, with Kesey immediately next to her. 'I want to see the body.'

Doctor Carter took a large colour image of the victim's face from a green cardboard file and placed it face down on her desk. 'I'd like you to take a good look at a photograph initially, if that's okay with you? If you think it's your daughter, we can progress matters from there. Does that sound acceptable?'

Williams took a paper hankie from her patent leather handbag, dabbed at each eye in turn, and said, 'Yes,' in a quivering voice reverberating with emotion.

'Are you ready?'

She grabbed DS Kesey's hand and held it tightly. 'Yes.'

Kesey nodded. 'Take your time, Mrs Williams. Take a good look. You need to be sure. Our brains can play tricks on us in circumstances like this.'

She released the officer's hand, picked up the photograph, studied it, and began weeping silent tears, which quickly became a torrent, as her chest heaved, and she gasped for breath. 'It's A-Amanda. It's my l-lovely girl. Why? Why would a-anyone want to hurt her? She was kind. Gentle. She didn't have an e-enemy the world. Why would …?'

Kesey reached out and squeezed the grieving mother's arm.

'I want to see her.'

Doctor Carter met her eyes. 'Are you ready?'

Williams blew her nose noisily and nodded. 'I'm ready. Where is she? I want to see her. I can't stand the idea of her being alone.'

'If you follow me, I'll take you straight to her.'

'Thank you.'

Carter lifted the sheet from Amanda Williams' cold and pallid face, and took a step backwards, allowing the mother to slowly approach her daughter's body. 'Is it okay if I kiss her cheek?'

Kesey met the pathologist's eyes and nodded. 'Of course.'

She leaned forwards and gently kissed her daughter. 'She's so cold. She hated the cold. She's gone. Hopefully to a better place.'

The doctor kept her counsel, allowing the officer to take the lead.

'Yes, no-one can hurt her now.'

'What did he do to her?'

'There's no easy way to tell you this… Your daughter was strangled.'

Mandy Williams paled as she swallowed hard and turned away. 'Like the other girls, the girls on the n-news.'

'Yes, just like them.'

'They were raped.'

Kesey's expression darkened. 'Yes, they were.'

'What about my Amanda? Did the bastard violate her?'

The detective paused before replying, wishing she had a very different answer to offer. 'Yes, we believe so. I'm so very sorry.'

Williams suddenly looked away from the two women and approached her daughter, seemingly oblivious to the unwelcome response. 'Was Amanda wearing her necklace?'

Kesey shook her head. 'No, no jewellery was found.'

'Amanda was wearing it when she left the house that morning. It was a Christmas gift from Simon. She loved it. There's no way she'd have taken it off herself. She was never without it.'

DS Kesey took her pocketbook from her handbag. 'Is it okay if we use your office, Doctor? I'd like to make some written notes.'

Carter placed the sheet back over Amanda's face. 'Of course, no problem. Take as long as you need.'

'Take a seat, Mrs Williams.'

'It's Mandy. Call me Mandy.'

'I really appreciate your help, Mandy. You're doing unbelievably well in the circumstances.'

She focused on the tiled floor. 'Just get on with it, Sergeant. Nothing you can say is going to make me feel any better.'

'Okay, just to be clear, before I commit anything to paper, are you certain that your daughter was wearing the necklace when she left the house the last time? If you've even the slightest doubt, now's the time to tell me.'

'She was wearing it. How many times do I have to say it? She always wore it. I can't be any clearer than that.'

Kesey opened her pocketbook and poised her pen above the first blank page. 'Can you describe it to me?'

'It's got a delicate sixteen-inch, nine-carat gold chain, with a heart shaped pendant encrusted with tiny blue sapphires and a single diamond. Simon worked overtime for weeks to pay for it. It's not like he earns a lot.'

'Thank you, Mandy, that's very helpful. Just one more question.'

'I'm listening.'

'Did she ever wear lavender perfume?'

'What?'

'Did Amanda ever wear lavender perfume?'

'No, never.'

'You're certain?'

'She thought it was an old lady scent. It reminded her of my mother.'

Kesey noted her response as the grieving mother gripped her hand and spat, 'You've got to get the bastard for me. I want him caught and locked up forever. I want him to rot. I want him to suffer like she did.'

The detective nodded. 'I won't rest until I find him, that's a promise. We'll lock him up for the rest of his miserable life.' She meant every single word.

Chapter 9

Charles Turner was keenly anticipating whatever the evening might bring, as he arrived at his Caerystwyth home. He discarded his winter coat on the bannister, on entering the spacious hall, and hurried upstairs to prepare himself with, what he considered to be, the appropriate degree of attention. Meeting the infamous DI Gravel and taking his daughter to dinner were significant developments in his eyes. He wanted to impress. And this, he assured himself, was the opportunity to do exactly that. Getting to know Gravel socially could provide valuable insight into the man, his methods, and the investigation itself. Keep your enemies close. Wasn't that how the saying went? He'd read it somewhere, or was it a film? Yes, yes, that was it, a film. Keep Gravel close and pump Emily for information at every opportunity. That was the key.

He showered, shaved, and dressed in a suitably impressive smart-but-casual outfit that he thought reflected his elevated status. He had to look just right. Perfect for the role. Preparation was everything.

Turner ran a hand through his still damp hair and stared in the full-length mirror on the back of his wardrobe door. He looked himself up and down, drinking in his image. He really couldn't have chosen better; that's what he told himself. The made-to-measure grey jacket, the white Egyptian cotton shirt, the tailored black trousers, and the highly polished slip-on shoes all screamed impeccable style and taste. Fabulous. No wonder his previous victims had put their trust in him so very quickly. No wonder they'd fallen for his charms like the bitches on heat that they were. He was a good-looking man – successful, affluent – and now, it was Emily's turn to fall under his Machiavellian spell. A tweak here, a tweak there, and she'd be an eminently suitable victim. It was nothing if not inspired – a win-win.

Turner checked his watch, for what he told himself was the final time, and smiled. Plenty of time. Being late wasn't an option, but neither was being early. Impressions mattered. Don't seem too keen; it could stink of desperation. Why not indulge himself? Yes, what the hell, take full advantage of the available time.

He strolled into his large and modernistic lounge, picked up his laptop from where it was charging, relaxed in a leather armchair, and sought out his film of choice. Ah yes, there it was: AW. He wouldn't have time to watch it all, more's the pity, but he could get a flavour of it to feed his fantasies for the evening ahead. Was it too soon to give Emily the necklace? Of course, it was. What the hell was he thinking? Get a grip, man. The long game was long for a reason. He had to play safe, however difficult, however frustrating.

The solicitor sat back in his chair and focused on the screen as Amanda Williams' last hours unfolded before him. She was huddled, cold, naked, and afraid, chained to a cast-iron radiator in a bedroom at the back of his house. A room, free of furniture or any other unnecessary adornments, that had been carefully soundproofed and fitted wall-to-wall with waterproof, beige and green plastic flooring that he considered practical and aesthetically pleasing.

Turner focused on Amanda's quivering, alabaster-white body and noted that she was crying as a stream of urine ran down one leg and pooled under her. Lovely, what an incredible sight to behold, providing not just enjoyment, but exhilaration, too; a level of euphoria no drug could engender. She was lost in torment and bereft of hope. The pleading had stopped, and she was seemingly resigned to her fate.

Perhaps she was in some psychological hell as she'd sat there and wallowed in her own filth. It certainly looked that way. Waiting for, and anticipating, whatever death may bring. Yes, the girl had been surprisingly insightful for such a limited creature. Interesting that she gave up the fight surprisingly quickly. She'd known she was approaching the end game; that he was a man devoid of empathy or virtue. Maybe kill the next one on film. Yes, why not? It was worth considering. Although, walking them to their place of execution had its undoubted advantages: a thing of beauty in a place of beauty; the body there for anyone to find and appreciate. He had to remember that. Everything for a reason. Why deviate from such a well-established and successful modus operandi?

Turner felt his penis engorge with blood as he pictured himself placing his hands around Emily's slender neck and squeezing, harder, harder, harder, as he looked in her doe-like eyes and witnessed her life-force draining away. He stroked his genitals and considered undoing his zip, but thought better of it. Time was getting on. He couldn't be late, not tonight, not the first time. What sort of impression would that give? Reliability mattered. Good timekeeping mattered. Where would society be if professionals such as himself let their standards slip?

He jumped to his feet, stretched, and strode purposefully into the hallway. Where the hell had he left his car keys? He had to concentrate. Focus. It was time to initiate his plan. To play the long game, for once. Time to get it done.

Turner parked his two-seater convertible behind Grav's aged green hatchback and walked down the concrete path towards the front door with a seductive smile on his face. He rang the bell, once, then again – not too briefly but not for too long either – and waited with increasing impatience until the detective eventually flicked on the light switch in the hall and opened the door.

Grav held out a hand in friendly greeting. 'Good to meet you, Mr Turner. Emily said she was expecting you. Why don't you come in and wait in the lounge? It's brass monkey weather out there.'

Turner followed him into the house. The pleb was almost as moronic as his bitch daughter. It seemed it ran in the family. 'Please call me Charles. There's no need for ceremony.'

'Take a seat, Charles. She shouldn't be too long. Do you fancy a drink while you wait? I've got a few cans of beer in the kitchen, if you fancy one?'

'A glass of water would be appreciated.'

'Water? I never touch the stuff myself. You're sure you don't want something a bit stronger?'

'Water will be fine, thanks. You know, with driving. It seems best.'

Grav returned a minute or two later with a glass of tap water in one hand and a can of bitter in the other. 'I don't know what the hell she's doing up there. Women, eh?'

Turner forced a smile. 'There's no rush; I wanted a private word with you, anyway. I'm rather glad of the opportunity.'

Grav's eyes narrowed. 'Something related to Emily?'

'Oh, no, no, nothing like that. You do understand that interactions between a client and his solicitor are privileged, don't you?'

'I've been a copper for a long time. What's this about?'

Turner moved to the edge of his seat. 'This has to be off the record. I can't stress this sufficiently. I'd likely be struck off if what I'm about to tell you becomes public knowledge. If I tell you, you didn't hear it from me. Are we agreed?'

'Where the hell's this going?'

Emily walked on to the landing and leant over the bannister before Turner had the time to respond. 'You're a little early, Charles. I'll be with you in another five minutes or so.'

Turner smiled and replied, 'No problem, take your time,' before returning his attention to Grav, who was tapping the first two fingers of his right hand on the arm of his chair. 'Am I correct in saying that you're the lead detective investigating the recent murders?'

'If you've got something to say, just say it, man. I think that's best, don't you?'

Turner wrung his hands together and paused for a beat, keen to make the moment as memorable as possible. 'This isn't something I've ever done before. I need you to understand that. I take my professional responsibilities extremely seriously, but I feel I have a moral obligation to share this information with you.'

'Okay, I'm listening.'

'It has to be on a strictly confidential basis, as I said. Do I have your assurances? I need to know I can trust you.'

Grav reached out and shook Turner's hand firmly, thinking he had nothing to lose. 'You have my word. Guaranteed. I don't break my promises.'

Turner relaxed in his seat. 'Do you know of a man by the name of Peter Spencer?'

'The wife beater?'

'Yes, yes, that's the man I'm talking about. I'm currently representing him.'

'And?'

'I think he may be the man you're looking for.'

Grav pondered Turner's information as Emily descended the stairs and entered the room, wearing fitted jeans, knee-high, brown leather boots, and a matching jacket.

'Ah, here she is, and looking even more radiant than usual if that's possible.'

Emily chose to ignore the solicitor's compliment. 'So, what have the two of you been talking about? It all seemed rather serious from the little I heard.'

Grav met his daughter's eyes. 'Can you give us a minute, love. There's something I need to discuss with Mr Turner.'

'Charles, please call me Charles.'

She looked at one man and then the other. 'Are you telling me you want to speak privately?'

'Please, love.'

Turner took his car keys from his trouser pocket and casually tossed them to Emily. 'My car's on the driveway, start the engine and put the heating on. This won't take too long. There's some CDs in the glovebox, if you're interested.'

She glared at him, turned on her three-inch heels, and strode towards the front door without the need for words.

'You were telling me about Peter Spencer.'

Turner nodded. 'It's nothing concrete. Nothing that would lead you to conclude he's a brutal killer, but some of the things he says have had me questioning if he could be. Does that make any sense to you?'

Gravel shook his head. 'Not really. What the fuck are you trying to say? It all sounds a bit nebulous, to be honest. Can you give me some specifics?'

'It's more a feeling than anything else. That's the only way I can put it. He seems to take pleasure in his wife's suffering. The man's a sadist; I think that's a fair way of putting it. I get the distinct impression that he likes hurting her. It gives him satisfaction. There's a glint in his eye when he talks about it. Why she stayed with him for as long as she did is a total mystery to me. Maybe some form of Stockholm syndrome would explain it.'

'That's it? The man's a scrote, for sure, but that doesn't make him a killer. There's a lot of them out there: wife beaters, men who get pissed and take their anger and insecurities out on their partner and kids. You know that as well as I do.'

'I'm sorry if you feel I've wasted your time.'

'You're sure there's not more to it? There's nothing you're not telling me? Now's the time to say if there is.'

They approached the front door with Turner taking the lead. 'Look, I think I may have said too much already. Maybe I'm overreacting. The last thing I'd want to do is misdirect the investigation. It's a terrible business.'

'You needn't worry about that. I'll check him out, it's easily done, and you know where I am if you've got anything else you want to discuss. You can get hold of me here or at work. Day or night, don't hesitate. Just pick up the phone.'

Turner smiled. 'I will, Inspector. I appreciate your understanding. I was beginning to wonder if I should have kept my mouth shut.'

'Not at all. And have a good night.'

'Oh, I'm sure we will. I feel certain that Emily's going to be an invaluable addition to our team. I'm glad to have found her. She's a credit to you.'

Grav beamed. 'You won't hear me arguing. She's a chip off the old block, for sure.'

'Right, I'd better make a move. I think the young lady's been waiting long enough.'

Grav called after Turner as he approached his car. 'If you have any further concerns, you'll tell me, yeah? Anything at all.'

Turner looked back and nodded before getting in. 'If there's anything whatsoever I can do to help you catch the man who killed those unfortunate young women, I'll do it. That's cast-iron guaranteed. A line's been crossed. You can count on me.'

Chapter 10

Emily was beginning to question the wisdom of agreeing to the arrangement, as they travelled west along the A40 in the direction of Laugharne – a small Welsh coastal town forever associated with the poet and writer Dylan Thomas. It had all seemed practical enough when Turner had suggested it that morning, but she was starting to have her doubts. She liked him well enough, on early impressions, and he was her new boss after all, there was no denying that, but the evening was beginning to feel more like a date than the business meeting he'd talked of earlier in the day. She wanted someone honest, someone predictable. Not another charmer who may only be thinking about one thing.

She pressed her knees together and gave the situation more thought. Was she overreacting? Worrying about nothing? Was she doing him an injustice, or were her misgivings justified? Yes, trust your gut, girl. They could be. He smelt strongly of a heady, masculine scent that she recognised but couldn't identify; there was passionate music playing on the car's CD player, and he seemed to be doing all he could to appear pleasant and amusing to the nth degree. A compliment here, a joke or clever comment there. Did he have an agenda she didn't want or need? Was it his way, his usual persona? Or was he putting on a performance for her benefit? That was what she asked herself as he manoeuvred expertly through the Welsh countryside, dulled by the attentions of winter, with one soaring, classical aria after another filling the car.

She wasn't the best judge in the world when it came to men. Recent events were a testament to that. Should she say something? Should she clarify matters, or should she go with the flow and avoid the risk of making a fool of herself again? He was nice enough on the face of it. And he held her career in the palm of his hands, that was undoubtedly true. Maybe this was an opportunity to get to know him a little better and curry favour. Turn the tables. Play him at his own game. What the hell, why not see how the evening progressed and re-evaluate from time to time? Yes, that made sense. Oh, God, was she overthinking things again? Probably. Relax, Emily. Just relax. What harm could a meal and a drink or two possibly do?

Emily adjusted her hair, pulled down the sun visor to check her lipstick in the vanity mirror, and swiveled slightly in her seat to face him. 'Are you a big classical music fan?'

He turned the volume down a notch and smiled. 'Would you like to listen to something a little more contemporary? I appreciate that opera isn't to everyone's tastes. I'm a little unusual in that regard.'

'No, really, I'm enjoying it.'

'You're sure?'

'What is it?'

'It's Verdi's *La Traviata*: a tragic love story. I saw it performed at the opera festival in Verona last summer. It was truly wonderful. Music fills me with joy like nothing else could. I think of it as food for the soul.'

'That's very poetic.'

'Do you think so?'

'I'd love to go to Verona one day.'

He smiled again as "Addio del passato" came to a sudden and dramatic end. 'Do you speak Italian?'

'Just English and Welsh.'

'"The joys, the sorrows soon will end. The tomb confines all mortals! Do not cry or place flowers at my grave. Do not place a cross with my name to cover these bones! Ah, the misguided desire to smile; God pardon and accept me, all is finished."'

'It's beautiful, tragic but beautiful.'

'Perhaps we could go together one day. I could translate for you. What do you think?'

She stiffened, thinking that things were moving too fast. Far too fast. 'How long have you been a solicitor?'

He paused. For fuck's sake, Charles, get a grip. 'My apologies if I've overstepped the mark somewhat. I felt we had an unstated connection. Perhaps I've misread the signals.'

She shrugged, searching for a response she couldn't find.

He suddenly switched off the CD player, turned into an unlit lay-by, and brought the car to a gradual halt. 'Look, the last thing I want to do is upset you. If I have, I can only apologise. I can take you home now, or we can carry on to the restaurant. It's up to you, you decide.'

Emily thought for a moment, considering her limited options.

'So, what's your answer? I can ring and cancel the table. It's no problem at all. Just say the word and it's done.'

She fidgeted with her cuff. 'No, no, I'm being too sensitive. A meal would be lovely. Let's get going. I don't know what on earth I was thinking.'

He patted her knee gently before restarting the engine. 'A meal it is. I'm glad we've got that little misunderstanding out of the way.'

'Me too. It's best forgotten. I'm sure we'll have a pleasant and productive evening.'

Turner already had a large glass of red wine waiting for Emily when she returned from the ladies', and he'd sat himself down at a table for two that was within touching distance of a smouldering log fire at the back of the room. 'I thought a nice glass of vino would help us relax after our minor misunderstanding. It's a good vintage. This restaurant has a surprisingly impressive wine list.'

She'd asked for mineral water, but decided to let it slide. 'Thanks.'

'It will only be the one glass for me, regrettably, with driving, as I explained to your father. Although, if that snow gets any heavier, we may have to consider travelling back in the morning.'

'It's started snowing?'

'I believe so.'

She rose without speaking and approached a large picture window with an uninterrupted view of the ruined castle and wild estuary beyond. It was snowing lightly, but the tiny swirling flakes were melting almost immediately upon contacting the warmer ground.

'So, how's it looking out there?'

She returned to her seat, feeling more relaxed. 'I don't think we've got too much to worry about.'

'Let's hope not. The car's handling suffers terribly on slippery roads. I think it must have been designed for sunnier climes. The last thing I'd want is an accident. Your father would never forgive me.'

Her facial muscles tightened. 'Look, I appreciate you making the time and effort to bring me here, it's very kind of you, but I hope I haven't given you the wrong impression. I've only recently split up from a long-term relationship. I like you, I respect you, but I'm not looking for a new man in my life at the moment. I hope I'm not speaking out of turn?'

He smiled sardonically. Who the fuck did she think she was? 'Message received and understood. Why don't we keep a close eye on the weather, and we'll leave immediately if it gets worse? How does that sound?'

She nodded and picked up the menu. 'Thank you, Charles, I'm glad you understand. The last thing I'd want to do is cause offence.'

He looked across the table. 'I've already ordered for us both. This establishment serves an excellent steak. Rare, of course. It's the only way to eat it; I'm sure you'll agree.'

'What?'

'Oh, dear, have I done the wrong thing again?'

She shook her head slowly. 'I'm sorry, I really don't like steak. I'd like to choose something else.'

The bitch, the total fucking bitch. 'If I've been presumptuous, I can only apologise. I just thought, with the threatening snow, it was a good idea to expedite matters.'

She perused the menu, looking at each option in turn and making a point of taking her time. 'I'll have the Welsh lamb, well done, with mint sauce.'

Oh, you will, will you, you fucking ignoramus? 'Are you sure? All the best chefs serve it rare.'

Emily stood again, approached the bar, and amended the order to her taste before returning to her seat. 'I was asking how long you've been a solicitor?'

It would feel so good to shut the self-important bitch up for good. Why were all the women in his life such a fucking burden? 'About twelve years.'

'You've progressed really quickly.'

'I'm not usually one to blow my own trumpet, but, yes, I'm good at the job. I'm a strong believer in doing things to the very best of my ability. I like to suck the juice out of life, whether it's work-related or recreational. Make the most of your opportunities, Emily, that's my advice. Experience everything you can of life's rich tapestry. It passes so very quickly.'

Emily had never felt more conflicted in her life.

'You're very quiet, is everything okay? I haven't said the wrong thing again, have I?'

'Sorry, I was deep in thought. How's the weather doing?'

Turner glanced towards the window. 'Oh, I don't think we need to worry about that too much. The snow seems to have stopped for the moment. It rarely settles this close to the sea.'

A part of her was relieved, but only a part. 'Where's that food? I'm absolutely ravenous.'

'Another glass of wine?'

She lifted her glass to her lips and sipped before responding. 'No, I'll just stick with this one, thanks. I'm a lightweight when it comes to alcohol.'

'It was good to meet your father this evening. He's an interesting man.'

'You hadn't met before?'

'I was aware of him, of course, our paths have crossed from time to time, but, no, not socially.'

'He's under so much pressure. It worries me sometimes. He's not getting any younger.'

Turner nodded. 'What do you think goes on in the head of a man like that?'

'What, my dad?'

He laughed. 'No, no, the killer. I was talking about the killer.'

'Perhaps it's best not to know.'

'I don't see it that way. The extremes of human behaviour fascinate me. From an academic perspective, you understand. What leads a man to abandon any semblance of a conscience, and enthusiastically embrace his dark side, as the killer so obviously has? What kind of person becomes a serial murderer? What kind of person becomes a merciless sexual predator? That's what I ask myself. Was he born to rape and kill, or have the attentions of cruel fate led him along that shady path? What do you think?'

Emily didn't hesitate. 'I think he's evil, a monster. How else can you describe him?'

'Maybe, in the right circumstances, we're all capable of almost anything. You and me included.'

'Not that, definitely not that.'

'He's killed four times in a matter of months. Do you think he feels any remorse? Or does he feel driven to do it again just as soon as he gets the opportunity? He must do, or why continue as he has? Maybe he's devoid of conscience. Maybe he feels no regret at all.'

'People like that bring nothing but misery into the world; nothing but death and destruction. I hope the bastard's caught, locked up, and left to die in prison.'

Turner's eyes shone brightly in the light of the glowing embers. 'I guess that's up to your father.'

'Yes, I suppose it is. And the other officers working on the case, of course. It's not just down to him. It's a team effort.'

'Yes, but your father's the lead detective. The buck stops with him.'

She nodded. 'Yes.'

'That's pressure, real pressure. I wouldn't like to be in his place. I'm certain there are more victims to come. Don't you agree? He's going to keep killing again and again, right up to the time he's forced to stop.'

'Why would you say that?'

'It's just an informed impression. I suspect the killer's enjoying himself rather too much to stop. It seems obvious. That's how his mind works.'

'You seem very sure?'

'People say these sorts of crimes are all about power. And they are, to a degree. But what they're primarily about is sex. He kills and rapes because it excites him sexually. It turns him on like nothing else can. He fantasises, he kills, and then he fantasises again. It's something I've read a great deal about. I like to understand the criminal mind.'

She felt a cold shiver up and down her spine as she sat contemplating the intensity of his statement.

'Oh, here we go, our food's about to arrive.'

Emily looked up and smiled as an overweight waitress wearing a tarnished silver nose stud, which looked more like a blemish than an adornment, approached their table with plated meals in hand. 'That all looks lovely, thank you.'

'You're welcome.'

Emily nodded her acknowledgement and returned her attention to Turner, who was in the process of cutting his steak. 'Can't we talk about something else? It's all rather depressing.'

He glanced around the room, from one male customer to another. 'Think about it for a moment longer. He could be here now. It could be any of them. The grey-haired man with the stick, the business man in the pinstripe suit and purple tie, one of the young friends chatting at the bar, seemingly without a care in the world. He could be with us right now and planning his next killing – scheming, manipulating. Have you considered that possibility? Everyone has to be somewhere. Why not here?'

She shuddered. 'Dad said much the same thing. He's hidden in plain sight.'

'Maybe the waitress is to his tastes. Or the barmaid with her ponytail, what about her? There are so many potential victims. So many for him to choose from.'

Emily shivered. 'This is all getting a bit too weird. You're starting to scare me.'

'How would you feel about legally representing a man like that? A man who's killed, without mercy, time and time again. What if he'd killed five, six, or even ten? It's not beyond the bounds of possibility. The Yorkshire Ripper killed thirteen; Ted Bundy, thirty-six; the Green River Killer, at least seventy-one – despite his apparent ordinariness. They gained a level of infamy that was lost to their victims. How many people could name even one?'

'Their families could. Their friends could. It's a sick world.'

'Yes, it is, Emily, but could you ignore your instinctive feelings of revulsion and disgust, and represent a man like that to the very best of your ability?'

The tension dissipated from Emily's body. 'Ah, I was wondering where this was going. You were beginning to freak me out for a minute there.'

He was more animated now, sweating, red in the face. 'So, could you do it? That's the question. Could you do it?'

She forked some garden peas into her mouth, chewed, and swallowed before replying, 'Yes, I guess so. It wouldn't be easy, but I'd have to. It's not like it's going to happen anytime soon.'

He smiled warmly. 'Very well said. That's the response I was looking for. Everyone's entitled to a defence, whoever they are, whatever they've done. We have to put our personal feelings aside, that's the key. It isn't always easy, as you've said yourself, but there it is. Such things are sent to try us. Our cross to bear, so to speak. A good lawyer sets their personal prejudices aside.'

'I understand that.'

'Yes, I believe you do… Now, tell me, do the police have any clues as to the killer's identity? Anything at all?'

'The investigation wasn't going particularly well, but it seems things may be looking up at last.'

Turner smiled. 'That is good news. Anything specific?'

'I think Dad's waiting on DNA results. I don't know the details. He didn't say any more than that.'

What a bunch of fucking idiots! 'Oh, that sounds hopeful.'

She nodded enthusiastically. 'He seems to think so.'

'How's your meal?'

'It's excellent, thanks. The lamb's so very tender, like butter. What about yours?'

'Not bad at all. We should come again.'

She smiled.

'Where do you see yourself in five years' time, Emily? Do you have a clear view of the future? Are you someone who plans ahead, or do you live in the moment?'

'We talked about that at my interview. You asked me the exact same questions.'

'Ah, yes, yes, of *course*, I did, I remember now. You're an ambitious young woman, and I respect you for that. I wouldn't have it any other way. I was much the same on leaving university.'

'Any more questions before I finish my meal? This is starting to feel a bit like being on *Mastermind*.'

He laughed, but his eyes portrayed his true feelings. 'Just the one.'

'Go on, then. Let's hear it.'

He tilted his head and studied her for a second. 'Have you ever considered a shorter hairstyle? Shoulder-length, with a fringe, something that frames your face?'

'Excuse me?'

'Your hair, have you thought about cutting your hair? And perhaps opting for a different colour? Something less severe than your current shade; strawberry-blonde, or ginger possibly. I think either would suit you perfectly.'

She lifted her glass and hurriedly gulped down half its contents as he continued to stare at her. 'I really don't know what to say. It's not something anyone's ever asked me before. I've never thought about it.'

He reached across the table and touched her sleeve, but withdrew his hand quickly when she pulled away. 'I'm sorry. I was thinking out loud, nothing more. I was being too personal, I didn't mean any offence. Please forgive me.'

Emily ignored the seemingly heartfelt apology and approached the window again. She peered out and swore crudely under her breath as she witnessed the scene. It was snowing heavier now. Heavier than had been forecast. Heavier than she'd anticipated. Large snowflakes appeared to be swirling in every direction at the bidding of an east wind and, much worse than that, it was beginning to settle on the ground. The dark tarmac was slowly disappearing under a blanket of white. She cursed again, more loudly this time, as the implications sank in.

Emily returned to their table but remained standing. 'It's snowing again.'

He looked confused, less sure of himself. 'Aren't you going to sit down and finish your meal? It's getting cold. It would be a shame to waste it.'

'Didn't you hear me? The weather's taken a turn for the worse.'

Turner stood and approached the door, opened it, and walked into the freezing night, returning to the restaurant a minute or two later with melting snowflakes on his head and shoulders. 'We're not going anywhere in that lot. There's a good two inches on the road in places.'

'I hope this isn't something you've planned.'

Turner laughed, head back, faultless teeth in full view. 'Oh, come on, I'm influential but not that influential. I can't control the weather. Don't you think you're overreacting just a bit?'

Emily flopped down into her seat and drained her glass. 'Yes, I'm sorry, me and my big mouth. I sometimes think I shouldn't drink at all. My ex-boyfriend let me down; he rather destroyed my faith in men.'

'Another glass of wine?'

She took a slow, deep breath in through her nose, and out through her mouth before replying, 'Oh, go on, then. Why not? If we're stuck here we may as well, make the most of it. It may even do me some good. Things have been a little fraught lately, to say the least.'

He smiled warmly. 'That's the spirit. Don't let the bastards grind you down, that's my advice. Red or white?'

'I'd better stick with the red, thanks. I tend to get a ghastly hangover if I mix drinks.'

'Very sensible, best not to overdo things. I'll bring a bottle.'

He returned to the table, refilled her glass to the brim, and poured one for himself. 'The barmaid tells me that rain's forecast for the early hours.'

'Thank God for that.'

'There's only one room available, I'm afraid. We really should have enquired earlier in the evening. Everyone seems to have had the same idea.'

Emily shook her head. 'We hardly know each other. I don't feel comfortable sharing a room.'

He licked his top lip, smiled, and met her eyes. 'I appreciate this isn't ideal, but it's a case of needs must. I'm told there's a three-seater settee. You can take the bed, and I'll sleep on the sofa. How does that sound?'

'There's definitely no more rooms?'

'No, I asked.'

'Then I guess it'll have to do.'

'I reached the same conclusion.'

'Will you drop me off at my dad's place in the morning? I'd like to change before work.'

'Of course I will. No problem at all. We can talk about your caseload as we go.'

'And you're certain there's a settee?'

He smiled without parting his lips. 'That's what the barmaid told me. One double bed and one settee. Guaranteed.'

'As long as you're sure.'

'Relax, Emily, I take my duty of care as your employer seriously. You can trust me. Now, tell me a little bit more about that unreliable boyfriend who let you down so very badly.'

Emily sipped her wine and began to unwind as the familiar effects of drunkenness clouded her thinking. 'Do you really think my hair's too dark?'

He refilled her glass for the third time. 'Are you sure you want me to answer that one?'

'Yes, I want to know.'

'Sure?'

'I said so, didn't I?'

He eased back in his seat and studied her for a moment with eyes that sparkled. 'You're beautiful as you are – of course – stunning; that goes without saying. But maybe beauty can become perfection.'

Emily laughed self-consciously and looked away, as he pictured himself placing his hands around her throat and crushing her windpipe. 'It's a pity my ex-boyfriend didn't think so.'

'The man's a fool!'

She lowered her head. 'He's a right bastard, completely untrustworthy. He'll screw anything with a pulse.'

Turner reached out and patted her arm, allowing his hand to linger for a little longer than was comfortable. 'Come on, drink your wine. There's plenty more where that came from. That's it, down it goes. Oh, what the hell. Let's throw caution to the wind. Here's to us. I'll order another bottle.'

Chapter 11

Twenty-five-year-old Tina Spencer had never felt more anxious as she dialed her social worker's direct office number and waited with bated breath until she eventually answered the phone. 'Hello, Mrs Larkin, it's Tina, Tina Spencer. I don't want to go to court. I w-want to withdraw my statement.'

'Slow down, Tina. Take a breath. Now, tell me, where's this coming from?'

'I've changed my mind, that's all. I just don't want to go through with it.'

'Oh, come on now, we've talked about this more than once. Nothing's going to change if you don't give evidence. Think about how badly he hurt you this time; he's going to do the exact same thing again if you give him the slightest opportunity. You know that as well as I do.'

'I can't. I just can't.'

'Now, look, Tina, we've had the locks changed, there's an injunction in place, and you've got a panic alarm installed in the house. You're as safe as you can be under the circumstances. I get that you're nervous about going to court, it's entirely understandable, but you seemed so very sure you were doing the right thing when we last spoke. It was only a day or two ago. What's changed?'

Tina lowered the phone and began weeping, her chest heaving as she struggled to breathe.

'Are you still there, Tina? Are you still with me?'

Tina lifted the phone. 'I'm s-still here.'

'Are you ringing from the house?'

'Yeah, where else would I be?'

'I'll be with you in twenty minutes. Please don't contact the police before we've spoken again. I want to talk to you, face-to-face, before you do something you later regret. Do you promise?'

She tugged at her lank, greasy, brown hair with her free hand. 'Yeah, I promise.'

'Hold on, Tina. Life's not always going to lurch from one crisis to the next. If you do the right thing now, there are better times ahead. I'll be on my way as soon as I've put the phone down.'

The social worker drove a lot faster than was sensible, as she negotiated the busy market day traffic, en route to the large, red-brick council estate on the edge of town. She parked half on the curb, almost directly opposite the Spencer family's semi-detached home, and avoided various piles of dirty grey slush as she made her way to the front door; her black woolen coat wrapped tightly around herself.

She knocked and kept knocking until Tina Spencer eventually peered out of the thin yellow curtains, nervously confirming the social worker's identity, before finally opening the glazed door and standing there with a despairing look of defeat on her face. 'You look exhausted, Tina. Have you been crying?'

The young woman poked her head out into the street and glanced from right to left and back again. 'You didn't see him, did you? He's not hanging around on the estate, is he? I keep thinking he's going to turn up. I'm a nervous wreck.'

'Slow down, Tina. If he comes anywhere near the house, he'll be arrested again. He wouldn't dare.'

Tina forced a gap-toothed smile. 'Well, thank fuck for that. He's probably getting pissed somewhere. He hasn't given me any money for the kids for weeks. It must be going somewhere. The pubs and the bookies are probably seeing most of it.'

'Can I come in, Tina? Something's happened – that's blatantly obvious. We need to talk.'

She turned and walked towards the ill-kempt lounge with the persona of a woman approaching the gallows. 'Make sure you lock the door and put the chain on.'

'Already done, safe and sound. Come on, in you go. Take a seat, and I'll put the kettle on. Tea or coffee?'

The young woman slumped into an armchair and hugged her knees to her chest. 'Tea, please, one sugar.'

The social worker handed Tina her mug, sat herself down on the frayed, velour sofa, and smiled warmly. 'You look as if you've lost weight. Have you eaten lunch? I can get you something if you like?'

'I'm good, ta. I had some toast and strawberry jam first thing.'

'Are the kids in school?'

'Yeah, I'm glad of the peace. They drive me round the fucking bend sometimes. Pete was good with the kids when he was sober, I'll give him that much.'

'But not so much when he's been drinking. I think that's safe to say.'

Tina exhaled noisily. 'When he's pissed, he's a fucking liability.'

The social worker sipped her coffee, savouring the rising vapour that was warming her face. 'Right, what's happening, Tina? What's changed since we last spoke? I know there's been something significant; I can see you shaking from here.'

Tina averted her eyes and focused on the multicoloured carpet at her feet. 'It's nothing. I just want to withdraw my statement, that's all. It's up to me. You can't make me go to court. Nobody can.'

'But you seemed so determined this time. If you're not going to give evidence for your own sake, do it for the children. You told me how badly they're affected by his behaviour towards you: the temper tantrums, the nightmares, the bedwetting. Domestic violence can have a devastating psychological and emotional effect on young ones. I've seen it more times than I care to count. Your children aren't immune. You know how his violence affects them.'

Tina slurped her tea. 'I just can't, that's all. I want to, but I can't.'

The social worker leaned forwards in her seat. 'What's he done, Tina? Has he been here? Has he broken the conditions of the injunction? Is that what this is all about?'

'He threatened me.'

'Ah, now it's all starting to make sense.'

'He said he'd hurt me bad.'

'That's not something he hasn't said before; it's not something he hasn't *done* before.'

Tina shook her head. 'This time was different.'

'Different how?'

'He was sober, for one. That's a first.'

'And? I know there's more. I can see it in your face.'

'He followed me back from town. He threatened the kids. He said he'd hurt them if I didn't withdraw my statement. He was so fucking angry, so hateful. I just can't risk it. I believed him. He's changed. He'll do it.'

'What a complete bastard, and after all his empty promises.'

'He'll do it, I know he'll fucking do it.'

'Now, look at me, Tina, deep breaths. I need you to try and relax, and to think this through properly. Let's not make any rash decisions that may come back to haunt you. It would be too late then; he'd be back with all that entails.'

Tina began shaking her head more rapidly. 'I have thought about it. I've thought about nothing else since getting back to the house. He means it. I haven't seen him like that before. He was cold, merciless. It's like he was a different person or something. He scared me shitless.'

'When was the first time he hit you?'

'What?'

'When was the first time?'

Tina rubbed the back of her neck. 'At the hotel on our wedding night, as soon as we were alone in our room.'

'And what did he say to you after assaulting you? What did he say when he'd sobered up and calmed down a bit?'

'The usual shit. How sorry he was, how he'd never do it again, you know, all the usual crap he comes out with when he's hurt me.'

The social worker nodded slowly. 'And how long was it before he hit you again? Days, weeks, months?'

'I've told you all this.'

'Remind me.'

Tina closed her eyes tightly, lost in thought as the past closed in and beat her down a little further. 'On our honeymoon. He punched me to the floor and started kicking me on our first night in Spain.'

'And did he say why? Did he try to justify his abhorrent behaviour?'

'He said I'd smiled at a waiter. That I must fancy him, or something. He didn't like that. He said it was my fault. That I'd driven him to it.'

'So, he's been violent towards you from the very beginning?'

'Yeah, right from the fucking start.'

'And how often did he assault you when the honeymoon was over?'

Tina opened her eyes and raised a hand to her battered face as her tears began to flow.

'How often, Tina? Tell me how often?'

'Most weekends, w-when he'd been out with his mates for a few pints.'

The social worker paused. 'And then, you lost the baby. You miscarried when he kicked you in the stomach. That's right, isn't it? That's what you told me.'

'Yes, I fucking well did!'

'And did he say that was your fault too? What terrible crime justified such an extreme reaction on his part? Surely you must have done something awful; something truly unforgivable.'

'I had terrible morning sickness. I just couldn't manage the housework. I was puking constantly. His meal wasn't ready when he got home from the pub. That's all it took. He beat the crap out of me.'

'He punched you to the floor and kicked you so very hard that you lost the baby. What sort of man would do such a thing? What sort of monster does something like that? To their wife? To their unborn child?'

Tina sat staring into space, choosing not to respond.

'And what happened when your first child was born? Did anything change? Did fatherhood have a positive impact on his behaviour?'

'He said it would. He promised it would. He was going to be a good father. He swore it on the baby's life. He swore he'd never do it again.'

'And did he keep his word? Was he a changed man?'

Tina hugged herself. 'No, it happened again about a week later.'

'And it's been happening ever since, that's the truth of it. He hits you, or kicks you, says it's your fault, and apologises when he's sobered up and calmed down. That's the pattern, isn't it?'

'Yeah, that's it.'

'He's been doing it for years. He's never going to stop hitting you. It's who he is. It's what he does. If you drop the case, if you have him back, how long is it going to be before he does hurt one of the children? Have you considered that? Those threats could become reality at any time – let alone the psychological damage he's already inflicted. The children are growing into little people now, individuals with developing personalities. He won't like that. He'll see it as a threat. The first time he perceives any element of rejection, or disapproval on their part, he's likely to hit out. You can see that, can't you? The risks are increasing with every day that passes.'

'I know exactly what you're doing. I'm not a complete idiot, whatever he thinks.'

'I never thought that for a second. I want you to make an informed decision, that's all. I want you to fully appreciate the impact of any resolution you come to.'

Tina shifted her gaze to the wall. 'I get it. I can't let him win this time. Enough's enough, I've got to stay strong for the sake of the kids. I know what you're telling me. I've heard it a thousand times before.'

The social worker reached out and squeezed her client's hand, before releasing it and sitting back in her seat. 'That's the spirit; he's bad news, always was and always will be.'

'I've got to put an end to it.'

'We'll do it together. I'll be with you every step of the way. You won't be on your own.'

'So, what happens now?'

'I'm going to ring the police child protection unit, and I'm going to tell the officer in charge exactly what's happened. She'll want to take a statement from you, and then the bastard will be arrested again. He's broken his injunction – that's contempt of court… He'll be locked up. It's your shout. Shall I make the call?'

Tina began rocking in her seat. 'For the kids, yeah?'

'Yes, do if for the children.'

'Do you know the number?'

'Yes, I do. Only too well.'

Tina rose to her feet and began pacing the room, shaking, nerves taut, hands clammy and mouth dry. 'Threatening to kill the kids. What the fuck's that about? He's gone too far this time. He's fucking dangerous.'

'You won't hear me arguing. Stay strong, Tina. It's the only way. Don't let him win.'

Tina paused mid-pace, her eyes flickering like a faulty bulb. 'Okay, this is it. The time's right, he's a vicious sod, an absolute bastard! Ring quickly before I change my mind, there'll be no going back this time.'

Chapter 12

Helen Smith was in the process of checking her, she liked to think subtle, makeup with a hand-held mirror, when the phone rang and made her jump. She wasn't in the best of moods as she picked it up and said, 'Hello, Mr Turner's secretary,' in a brisk and business-like Welsh accent that she'd cultivated for the purpose.

'Is Turner in?'

She took a deep breath. 'Who's speaking, please?'

'It's Peter Spencer. I'm at the police station. I've been fucking arrested. Just get him on the phone. It's his fucking fault I'm here in the first place.'

'Mr Turner is unavailable at present. If you tell me which police station you're at, I'll pass on a message as soon as I can.'

'Are you trying to be funny? This is my one fucking call!'

'It's the best I can do.'

He snorted. '"Threaten her," he said. "Shut the bitch up," he said. Well, that worked fucking brilliantly. And that's sarcasm, in case you were wondering. The missus grassed me up. He's dumped me right in the shit.'

'I've got no idea what you *think* Mr Turner told you to do, but you've clearly got it very badly wrong. There is no way he'd say those things.'

'Are you calling me a fucking liar? Is that what you're doing? I'd watch your mouth, if I were you.'

She tensed her jaw. 'I do not appreciate your attitude.'

'Like I give a toss. You're the monkey, not the fucking organ grinder. You're not all that. It might be an idea to remember that.'

She took a deep breath and counted to five in her head. 'I'm going to ask you for your location one last time. I can pass on a message, or you can ask the police to contact the duty solicitor. It's up to you. Any more abuse, and I'm putting the phone down.'

Spencer spoke in softer tones this time, sounding less confrontational. 'I don't want to be interviewed without legal representation, and I don't want to be represented by some underqualified duty solicitor who doesn't know their arse from their fucking elbow. Tell Turner that if he doesn't get down here within half an hour, I'm telling the pigs exactly what he told me to do, word for fucking word. I'll get the bastard struck off if he doesn't help me, and that's a promise.'

'Where are you exactly?'

'Caerystwyth Police Station, where the fuck else would I be?'

Helen poked out her tongue and gave a flamboyant V-sign to the phone. 'I'll pass on the message as soon as possible.'

'Make sure you fucking well do. Turner's job's on the line, and the clock's ticking.'

Chapter 13

Grav shoved the incident room door open with his right shoulder and stumbled into the room weighed down by paperwork he planned to work through that day. 'Morning, love, Put a smile on your face. You've got a long day ahead of you.'

Kesey looked up from the two-page report resting on her desk and forced a smile as her boss dumped the various files on his desk and bent down stiffly to switch on the kettle. 'Mine's a coffee, if you're offering, boss.'

'White, no sugar?'

She sat upright in her chair. 'What, don't tell me you're actually going to make one for a change? Wonders never cease. I'll have to mark it on the calendar for posterity.'

'What the hell are you talking about? I'm the very definition of a new man. My missus used to tell me that on a regular basis.'

Kesey laughed. 'Oh, yeah, I'm sure she did.'

Grav poured boiling water into two reasonably clean mugs, added a splash of full cream milk to both and five sugar lumps for himself. 'There you go, love, make the most of it. I won't be making another one for a while.'

She accepted her mug with an outstretched hand. 'Do you want the good news or the bad news?'

'Surprise me.'

'We've got the results of the DNA tests. The lab rushed them through.'

Grav lowered himself into his seat and began massaging his arthritic right knee as it began to throb and swell. 'So, what's the news?'

'There wasn't any spermatozoa in the sample to get a DNA profile. I'm sorry, boss. They've drawn a blank.'

He winced. 'Oh, for fuck's sake. I really thought we had him. The bastard's had a vasectomy.'

'Yeah, it's looking that way, but there's better news on the cigarette butt.'

'Well, thank fuck for that. Tell me more.'

'Not only did they get viable DNA, but there's a match on the National Database.'

'And?'

Kesey took a deep breath and paused for a beat, milking her moment in the spotlight. 'Peter Spencer. He lives on the big council estate on the outskirts of town.'

'Well, fuck me. His name was mentioned to me by someone Emily works with. I didn't think there was anything in it.'

'I ran a PNC check, but there's not much on record. What do you know about him?'

'I've not dealt with the scrote personally, but I've heard his name mentioned a few times over the years. Domestic violence. He's an obnoxious little git who likes to hit his missus when he's pissed. He needs a fucking good hiding, in my opinion.'

'So, he's violent?'

'Oh yeah, but I didn't see him as a potential murderer.'

'Well, he's right in the frame now.'

'It could be something and nothing, but we've got fuck all else to go with. He's got to be worth a look. And stranger things have happened. Maybe one discarded fag butt's given us our killer.'

'He's got to be worth talking to.'

Grav pushed himself upright, stretched, and delved into one trouser pocket then the other for his car keys. 'So where do we find him?'

She smiled. 'You're going to love this.'

'Try me.'

'He's remanded in Swansea nick after breaking the conditions of an injunction.'

'Since when?'

'It only happened yesterday.'

'Who dealt with it?'

'Child protection.'

'So, the dates fit. He could have killed her.'

'Yeah, it's possible.'

'Well, at least he's not going anywhere, small mercies and all that.'

'That's what I thought.'

Grav opened a metal filing cabinet and took out a notepad. 'Come on, let's pay the scrote a visit. You can do the driving. I didn't get much sleep last night; my back's fucking killing me.'

'I've got some painkillers in my bag, if you need them?'

He shook his head. 'No, you're all right, I took some before leaving the house. I mustn't overdo it. They play havoc with my stomach.'

'Are we going to interview Spencer at the prison?'

'Yeah, we'll have a quick chat with him and bring him back here to question him on tape, if we think there's anything in it. I'll give the nick a quick call en route and tell them to expect us. Let's see what he's got to say for himself and proceed from there.'

Kesey picked up her wax jacket. 'The way I see it, the butt hadn't been on the riverbank long – it was relatively fresh, we know that. It would have been significantly more degraded, if it had. Spencer may have killed her, he may have been an accomplice or, at the very least, he was there at the scene of the crime shortly before, or very soon after, she was killed.'

Grav followed on as they approached the lift. 'You're not wrong, love. I couldn't have summarised the situation better myself. Let's hope the bastards had a vasectomy. If he has, we've got him.'

Chapter 14

It took Kesey just over an hour to drive the approximate forty miles to HMP Swansea in the Sandfields area of the sprawling Welsh seaside city. She parked the Mondeo in Oystermouth Road, directly below the high Victorian granite walls, and the two officers hurried to the main entrance as the grey skies filled the air with icy drizzle that threatened to turn to snow at any minute.

The enthusiastic young guard on the main door checked the officers' names against a list of expected visitors and waved them through almost immediately, rather than engaging in the potentially lengthy security procedures that could accompany such visits.

DI Gravel led the way through the prison's familiar corridors to interview room two as instructed, and they waited while a less than enthusiastic prison officer escorted Peter Spencer from the remand prisoners' unit.

The police officers remained seated behind a small rectangular table when the two men entered the starkly lit room a short time later. Grav glared at Spencer, introduced himself, gave DS Kesey time to do likewise, and gestured for him to take a seat opposite them.

As Spencer sat in brooding silence, Grav turned to the guard who was still standing a few feet to their left. 'We don't need you to stay, thanks, mate. I'll give you a shout when we're done.'

The prison officer approached the door and spoke without looking back. 'Okay, ring the bell on the wall behind you when you're finished. I'll need to get him back in his cell.'

Grav rested his palms on the grimy table and stared directly at Spencer, who held his gaze for a moment before suddenly looking away. 'I hear you're not particularly enjoying your stay at the tax payers' expense, Peter. Aren't the facilities up to your exacting standards? Five-star for the criminal classes.'

'I'm only here because of my fucking solicitor. The man's a git.'

Grav sneered. 'Oh, give me a break. You're a nasty little slimeball. A waste of fucking space. It's about time you were banged up. You've avoided justice for long enough.'

Spencer looked ready to explode. His eyes popped. 'That cunt Turner caused all this shit. He told me to threaten the missus to shut her up; he told me to threaten my own fucking kids, and then, he didn't even bother turning up at the police station when it all went tits up. What the fuck's that about?'

'Are we supposed to believe that crap?'

'And that bitch social worker persuaded Tina not to drop the case. She always drops the fucking case. It never gets this far.'

Grav laughed, head back, mercury fillings in full view. 'I'll have to find out who this social worker is and thank her personally. I'd like to shake her by the hand. I like her already.'

'I want to make a formal complaint about Turner. He stitched me up. I want his fucking job.'

Grav shook his head dismissively. 'We don't give a toss about Turner. He's not our problem. If you want to make a complaint, talk to the Law Society. We're here to talk to you about something else, something a lot more serious.'

Spencer winced, hunching his back and making himself smaller. 'I've been charged. I'm waiting to go back to court. I've got fuck all else to say.'

Grav relaxed in his seat and focused on the prisoner with veined, bloodshot eyes, as Kesey took the lead, speaking in soft Brummie tones that contrasted dramatically with the inspector's brash approach. 'Where were you last Sunday night and early Monday morning?'

'I had a few pints in the White Horse and went back to my mother's place at about ten o'clock to crash out. I picked up a curry at that Chinese in King Street. Plenty of people saw me, if you want some names. It's not a problem.'

'Did you go out again?'

'Not until Monday morning. What's it matter?'

'What time Monday morning?'

'About eleven o'clock. Maybe a bit later. I felt like shit.'

'Can your mother confirm that?'

'She was staying at her sister's place. There was just me and the dog.'

'So, you haven't got an alibi?'

'Alibi? Why the fuck would I need an alibi? I didn't go anywhere near my missus if that's where this is going.'

'Have you had a vasectomy, Peter?'

He looked puzzled. 'What the fuck are you asking me that for?'

'Just answer the question. Being obstructive won't achieve anything. We can always check your medical records, if we need to. You're just going to piss off my DI even more than you already have.'

'All right, yes, I've had a fucking vasectomy. Are you happy now? The missus didn't want any more kids. The GP arranged it. There's no crime in that, is there? What's the problem?'

She hid her excitement as best she could. 'And do you smoke, Peter?'

He sat up in his seat as his desire for a nicotine hit became virtually unbearable. 'Yeah, I'm fucking gagging. Some big bastard nicked the last of my fags.'

'You smoke, don't you, boss?'

Grav met her eyes. 'Yeah, cigars. Why do you ask?'

'Perhaps Mr Spencer could have one when we're finished, what do you think? Have you got one to spare?'

Grav took a packet of five from the inside pocket of his tweed jacket, opened it slowly, and peered in. 'I've only got three left.'

She smiled. 'You could spare one, couldn't you, boss?'

He paused. 'Maybe, if he fully cooperates.'

Kesey turned her attention back to Spencer, who resembled a hungry mongrel begging for a treat. 'Do you ever walk on the riverbank, Peter?'

He tensed as the interview took another unexpected turn. 'What the fuck are you talking about? Where's this going now?'

'It's a simple enough question. Do you ever walk along the bank of the Towy near Caerystwyth?'

He stared into space for a few seconds before responding. 'I used to do a bit of fishing. Sewin, salmon, bass, that sort of thing. And I had a fucking licence, if that's what you're wondering. Poaching's not my thing. You can't get me on that one.'

'When was the last time you went fishing?'

He shook his head slowly, once to the right and once to the left. 'It was fucking years back. Why'd you ask?'

'How many years are we talking? One, two, three, more?'

'More, fucking more. I haven't been fishing since the first kid was born. I lost interest. What the fuck does it matter?'

Kesey paused briefly before asking her next question. 'So just to be clear, you're claiming you haven't been on the riverbank more recently?'

'No, I fucking well haven't. How many times do I need to say it?'

She pressed her lips together. 'Do you need time to think, Peter? Take your time. No pressure. This matters.'

'I haven't been near the river. You can ask me the same fucking question for the rest of the day, if you want to, but the answer's not going to change. I have not been anywhere near the fucking river, not for years. Is that clear enough for you?'

Grav moved with surprising speed for a man of his age and fleshy build, crashing a palm down on the table and causing Spencer to retreat in his seat. 'You're lying to us, Peter. That's never a good idea; I'm not a forgiving man.'

Spencer was close to tears now, twitching like a junkie in need of drugs. 'I want to go back to my cell.'

Grav reached out, grabbed him by his shirtfront, and dragged him across the table. He held him there, with their noses almost touching, relishing the up-close and personal fear in his eyes, before throwing him back in his seat.

'I want to go back to my fucking cell.'

Grav stood, formed his right hand into a tight fist, and winked at Kesey who grabbed his arm and pulled him back. 'Let me talk to him alone, boss. There's no need for all that. He told us about the vasectomy. He's not being uncooperative. You're not, are you, Peter?'

'No, I'm fucking well not!'

Grav stood there, panting hard, his blood pressure slowly reducing from its dangerous high. 'You talk to the bastard; I need some fresh air. His stink's starting to get to me.'

Kesey waited for her boss to leave the room and close the door behind him, before speaking again in breathy, urgent tones. 'It would be a really good idea to tell me everything before he comes back, Peter. I can only control him for so long. He's got one hell of a temper – he's handy with his fists. I've seen him give people a serious hiding before now.'

'The man's a fucking maniac.'

'I'd advise you to start talking. He'll come back. There's no way of avoiding it. He always comes back.'

Spencer was close to panic now, his voice betraying his emotions. 'I don't know what the fuck the two of you are talking about. Have I had a vasectomy? Do I smoke? Have I been near the fucking river? I'm here for giving my missus a few slaps. What the fuck's that lot got to do with anything?'

'Now, I want you to think carefully. I'm going to ask you one last time. Have you been on the bank of the Towy, anywhere between Caerystwyth town and Johnstown Railway Bridge recently?'

He shook his head frantically and shouted, 'No, I fucking well haven't,' as Grav listened outside the door.

'Is that your final answer? You're absolutely certain?'

He replied in the affirmative as Grav burst into the room. 'Then how do you explain the fact that a cigarette butt with your DNA on it was found there by DS Kesey? A fresh butt. Thrown to the floor and discarded not long before you were banged up. Can you answer that one for me before I punch your face in?'

Spencer cowered in his seat. 'It's a fag butt. Just a fag butt. What's it fucking matter?'

Grav lowered himself back into his seat and leaned towards the prisoner. 'Oh, it matters, Peter, because it was found immediately next to the body of a murdered girl. Can you explain that for me? Now would be a good time to start talking – I'm not a patient man.'

Spencer stared open-mouthed, attempting to register and compute the unfathomable. 'That can't be. I haven't been anywhere near the fucking place. It's got to be a mistake.'

Grav laughed dismissively. 'Oh, I think I'll trust the DNA results. They tend to be a lot more reliable than lying gits like you. If that's the best you've got, you're well and truly screwed.'

'I want a solicitor. I'm saying fuck all else until I've got a solicitor.'

'Have it your way. We can talk more at the station.'

'I'm going nowhere.'

Grav reached out and grabbed Spencer's sleeve, clutching it tightly and not letting go. 'I'm arresting you on suspicion of murder. You do not have to say anything. But it may harm your defence, if you do not mention when questioned something that you later rely on in court. Anything you do say may be given in evidence.'

Spencer was weeping now, the tears running down his pasty, sun-deprived face. 'This is fucking m-mad. I haven't done anything. I'm innocent. I didn't touch the bitch.'

The DI glared at him with a look of undiluted disdain. 'Put the cuffs on, Sergeant, nice and tight until the bastard's squirming. Mr Spencer's going to join us in Caerystwyth Police Station. I'll just sort out the necessary paperwork, and we'll be on our way.'

Chapter 15

Grav hurried across the car park at Caerystwyth, dragging Peter Spencer towards the cells, as Laura Kesey locked the car and followed close behind. Their prisoner had said very little during the journey – beyond repeatedly protesting his innocence with increasing desperation, as his words fell on predictably deaf ears.

The DI opened a cell, flung his prisoner inside, and stood at the open door. 'You may never see the outside world again. A whole life sentence without any chance of parole. Tina shacked up with someone new; your kids calling him Dad. How do you fancy that?'

'I haven't fucking well done anything.'

'It might be an idea to start cooperating before I throw the book at you. You're going down, Peter. It's just a matter of for how long, and what happens when you get there. It would not be a good idea to piss me off more than you already have. You're still a young man. A whole life sentence could be a very long time.'

Spencer retreated to the very back of his cell that stank of stale urine. 'I want a solicitor. I'm saying fuck all else until I get a solicitor.'

Grav slammed the door shut, peered through the open hatch, and grinned. 'And which particular legal genius did you have in mind? I'm assuming Charles Turner won't be required, given your recent slanderous claims. He may well be suing you for the little you've got left.'

'It was the truth, nothing but the truth. Get that into your thick head.'

Grav grinned. 'Of course, it was. You're a fucking comedian.'

Spencer kicked the wall hard and yelped. 'Just get me someone else, anyone other than Turner; I'm going to have that fucker's job.'

Grav raised his hand to the side of his head in mock salute. 'Yes, sir, anything you say, sir. I'll contact the duty solicitor as soon as I've had a bite to eat and a nice cup of tea. They're usually next to fucking useless, but we'll hang on and make a start once they arrive. Anything to please a valued guest like yourself.'

'You do that, you snarky bastard.'

'You're a killer, Peter, and I'm going to prove it. You're going down for a long, long time.'

Spencer glared at the cell door, lost in a sea of despair, as Grav turned and walked away. 'I haven't done anything. How many times do I have to tell you? I haven't fucking well done anything.'

The two officers sat opposite their prisoner and an exhausted-looking duty solicitor in a badly creased business suit, who couldn't have appeared less enthusiastic if paid to. 'Put the tape on, Sergeant. I think we'll make a start.'

Kesey reached out and flicked the switch. 'It's done, boss.'

'It's five twenty-five p.m. on Thursday the eleventh of January 2001. I'm Detective Inspector Gareth Gravel, also present is Detective Sergeant Laura Kesey, the interviewee, Mr Peter Spencer, and his solicitor, Mr Jeremy Ward. I need to advise you, Mr Spencer, that you are still under caution. Anything you say could be used in evidence against you if the case comes to court at a future date. Do you understand?'

Spencer nodded his reluctant confirmation.

'For the tape please, Mr Spencer, we need to hear you say it.'

'I'm not a fucking idiot.'

'So, you understand?'

'Yes, I understand.'

The DI took a glossy colour photo from a cardboard file and pushed it across the table. 'Take a good look at that, Peter. The young lady was found murdered, on the bank of the Towy near Caerystwyth, on the eighth of this month. She'd been raped and strangled. We have very good reason to believe that you killed her.'

Spencer glanced at the photo and quickly looked away. 'No fucking way! That's got fuck all to do with me.'

'The killer's had a vasectomy. You've had a vasectomy, haven't you, Peter? You told us that yourself.'

'You know I fucking well have, but that doesn't mean I killed the bitch. I'm not the only man in Wales to have had the snip; there must be loads of us.'

Kesey placed a clear plastic evidence bag, containing a single cigarette butt, on the table. 'This was found close to the victim's head. It has your DNA on it. Please explain.'

'How many times do I have to say it? I haven't got a fucking clue how it got there. It's a fucking stitch up.'

Grav leaned towards his prisoner. 'You're going to have to do a lot better than that. It didn't materialise out of thin air.'

'I haven't been anywhere near the river, not for years. I haven't even been in that part of town. Either it's a mistake, or someone put it there.'

The DI handed him the second photograph and watched his reaction. 'What size feet have you got?'

Spencer stared at the image of a faint footprint in the dark river mud. 'That's not mine. No fucking way is that mine.'

The DI grinned. 'So, what size are your shoes? It's a simple enough question. What's the answer?'

'Eight, size fucking eight, if you must know.'

The two officers glanced at each other knowingly before Grav spoke again. 'A size eight footprint was found immediately next to the murdered girl, within inches of her cold and battered body.'

'It's not fucking mine!'

Grav met his eyes. 'Perhaps now would be a good time to summarise: there's your long history of violence towards women, the semen sample, the cigarette butt, and now the footprint. This isn't going well for you, Peter. It might be an idea to start talking.'

The duty solicitor shuffled some papers to no effect. 'I'd like to consult with my client privately.'

Spencer jumped to his feet. 'This is a setup. It's mad. I've done fuck all. It's a fucking setup.'

Kesey took his arm. 'Sit down, Mr Spencer. Just answer our questions. That's all you've got to do.'

The duty solicitor spoke out again, more insistently this time. 'I'd like some time alone with my client.'

To everyone's surprise, Spencer glared at Ward and shook his head. 'No. I've got nothing to hide; I'm an innocent man. I just want to get this shit over with.'

Grav couldn't believe his luck. 'You want to continue?'

'Just get on with it.'

'You don't want a break, despite your solicitor's advice?'

'Just ask your fucking questions. The quicker I'm back in Swansea nick, the happier I'll be.'

Kesey took three further photographs from the file and lay them side by side about an inch apart. 'We believe that these young women were victims of the same killer. As of now, you're our most likely suspect.'

Spencer dry gagged, swallowed, and gagged again. 'This is fucking ridiculous. I gave my missus a few miserable slaps when I was pissed and threatened her, I'll put my hands up to that.' He pushed the photos away from him. 'But that lot's got fuck all to do with me.'

The DS returned the photos to their original positions. 'Look at them. Take a good look at what you did; that's down to you.'

'No fucking way!'

'Where were you on the third of October last year?'

Spencer was repeatedly blinking now. 'How the fuck am I supposed to know the answer to that?'

'What about the sixth of November, can you give us an alibi for that date?'

He shook his head forlornly as Grav glared at him and said, 'You're not doing very well are you, Peter? How about I give you one last chance before we charge you with murder?'

Spencer looked ready to puke.

'Where were you on the fifth of December? It's only a few weeks back. Surely even you can answer that one. Go on surprise me.'

Spencer relaxed in his seat as his tension melted away. 'Are you saying that's when one of the girls was murdered?'

'What's your point?'

He laughed out loud. 'Are you saying the bitch was murdered here in Wales?'

Grav glared at him and hissed through gritted teeth, 'What's so funny about a young woman losing her life so tragically? Does her death amuse you? It seems that way to me.'

'She was killed here, wasn't she? Or you fucking jokers wouldn't be investigating the crime.'

'Her body was found in Trinity Field. That's about ten minutes' drive from your home address. We believe you killed her there. Do you find that as funny? Are you laughing now?'

Spencer broke into a smile that gradually evolved into a full-blown laugh that caused his chest to heave as he guffawed loudly.

Grav formed his hands into tight fists below the table. 'What's so funny, Spencer? You are seriously winding me up.'

'We were visiting the missus' mother's place in Newcastle. It was her seventieth birthday on the fourth. We travelled up on the third and stayed for a week. That's an alibi, isn't it, Inspector? There's witnesses, lots of them, and not all family. You've got fuck all.'

Grav reached across the table and switched off the tape. 'Get this bastard back to Swansea, Laura. He's wasted enough of our time already.'

'You don't want to keep him here until we've checked his story and searched his mother's place?'

'Oh, we'll do that all right; we'll check everything. We'll search the house, we'll interview the witnesses, and we'll check any cameras between here and Newcastle. I can promise you that. If the bastard's lying, we'll drag him back here, kicking and fucking screaming.' In his heart, though, he knew his prisoner's claims would prove to be true. Peter Spencer wasn't the man they were looking for.

Chapter 16

Grav sat opposite Doctor Jenny Rees, his GP for over twenty years, and unbuttoned his shirt as instructed. She listened to his heartbeat for thirty seconds or so before returning to her seat with the hint of a frown on her heavily lined face. 'You can do your shirt up.'

Grav fastened three buttons, left the top one open, and stuffed his polyester tie into his trouser pocket. 'What's the verdict, Doc? Have I passed the MOT?'

'You've got angina. You know that. And you're not looking after yourself like you should be. You need to take this seriously if you want to live for very much longer.'

'I'm taking the tablets you gave me. What more do you want?'

She shook her head, exasperated to be having the exact same conversation yet again. 'Come on, up you get. Let's get you weighed.'

'Oh, do I have to? You weighed me the last time I saw you.'

'Let's just get on with it, shall we? Is there really a need to be so damned awkward every single time?'

He stepped on the scales.

'You've put on another four pounds.'

'Only four? It could be worse.'

The doctor returned to her seat for a second time and waited for Grav to do likewise. 'Morbidly obese is the technical term. You're about five stone overweight. It's time to do something about it.'

'Yeah, but I had my shoes on.'

'They're not made of lead, are they? What happened to the diet sheets I gave you?'

'They're in the house somewhere.'

'Have you thought of actually reading them?'

Grav shook his head. 'It's this case I'm dealing with. It's all-consuming. I'll focus on the diet once we've caught the bastard. There's too much happening just now to think about losing weight.'

'There's always some excuse. You've been saying the same thing for years. How much beer are you drinking these days?'

'Seven or eight pints.'

'A week?'

'A day.'

She shook her head and scowled. 'What about the whisky?'

'One or two a week.'

'Glasses?'

'Bottles.'

'For goodness sake, Grav, how you've survived for as long as you have is a complete mystery to me. You're in a high-stress job; your blood pressure's through the roof, and your lifestyle's tantamount to suicide. Please tell me you've cut down on the cigars?'

This time it was his turn to shake his head. 'I've tried, but with the pressures of work and all that, I need them like food and drink. They keep me sane.'

The doctor's glasses slipped to the tip of her nose. 'Why have you bothered coming to see me? You don't listen to a single word I say. If all my patients were as stubborn as you, I'd give up and go and lie on a beach somewhere warm for the rest of my life.'

'I need some more tablets.'

She picked up her prescription pad and sighed. 'Is that it?'

'Yeah.'

'Just ring in next time. There's a good lad. Don't waste my time unless you're willing to take some responsibility for your health. I haven't got a magic wand I can wave. The tablets can help, but they're not enough in themselves.'

'What good did it do Heather? She was doing all the right things, but she was the one who died.'

'Fucking cancer! There, I've said it for you.'

Grav smiled thinly. 'Precisely.'

'Have you thought about retirement?'

'Funnily enough, my detective chief superintendent asked me the exact same thing fairly recently. I think she wants me gone.'

'And what did you say in reply?'

'That they'd have to drag me out of the police station when the day finally comes. If I'm not a copper, what the hell am I?'

'You might live a bit longer, if you pack the job in. Have you thought about that?'

'Yeah, but would I want to, Doc? You know exactly what I'm talking about. You're still here, after all these years. You're even older than I am.'

Jenny Rees scribbled her virtually indecipherable signature in black ink and handed him his prescription with a trembling hand. 'You'll be looking for a new doctor, if there's any more of that. There's only so much of your cheek I'll take, however long we've known each other.'

He stood up and smiled. 'Thanks, Jenny, it's appreciated as always.'

'Look after yourself, Grav. And get yourself straight to casualty if those chest pains get any worse. You're a heart attack waiting to happen.'

Chapter 17

Charles Turner loved the world wide web. It provided opportunities. Easy access to potential victims, that's what he told himself, and he used it to his full advantage at every opportunity. He'd created numerous false identities, being careful to protect his identity, and targeted carefully chosen young women who met his preferred victim profile perfectly. They had to be just right. No compromises. The right height, the right build, the right level of intelligence – that was especially important. What was the point of a victim who didn't fully appreciate the hopelessness of her predicament when she finally faced death? The hunt was amusing; the period of imprisonment entertaining and informative as they struggled and begged and pleaded for release, but it was that final moment that made all the risks worthwhile. The shock, the disbelief, and then, their final resigned acceptance. Wonderful! And it was time to do it all again. Time for the next in line. Yes, the long game provided an acceptable distraction; Emily's time would eventually come – when it best suited him. When she'd fully served her purpose. But what about the now?

The solicitor lay back on his king-sized bed, opened his laptop, adjusted his reading glasses, and stared at the screen. There were four candidates on his current shortlist. Four young women ideally qualified to fulfil his wants and needs. But which one to choose?

He unfastened his trousers and slipped a hand into his underpants as he studied the first profile. Sally, lovely Sally. Her hair was right, her figure just about spot on, and she was a graduate too. That was in her favour. But was it worth driving all the way to London to collect her? It wasn't totally out of the question, but surely there had to be a more convenient alternative online, or in the red-light districts he'd hunted to good effect in the past. Someone who lived outside the immediate area, but not too far away.

He began moving his hand up and down, increasing his rhythm, as he studied option two: Zoe, a nice enough name. She met all his requirements. A neck that needed squeezing, and she lived in Cardiff. An art student, she'd do, wouldn't she? Of *course* she…would. Ah, she was almost perfect. Why look any further? The remaining three could wait for another day. It wasn't as if they were going anywhere.

He moved his hand faster still, let out a loud, wide-mouthed groan as he ejaculated, and wiped himself with the corner of the cotton quilt cover before picking up his laptop and typing:

Hello Zoe, it's Michael. How are you doing?

Her reply was almost instantaneous.

Oh, hi, Michael, I was hoping to hear from you again. How's life with you? Are you still managing the gallery?

He laughed. It was easy, almost too easy. She was like a lemming: rushing towards a cliff edge, desperate to jump off.

All's good, thanks. Couldn't be better. And, yes, that's why I'm contacting you. I've had a cancellation. If you'd like an exhibition, now's the time.

Really? I haven't sold a single painting yet. Not even one!

Well, now's your chance to change all that. Van Gogh had the same experience. He was ahead of his time.

I love his stuff.

I was very impressed by the digital images you sent me. You're a unique artist, a new fresh and innovative talent in the world of art.

LOL. My lecturers don't seem to think so.

You know what they say. Those who can't do, teach. They're fools. They lack the required insight to identify real talent. Ignore them. I'm glad to have discovered you. An exhibition would be good for you and good for the gallery, I'm certain of it. We'll get your name out there and make a few quid in the process. It's time to let the art-buying public know all about you. It's your time.

Thank you so very much. I really can't believe my luck. When have you got in mind?

It's a last-minute cancellation. We'll need to act quickly if you'd like to make the most of the opportunity. It'll take a couple of days to display your work to its very best advantage. Can you get to Caerystwyth tonight? We badly need to get on with things, if you want to go ahead with an exhibition.

Oh, I'm a poor student. I haven't got a car.

What about a bus, or a train?

I could catch a bus, but what about the paintings? Some of them are a bit on the large side.

Ah, yes, of course, I should have thought. But no worries, if you get the paintings ready, I could pick you up in a couple of hours and take everything straight to the gallery. How does that sound?

She paused for a second or two before responding.

Is this for real? I can't believe it's happening. Things like this just don't happen to me.

Well, it's happening now, but no pressure. It's up to you. Shall we go for it?

Oh, why not? It means missing a few lectures, but I'd regret it forever if I didn't take advantage of such a great opportunity. They don't come along very often. My friends are going to be seriously jealous. They'll wish it was them.

That's excellent, Zoe, you've made the right decision. I'll pick you up at eight o'clock sharp, if that's convenient?

That would be great. Thank you!

How many paintings are we talking?

I've got twenty-one altogether. I hope that's not too many?

Twelve would be ideal, given the wall space, but let's bring them all. We can decide which to display to your best advantage once they're in situ. I'll borrow a van from a friend, rather than bring my car. That seems best. We wouldn't get the bigger ones in my convertible.

This is all very exciting. I can't wait!

I just need your address.

She began typing again and sent it with the click of a button.

Got it. I'll see you at eight sharp. I'm glad to be a part of your journey from obscurity to fame in the art world. We're all provided with signposts that lead us towards our destiny. You've had the wisdom to follow them. Not everyone has the courage or foresight to do that. Congratulations! Your life's about to change forever.

The aged, ill-kept van, on indefinite loan from a criminal contact who owed him, wasn't the most reliable form of transport, but it served its purpose with its unremarkable appearance and cloned number plates. It took Turner approximately ninety minutes to reach Cathays, the heart of Cardiff's studentville, and another ten to finally locate Zoe's shared lodgings in a surprisingly quiet side street, with adequate parking spaces on both sides of the road. He switched off the tired engine and exited the vehicle, raised his coat collar high, and pulled his peaked cap low to cover as much of his face as possible.

Turner approached the three-storey student abode in the orange sodium glow of the street lamps and pressed the middle of five bells as instructed. He only had to wait a matter of seconds before a slim, nineteen-year-old student, with purple hair, opened the door with a beaming smile on her pretty face.

He stood and stared, momentarily unsure of what to say or do.

'Is that you, Michael?'

'Yes, yes, it is.'

'Is everything all right? I've got the paintings ready; just like you told me to.'

He swallowed twice, resisting the impulse to scream at her and hit out. 'You've done something different to your hair. It was ginger in your photo.'

Her smile disappeared as quickly as it had appeared. 'Is there a problem?'

The bitch, the total fucking bitch. 'No, not at all, I just didn't recognise you at first, that's all.'

She smiled again. 'Are you going to come in for a cup of something before we head off? I could introduce you to my friends. They'd love to meet you.'

He pushed up his sleeve and made a show of checking his watch, looking at it for a second longer than necessary. 'No, we'd better make a move. The quicker we get to the gallery, the better. I don't want to leave it too late. I've an early start in the morning.'

Zoe glanced behind her into the dimly lit communal hallway. 'Okay, everything's ready and waiting. Where did you park the van?'

He considered walking away in search of more suitable prey but decided to stand his ground. The purple colour could pose potential difficulties – the dyeing process may prove more complicated than usual – but it was far from insurmountable. The purple-headed caterpillar standing before him could morph into a beautiful butterfly in his hands. A Red Admiral ready to die.

'Are you okay, Michael?'

He shook himself, suddenly back in the present. 'Sorry, I was lost in thought. It happens sometimes. I was just wondering about the best places to publicise your work. I can get the local papers involved easily enough, maybe even the nationals. We can have a chat about it on the way.'

She beamed. 'Shall we take the paintings to the van? The rain seems to have stopped.'

He nodded and followed her into the hallway. 'Yes, time's getting on, and it's a good omen. The universe is smiling on us. The van's just outside, let's get it done.'

Chapter 18

Grav stretched out on his three-seater settee, closed his veined and bloodshot eyes, and waited for the debilitating pressure in his chest to subside. He manoeuvred himself upright, placed a soluble aspirin on his tongue, and washed it down with a generous slurp of twelve-year-old Scotch whisky. He wasn't getting any younger. He'd seen and heard too much. Maybe retirement wasn't such a bad idea after all.

He looked across the room to where a silver-framed photo of his deceased, much loved wife of thirty years sat in pride of place on top of the television. 'I've been to see the doc again, love, like you told me to. She gave me some more of those tablets I've been taking. Not that they're doing much good. The chest pains are getting worse by the day.'

He lifted the bottle to his mouth and gulped down another generous measure, savouring the malty spirit as it warmed his throat. 'You're quiet this evening, love. Nothing to say for yourself?'

He took off his shoes, lay back down, and rested his head on the armrest. 'So, what do you think about Emily coming back home? That was a turn up for the books. The killer's still on the prowl; she could have timed it better.'

He closed his eyes and heard her whispering in his ear, as if she was still with him, as if she hadn't died. *Don't go changing the subject. I know your game.*

He smiled, picturing her face as clear as day. 'What the hell are you talking about, woman?'

If you put on any more weight, you'll have trouble getting through the door.

'Yeah, that's what the doc said. I've put on another four pounds, apparently.'

So, what are you going to do about it, Grav?

He sighed. 'Maybe I'll be with you sooner than you think.'

What about the investigation? What about those poor girls? You need to think about them before giving up on life. They deserve justice. It's your job to give it to them.

Grav took another slurp of whisky. 'I'm struggling, love. Maybe I'm losing it. My mind's not as sharp as it was. I've been in the job too long.'

He pictured her, shaking her head and wagging her finger in that familiar way of hers, and he knew what was coming next. *Oh, come on. That doesn't sound like the Grav I know and love. You've got a murderer to catch. Now's not the time for wallowing in self-pity. You need to focus and get on with the job.*

'I know, love, believe me, I know.'

Well, do something about it, then. Put down that bottle and concentrate on the investigation. You've put away a lot of serious villains. You're a good detective. You need to remember that.

He threw aside the bottle, spraying the carpet with golden liquid. 'I was good, one of the best, but maybe not so much anymore. Maybe I've lost my edge. Perhaps it's time to pack it all in.'

He opened his eyes and saw her, drifting in and out of focus, with a frown on her girlish face. *Right, it's time to get off that sofa, take a shower, and get back to work. If this is going to be your last case, you've got to go out on a high. Catch the swine. People are counting on you. I'm counting on you. I don't want you to let anyone down.*

Grav lowered his legs to the floor and lifted himself upright. 'All right, love, I hear you. One last time. I'll nail the bastard if it's the last thing I do.'

Chapter 19

Charles Turner took Zoe directly to his imposing Victorian home on returning to Caerystwyth, alleviating her initial concerns with what he considered surprising ease. 'I've forgotten the keys, Zoe, but not to worry. Collect the keys, a quick cup of coffee, and we'll be at the gallery in no time at all. It's only ten minutes away.'

Her breathing quickened as she questioned his motives, but she relaxed immediately on first sight of his house. 'Wow, nice place. Impressive!'

He smiled. 'Yeah, it's not bad. I bought it for cash about five years ago. I like to think of it as a reward for the gallery's success. All the hard work paid off for me, and it can do the same for you.'

She'd had her doubts during the journey. Nagging doubts that wouldn't let up, whatever she said to herself. But the house, and the stylish two-seater convertible sports car parked on the sweeping driveway, silenced Zoe's feelings of anxiety. 'It's huge. The garage is almost as big as my parents' place.'

Turner opened the garage's double doors with the click of a button and drove straight into the roomy concrete building before switching off the diesel engine and closing the doors behind them. He led Zoe through a side door and into a spectacular kitchen that was meant to impress, and invariably did. 'Take a seat at the table; tea or coffee? I drink double espresso with a little local cold-pressed honey myself. It's delicious. Do you want to try it?'

She glanced around the room with a quick turn of her head. 'That'll be lovely, thanks. What a great place. It's like something out of a glossy interior design magazine.'

'I like to think so.'

'Is there a bathroom I can use?'

He smiled warmly. 'Second door on the right. No need to go upstairs. Do you fancy a quick bite to eat? A sandwich perhaps, or some biscuits?'

'No, I'm good, ta. I had something before you picked me up. I've never got much of an appetite.'

Turner poured the strong coffee into two cups and took a small, plastic bottle, containing a thick green syrup, from a cupboard next to the range cooker. He glanced behind him, confirming that Zoe hadn't returned, before adding what he considered to be just the right amount of benzodiazepine medication to one of the cups, and stirring it vigorously.

Zoe flushed, washed her hands with scented soap and checked her appearance in the illuminated wall-mounted mirror above the sink. She smiled nervously as she re-entered the kitchen. 'You've got a lovely home, the nicest I've seen, but I'm surprised there's no art on the walls. I'd have thought it would be covered in the stuff. Aren't you a collector?'

He stared at her, searching for the right words.

'Are you okay, Michael?'

He picked up her cup and walked towards her. 'Yes, sorry, I was thinking about the exhibition. I'm surrounded by art all day at work and tend to keep my walls blank at home. I think that's a creation of sorts itself, don't you?'

She looked at him with a puzzled expression that evaporated as he handed her coffee to her. 'Yes, I guess so, a homage to minimalism.'

He lifted his cup to his lips and sipped, hoping she'd do likewise. 'I knew you'd understand. You're special; not everyone's blessed with your degree of insight.'

Zoe blushed. 'That's very kind; I don't know what to say.'

'Try your coffee.'

She lifted her cup to her mouth. 'It tastes a little strange.'

'It's a special blend that's not available in the shops. I import it directly from Columbia. I felt sure you'd like it. You seem like a girl who appreciates the finer things in life.'

Zoe laughed. 'Chance would be a fine thing.'

'Oh, your life's about to change forever. That I can guarantee you. I'll introduce you to a world you can't even imagine.'

She sipped her coffee again. Wanting to like it. Desperate to like it.

'Is it growing on you?'

'Yes, I think so. Do you mind if I add a little cold water?'

He pointed towards the Belfast sink. 'Of course not, help yourself.'

She turned on the tap, added a splash, and tasted it again. 'Yes, that's better. It's got an interesting aftertaste, almost medicinal.'

He sat at the breakfast bar and gestured for her to join him. 'Are you sure you won't have something to eat? It's no trouble. I've got a nice vegetarian quiche in the fridge, if you fancy it. I could heat it up, or serve it cold with a light salad and some chutney?'

She raised a trembling hand to her face and rubbed her eyes, which were slowly closing. 'I'm feeling a little lightheaded, would you mind opening a window? I could do with some air.'

He stood and slowly approached the back door, opened it an inch or two, and returned to his seat. 'Is that better for you?'

She yawned expansively. 'Yes, thanks. I'm feeling a little overheated.'

'Finish your coffee. The caffeine should help. It must be all the excitement. You'll be feeling better before you know it.'

She took another gulp as the room became an impressionist blur of bland colours that made no sense at all. 'I'm not feeling very well.'

He studied her carefully. 'Just sit there and rest. There's a good girl. That's all you have to do.'

Zoe attempted to stand, but her legs gave way, and she fell, slowly at first, like a gradually deflating beach toy, and then quickly as she lost her grip on the table's edge and hit the tiled floor, hard. 'What's … what's hap-happening to me?'

Turner jumped to his feet and rushed towards her. He bent down and took her arm in his before dragging her to her feet. 'Come on, up you get. You don't want to sleep down there on the cold tiles. Let's get you upstairs to your room. You'll feel much better in an hour or two after you've had some sleep.'

Turner nudged her with his foot when she didn't respond. 'Come on. You need to make some effort. I'm not in the mood to carry you.'

She turned her head stiffly and looked at him as the room began to spin. 'What ab-bout the…the g-gallery?'

'All in good time, Zoe. You just have to do what you're told for now, nothing more and nothing less. It won't go well for you if you try to struggle – that's never a good idea.'

She was drifting in and out of consciousness now, stumbling repeatedly as he shoved her down the hallway towards the stairs. 'Come on, up you go. For fuck's sake, girl, stay on your feet. One step at a time. Get up there.'

Zoe climbed one step after another as Turner ascended the stairs behind her, shoving her repeatedly and swearing when she slowed, or lost her footing.

'Come on, bitch. Up you go. Two more steps and you're almost there.'

She fell to her knees on reaching the landing and screeched loudly as he grabbed her by the hair and dragged her into the room.

Turner threw her against a cast iron radiator, and slapped her hard when she came around momentarily and tried to pull away. He watched Zoe closely as she drifted into a deep, drug-induced sleep; he screamed in her ear when he thought the time was right, and smiled when she didn't react.

He stood in front of her, spread his legs wide to provide optimum stability, and took each hand in turn, dragging her wrists up towards the black steel shackles that were secured to the wall, above the radiator. It took a lot of effort on his part, but he was a relatively strong man for his size, and within a few minutes, she was hanging, limp and pale, as others had before her.

When Zoe first stirred in the semi-darkness several hours later, she thought, for a glorious but all too fleeting moment, she was waking from a frightening and unpleasant dream that she couldn't begin to comprehend. But all too soon, the pounding in her head and the searing pain in her wrists, arms, and shoulders brought her new reality into sharp, unrelenting focus.

She shouted out, calling for help with increasing volume and urgency, but outside the room, the results were limited to muffled sounds that would be impossible to hear beyond the immediate vicinity. She tried to stand as her blood pressure soared, but both arms jarred against the tight steel cuffs securing her thin wrists, and she fell back to the floor. She hung there shaking, twitching, with a thin stream of yellow urine running down one bare leg and pooling under her. She searched her troubled mind for any potential means of escape and narrowed each hand in turn, attempting to slip them through her manacles. But it was hopeless, utterly hopeless.

Zoe closed her eyes and screamed. The man was a maniac. Why had she trusted him? Despite her misgivings, despite the alarm bells in her head that had gotten louder and louder until she had finally silenced them. She'd been like a child in a sweet shop, clamouring for candy – greedy, needy, desperate for fame.

Turner checked the time, listened intently to the baby alarm, which was plugged in, in one corner of the lounge, and heard more than enough to know she'd finally woken. He jumped from his seat, ran down the hallway, and ascended the staircase two and three steps at a time until he reached the top. He stood outside the door and listened again, amused and gratified to hear the faint sound of weeping coming from inside.

He was laughing as he opened the door and slowly approached her, one considered step at a time, until at touching distance. 'It might be an idea to stop all that pathetic snivelling if you want to survive for very much longer. Just shut up and listen. There's a good girl.'

She screamed out again, and he laughed in response, before suddenly stopping and meeting her eyes. 'I wouldn't waste your energy, if I were you. There's no escape. There's never any escape. My previous guests could tell you that – were they still alive and breathing.'

'Let me g-go. Please l-let me go. I won't t-tell anyone.'

He paused before responding, savouring her increasingly desperate persona. 'Oh, I don't think so. Not after all the trouble I took getting you here in the first place. And you can scream for the rest of the day, if you want to. Scream your little heart out as loud as you like. It won't do you any good, not in the slightest. This room's been comprehensively soundproofed at great expense and to the very highest standards. Only the best will do for my girls. Scream away, Zoe. There's no one to hear you but me.'

She dropped her head and began whimpering as he loomed over her.

'Right, if you'll shut the fuck up and stay still for five minutes, I'm going to dye your hair a lovely shade of copper-blonde. Or at least that's what it says on the box. How does that sound? The mother who abandoned me had much the same hair colour in my recurrent recollections. I can remember her face, her hair, her lavender perfume, and the sound of her voice before she walked away and left me. You want to look your best when they find your body, don't you? I can't strangle her, so you'll have to do.'

Zoe lost control of her bowel as he grabbed her hair tightly and jarred her head towards him. 'Not to worry. It's nature's way of confirming that my methods are working as intended. You're not the first, and I'm sure you won't be the last. I stripped you naked while you slept, so no need to worry about soiling your clothing. And you won't need them again, anyway. I have a rather stylish vintage dress for your final journey. Just wait until you see it. What a way to bow out.'

'Please, I'm b-begging you.'

'I was thinking about leaving your body on a remote beach. What do you think? There's plenty in the area, some within a short drive. But we're getting ahead of ourselves. There's a day or two before then. There's no point in rushing things unnecessarily.'

'Please, no!'

Turner pulled on a pair of rubber gloves and pinned Zoe's head against the wall with one hand while smearing Vaseline over her neck and forehead with the other. 'Hold still, you want to look your best, don't you? It's going to be a lot worse for you if you move even slightly. I could have done this while you slept, but it's a lot more fun this way. I want you to fully appreciate the entire process. I want you to understand exactly what's happening to you.'

She stilled herself, closed her eyes, and held her breath for as long and as often as she could until he finished, loathing the feeling of his fingers on her skin. 'Right, that's done. I'll just mix the dye, and then, we're good to go.'

Zoe opened her eyes wide and stared at him. 'You're totally fucking mad.'

He began running both hands through her hair, applying the mixture, concentrating on the dark roots initially then moving along the entire length of her hair. 'I'm not sure we've got the colour quite right. But, not to worry, we can always repeat the process. I always keep plenty of dye handy. Attention to detail.'

Zoe opened her mouth to speak, but then closed it again when no words came.

'It's nice to chat, don't you think?'

'Water, p-please. I n-need water.'

'My name's Charles, by the way, Charles Arthur Turner; Michael's fiction, a subterfuge; I think it's respectful to introduce oneself properly when appropriate, wouldn't you agree? Society would disintegrate without its mundane niceties.'

'Please, I n-need a d-drink.'

'Why would any mother leave her child? Can you explain that for me? Even animals provide adequate care for their offspring. What made her so very different? Was I really that unlovable?'

'Water, p-please, water.'

He began massaging her head more vigorously and then suddenly stopped and grabbed her throat. 'I think you'll find it's to your advantage to answer my questions with due forethought. That's why I brought you here in the first place. That's why you're still alive, rather than lying somewhere blotchy and cold in a makeshift grave. Please remember that.'

She indicated her reluctant compliance and hated herself for it.

'If you can help me understand, if you can help me explore my caustic past and reach an adequate resolution, I may conclude that you're not as worthless as she was. It's up to you.'

'I'm s-sorry. I don't know what you want me to s-say.'

He gripped either side of her chin between his thumb and fingers and squeezed hard. 'Try again, Zoe. I'm sure you can do much better than that, if you apply yourself properly. Your life depends on it.'

'I'm bleeding. My mouth's b-bleeding.'

He squeezed harder, increasing the pressure and cutting her skin with his thumbnail. 'Answer my questions, bitch. Your non-compliance is starting to anger me, and that's not good news for you. I can be surprisingly unpleasant when provoked. If you're not careful, you'll find out what I'm talking about.'

She tried to pull away as the warm blood ran down her chin and dripped on to her bare chest. 'She m-must have had her r-reasons.'

He began pacing the room. 'Ah, so she had her reasons, did she? That's your considered hypothesis? Are you suggesting that any mitigation she could claim would justify abandoning her only child? Is that what you're trying to say? I really hope it's not, for your sake.'

Zoe searched her troubled mind. 'I'm sure she m-must have loved you.'

He stopped mid-step, turned, and glared at her with a reptile like coldness. 'Oh, you think so, do you? I can't see things going well for you, if that's the best you can come up with. I suggest you think again. Do you hear me? Think again.'

'Maybe she h-had no choice.'

He nodded. 'Interesting, one of my previous guests suggested much the same thing before she died. Perhaps you can come up with something a little more original. Something worth my time and effort; something meaningful.'

'Water, please, c-can I have s-some water. My throat's so d-dry.'

Turner walked towards her and began stroking her face. 'We'll need to leave the dye on for about half an hour, that should suffice. We can decide if we need to repeat the process after we've washed it off. The final results are sometimes affected by the base colour. Frustrating, but that's the way it is. Such things are sent to try us.'

'Please can I h-have a glass of water. My head's p-pounding, and my throat's s-so sore. I'm begging you.'

He held out his hands in front of him and mimicked a panting dog. 'Oh, poor you. That'll be the effects of the drug, I suspect. But, not to worry, I'll tell you what I'm going to do. I'll be heading off to work once we're finished here. There are things I need to do, tasks that require my attention. That should give you more than enough time to come up with something that's worth listening to. If you please me, you can have some water; if you don't, you can't.'

Zoe pulled on her chains in a further hopeless attempt to free herself. 'Let m-me go. Please l-let me g-go.'

He laughed as he approached the door. 'Don't bother trying to escape. No one ever escapes. Save your energy. If you have something worthwhile to say on my return, I'll consider giving you something to eat and drink. How does that sound? I think it's more than reasonable, don't you?'

Zoe gagged, swallowed, and gagged again.

'Aren't you going to thank me? I'm sure Mummy would thank me, were she in your place.'

'Sorry?'

'Where are your manners? You need to say thank you before I go.'

She looked up at him. 'Thank y-you.'

'Again.'

'Thank you.'

'Louder.'

'Thank y-you.'

'Louder.'

'Thank you!'

He broke into a smile that unnerved her further. 'Now that was much better. I do like a cooperative guest. Use your time productively. Think hard about what I've asked you.'

'Please l-let me go.'

He turned away and entered the bathroom, filled a plastic bucket, and returned to his makeshift prison to pour it over her head. 'I'll see you later in the day, Zoe, lovely Zoe. You'll no doubt be pleased to hear that we can talk more then. Hopefully, you'll come up with some answers that satisfy me; something original, something inspired. Think of it as an exam you have to pass with flying colours. Succeed, and I may let you live for a time. Fail, and you die.'

Chapter 20

Grav knocked on Detective chief superintendent Hannah Davies' door and walked into her roomy office without waiting to be invited. 'All right, ma'am, I thought it was time for a catch-up.'

'You took your time.'

'What are you getting at?'

'Didn't Laura give you my message?'

He shrugged. 'Yeah, she said something, but there was a lot of background noise. I must have got the wrong end of the stick. It's easily done.'

'Take a seat, Grav. And you can drop the bullshit. I might not have your years of frontline experience, but I'm not a complete muppet. I suggest you remember that. You're on very thin ice as it is.'

Grav sat as instructed. 'What's this about?'

'The chief constable's had the Home Secretary on the phone. He's not a happy man, and that's putting it mildly. He wants the killer caught, and quickly.'

'What does he think we're all trying to do twenty-four hours a day, seven days a fucking week? I'm practically living here.'

'It's results that matter in today's world. You know that as well as I do. We need something positive to say. Have you made any significant progress?'

'I thought we'd cracked it for a time, but, no, we're back where we started.'

'But you've identified the four victims, yes?'

He nodded. 'Three with certainty, the fourth maybe. We're still trying to track down a relative or someone who knew her well.'

'What about dental records?'

'The Manchester force has been making some enquiries for us, but no joy.'

'Have the victims got anything in common? Any links that could point us in the right direction?'

'Well, two of them were sex workers; you know that. Girls who'd had problematic childhoods, spent time in local authority care, and become addicts as teenagers. But our local girl had no history of drug use or prostitution, not a hint. They're young women, unlucky enough to be targeted by a predatory killer; that's the common factor. He's casting the net wide, hunting in various parts of the country and killing them on our patch. Unless we get a lucky break, it's not going to be easy to identify him.'

'Do you think he's a local man?'

Grav nodded. 'He knows our area well, that seems obvious enough. He either lives here, has lived here, or comes here on a regular basis. We've got to consider itinerant men who move from place to place; men whose employment lends itself to travelling around the country, such as lorry drivers, salesmen, or those in military service. There's the bases in Pembrokeshire, and the Irish ferries. We're not short of military personnel and HGV drivers passing through the force area. It could be any of them.'

'What's your gut feeling?'

'Profiling suggests it's likely that we're looking for a local white man in his twenties or thirties of average intelligence.'

'Yes, I appreciate that, but what do *you* think? You've been a detective for a long time. This isn't the first murder case you've dealt with. You must have your own opinions?'

'Profiles are a starting point, nothing more. They're not always as helpful as you'd want them to be.'

Davies sighed. 'Yes, I was thinking along the same lines... Have you got time for a coffee?'

He glanced at the wall clock to his right. 'Yeah, why not?'

She picked up her phone and dialled her secretary's number. 'Two coffees, please, Abby; my usual, and white for the inspector.

And bring the sugar bowl.' She turned back to him. 'Tell me, Grav, did you read my latest press release?'

'Yeah, no problem, it said everything it needed to say.'

'It's been all over the media. Has anyone contacted us?'

'We've had the usual nutters ringing in – confessing to being Jack the Ripper and the like.'

'But nothing useful?'

Abby Fairbrother suddenly appeared from an adjoining office, carrying a silver tray laden with two overly fussy porcelain cups, a matching cream jug and sugar bowl, and a pot of steaming coffee. 'Shall I pour it, ma'am?'

'Just leave it on the windowsill, please, Abby. I'll manage from there. How's your little girl? Is she feeling any better?'

Abby spoke as she walked. 'She's on the mend, thank you, ma'am. She'll be back in school next week.'

'I'm glad to hear it. If you could close the door on your way out, that would be marvellous.'

'Will do, ma'am.'

The chief superintendent rose to her full five feet ten inches and glided across the room on her heels. 'How do you take your coffee?'

'Half and half with five sugars, please.'

She looked back at him. 'Five? They're only small cups.'

'Make it four, then. I've been meaning to cut down.'

She handed him his cup and returned to her seat. 'You've put on a bit of weight, Grav. When was the last time you had a medical examination?'

'Just a couple of days ago, as it happens.'

'Any problems? Anything I need to know about?'

He took a gulp of coffee and smiled. 'A-one, no problems at all. I'm as fit as I've ever been.'

'Really?'

'Apparently, I've got the blood pressure of a man in his twenties.'

She was less than persuaded but decided not to pursue the matter. 'Right, back to business; I think it's time for a full-blown press conference. One of the Chief's golfing friends is offering a £20,000 reward for any information resulting in the killer's arrest. I think we need to take full advantage of the opportunity. I suggest we go for maximum publicity. Let's recirculate photos of all the known victims, details of what they were wearing when found, and ask for the public's urgent help. What do you think?'

'The bastard's going to love the attention, but we're short of options. Let's go for it, and I think we need to consider making an appeal direct to the killer. Ask him to contact us. It's worked before. Why not again? Maybe his ego will get the better of him.'

Davies drummed her desk with a polished fingernail. 'I'd need to sound it out with the chief.'

'Fair enough. What sort of timing have you got in mind?'

She sipped her coffee and placed her cup back on its saucer. 'The end of next week. That should give you sufficient time to make the necessary arrangements.'

'Why not sooner?'

'I'd rather we take our time and get it right, rather than rush things.'

'We're not going to need that long.'

'I'm going to be out of the country for a few days. It's a personal matter. It's not something I can cancel.'

'I could handle it myself. Just leave it with me.'

'The chief constable wants me there. The decision's made. I'm in regular contact with the press. It's not an issue. There'll be no surprises on the day.'

He rolled his eyes and nodded. 'Do you want the victims' families involved? It would take some coordination and management.'

'No, I think not, but keep them fully informed.'

Grav tilted his head back and drained his cup, savouring the intense sweetness at the bottom. 'Are we done? I've got things to get on with.'

'We are, Inspector. I want to be kept fully informed of any significant developments as and when they happen. No surprises. Am I clear?'

He rose slowly to his feet, silently cursing his chronically painful knees. 'Message received loud and clear, ma'am. Your word is my command.'

'I could do without the sarcasm.'

'I'll keep you informed.'

'I hope that's true this time. If this goes awry, you're going to need me to cover your back. I'll only do that if I've learned to trust you.'

He reached out and shook her hand firmly. 'I'll keep you in the loop from here on in, that's a promise.'

Chapter 21

Emily looked up from her paperwork as Charles Turner opened the door to her claustrophobic office and smiled. 'Hello, Charles, did you have a good weekend?'

'Not bad at all, thanks. A friend came to stay. Someone I was happy to entertain. What about you?'

'Yeah, pretty good, all considered. I was house hunting.'

'Any luck?'

'Yeah, I did see one I liked. A two bedroom flat overlooking the river. It's a little expensive, but Dad's offered to help with the deposit.'

He stood and stared at her, meeting her hazel eyes with his head cocked and lingering. 'Have you done something different with your hair?'

She looked away and shuffled some papers. 'Oh, just a quick cut. I fancied a change.'

The fool was as malleable as warm putty. 'And a subtle change of colour, if I'm not mistaken. I'm sure it's a little lighter than it was.'

'Yes, it's a different shade.'

'Ah, I thought so. It suits you perfectly. My mother favoured a very similar style as a young woman.'

Emily picked up her desk diary, keen to change the subject. 'Can you spare some time this week to discuss my caseload? There's one or two things I'd like to clarify.'

'Yes, why not? Come into my office; I've got a few minutes, we'll do it now.'

She picked up a pile of files and followed him into reception, where Helen was watering the various potted plants from a white plastic jug.

Turner smiled at his young secretary as he approached his office door. 'We'll be in conference for about thirty minutes. Please ensure there are no interruptions, unless it's the call I mentioned. That's the one thing that can't wait.'

'Understood, Mr Turner. How about some coffee?'

The pleb bitch was so desperate to please; it was fucking pathetic. 'What would we do without you, my dear girl? Coffee would be marvelous. You know how we like it.'

'And a biscuit?'

If she forced her nose any further up his arse, she'd need a miner's lamp. 'What do you think, Emily, shall we indulge?'

'Not for me thanks. I had one of Dad's cooked breakfasts.'

He pictured his hands on her throat and stifled a laugh. 'Come on, in you come. Just a coffee will be fine, thank you, Helen, but kind of you to offer.'

Turner sat at his desk and invited Emily to sit in the only other available chair, directly in front of his own. 'Look, before we make a start, I was wondering if you'd like to come to the Law Society dinner with me on the twenty-sixth of this month? It's a somewhat pompous affair, to be honest, but there'll be a three-course meal and dancing. I'm sure we'd find a way to enjoy ourselves.'

She didn't reply nearly quickly enough for his liking.

'You were about to tell me if you'd like to come to the dance. I'm very much hoping you will.'

'Um...I don't know.'

What a fucking bitch! 'We had a rather enjoyable time on our adventures in Laugharne, didn't we, despite the snow? I thought you enjoyed yourself in the end?'

'Oh, I did.'

'So, what's the problem?'

'Maybe mixing work and pleasure's not such a good idea.'

He shook his head as it began to ache. 'Oh, come on, we're both grown-ups. I'm sure it wouldn't pose too much of a problem.'

Emily sipped her coffee and considered what to say next. 'There's something I haven't told you.'

'What's that exactly?'

'My ex-boyfriend's been back in touch, Richard, the one I told you about. He's been attending a sex addicts group run by a psychologist in Cardiff. He's made good progress, apparently. He wants us to get back together.'

Was she really that fucking gullible? 'Oh, come on, you're not going to fall for that crock of shit, are you?'

She smiled, touched by his apparent concern. 'Crock of shit? I've never heard you swear before.'

Focus, Charles, focus. Stay on plan. 'I'm fond of you. I wouldn't want to see you hurt again. That's reasonable, isn't it?'

'I still love him.'

He scowled as another obstacle raised its ugly head. 'Really, after everything he did?'

'I can't help my feelings.'

'Well, remember, I'm here if you need a shoulder to cry on.'

'That's very kind of you, Charles, I will, and thank you for being so very understanding.'

He paused before speaking again, weighing up his options. 'So, tell me, has your father made any further progress with the murder investigation since we last spoke?'

'I don't know how much I can tell you. Dad shouldn't really be talking to me about it as much as he does. He said that himself.'

He smiled broadly. 'We've all got to talk to somebody. It's what keeps us sane, and for him, that someone's you.'

'Yeah, I guess so. He used to confide in Mum before she passed. They were so very close, inseparable.'

Turner paused for a beat as his blood pressure began to spiral. 'For me, it was my mother. She was a wonderful woman, my rock. I miss her terribly.'

Emily appeared touched by his apparent honesty. Surprised by his seeming vulnerability. 'You said *was*. Is she no longer with us?'

Was she suspicious? Was his mask slipping? 'She died. I'm still grieving. I'm not sure I'll ever get over my loss.'

'Time's a great healer. It sounds like an empty platitude, but it's true. I still miss my mum, but the pain's less intense than it once was. It fades as the years pass. Yours will, too, given time.'

Turner lowered his eyes. 'I'm really glad we've had this heart-to-heart, Emily. If we can't date, I do at least like to think we can be good friends – as well as workmates. We can, can't we? We've got a lot in common after all.'

She wiped away her tears with the sleeve of her satin blouse, leaving a small damp patch on the cuff. 'Of course, we can. If it wasn't for Richard, well, you know what I'm saying. I'm sure we'd be more than friends.'

Richard, fucking Richard, blah-de-fucking-blah. 'You trust me, don't you?'

'Of course, I do.'

'So, tell me about the case. I shared some information with your father when we met; it's not something I've ever done before. I'm wondering if it came to anything.'

'They had a suspect, but he's got an alibi for one of the relevant dates. Dad was so sure, I've never seen him as gutted. He really thought he had him.'

'So, the killer's still out there?'

'It seems so. Unless the witnesses were lying.'

'Does your father think that's likely?'

She shook her head. 'No, I was just thinking out loud, clutching at straws.'

His raised a hand to his face as his right eye began to twitch. 'Look after yourself, Emily. Don't take any risks. I've said much the same thing to Helen more than once. I don't know what I'd do if either of you were harmed in any way.'

'I'm being careful. I'm sure Helen's doing the same. No woman feels safe.'

'Do you find the extremes of human behaviour interesting?'

Emily paused, wondering why he'd returned to the subject so very soon. 'We talked about that at the restaurant; I told you about Dad working with the FBI profiler a few years back. Remember?'

Turner nodded. 'Ah, yes, now, there's a man I'd like to talk to. Can you imagine the things he's seen and heard?'

'He was only in the UK for a short time on a lecture tour. I'm sure Dad would be willing to discuss it with you once the case is over.'

He was about to respond when the phone rang and broke his concentration. 'Ah hello, Mr Roberts, give me a second.' He pointed towards the door. 'Sorry, Emily, I'm going to have to take this. I should have an hour free later in the week. Ask Helen to check the diary for you. And give some more thought to my dinner invitation. We can go as friends, I won't take no for an answer.'

Chapter 22

Charles Turner was met by the familiar stench of human waste as he opened the door. 'Zoe, lovely Zoe, nice to see you hanging there. I've had a rather exasperating day. That's not good news for you, I'm afraid. I'm a man who likes to work through his frustrations.'

Zoe pulled against her chains and wept. 'Why a-are you doing this to m-me? Let me g-go. I won't t-tell anybody. I'm b-begging you. Please, let m-me go.'

Turner reached up and switched on the wall-mounted camera before slowly approaching her. 'Just shut the fuck up, girl. You said much the same thing this morning, and it's becoming rather tedious. You'd be well advised to shut your mouth before I shut it for you.'

She was weeping uncontrollably now, drowning in a sea of tears. 'Please. I'm begging you, p-please.'

He drew his arm behind him and swung it forward in a rapid sweeping arc, connecting forcibly with the left side of her jaw. 'Which part of shut the fuck up didn't you understand? Go on, say something else, I dare you.'

Zoe lifted her knees to her chest and hung her head to meet them.

Turner lowered himself to the floor, gripped her face between the fingers and thumb of one hand, and looked deep into her eyes. 'Now, tell me. Why was my mother such a total bitch? You've had plenty of time alone. Have you thought about it? I really hope you have.'

She began whimpering pitifully. 'I d-don't know w-what to say.'

He pressed his forehead against hers and held it there. 'I think it's probably best if you come up with something worthwhile, don't you? I was a good son, a loving son. Why did she let me down so very badly?'

'She m-must have had a v-very good reason.'

His expression darkened, and for a moment, he considered killing her right there and then. 'What the hell's that supposed to mean? Are you trying to justify her abhorrent failures? I hope you're not, for your sake.'

Zoe choked back her tears. 'No, n-not at all. I'd never d-do that. I never thought that, not e-even once.'

'So, give me an answer; an answer that makes sense, something I haven't heard before.'

'I don't know. I just d-don't know.'

He jumped to his feet and stood over her with the front of his right shoe pressing down on her bare toes. 'One last chance.'

'Please let me g-go. I'll do anything. Anything y-you want me to. Just l-let me go.'

He turned away without responding, strode out of the room, and returned a short time later with a glass of cold tap water. 'Right, listen carefully. I want you to follow my instructions to the letter. Just nod if you think you can do that without screwing up again? I don't want to hear your voice.'

She glanced up and nodded, desperate to quench her thirst.

'I'll give you some water when I'm ready, not before.'

'Thank y-you.'

'Very good, Zoe, it seems your manners are improving. It will be easier for you if you cooperate. The end will be quicker, less painful.'

He took a small, brown plastic medicine bottle from the inside pocket of his suit jacket and unscrewed the top; dropped two tablets in the palm of his hand and held them to her lips. 'Put them in your mouth and chew them well.' He slapped her face hard when she hesitated. 'You can take the tablets, or I can ram them down your fucking throat. Make your choice. You're taking them one way or the other, it's up to you.'

Zoe opened her mouth, he placed them on her tongue, and she began chewing.

He held the glass to her mouth. 'You wanted water, now's your chance to have some. Come on, wash them down. I haven't got all day. Wash the fucking things down.'

She followed his orders.

'It usually takes my guests about five minutes to nod off, although it's sometimes quicker. All you've got to do is hang there and relax. Just close your eyes and drift into oblivion. I'll wash you and attend to your appearance while you sleep. I'll present you at your best; it'll be your greatest achievement. Your only achievement. Mediocrity will become marvel. How does that sound? You'll be a work of art.'

Zoe fought the impulse to sleep, but it was hopeless. Her eyes closed tight and she dreamt of happier times. Goodnight, Mum, goodnight, Dad, see you in the morning.

Chapter 23

Twenty-six-year-old Richard Griffiths walked down Grav's concrete driveway with a dark and sullen expression on his face. He'd seriously considered avoiding his erstwhile future father-in-law for as long as feasibly possible, but had finally decided that if he was serious about winning back Emily's affections, he had to man up and face the inevitable shitstorm coming his way. And coming it was, like an irresistible flood, of that, he had no doubt.

He knocked reticently at first, half hoping he wouldn't get an answer, but all too soon, a bright light shone in the hallway, and Grav stood to face him, like an obstructive doorman at a Cardiff nightclub. 'What the fuck do you want? I was hoping never to see your ugly face again.'

Richard cleared his throat. 'I'm sorry, Grav.'

'It's Mr Gravel to you.'

'Look, I know I've been an arsehole.'

'You won't hear me arguing. It's as much as I can do to stop myself punching you in the mouth.'

'Can I come in and talk?'

Grav didn't move an inch. 'You've got some bottle. I'll give you that much.'

'Please, Mr Gravel, just five minutes.'

'Emily's said fuck all about you visiting. Is she expecting you?'

'We've spoken on the phone, but, no, I didn't tell her I was coming to the house. It was a spur of the moment thing. I miss her like hell.'

'You should have thought about that before shagging anything in a skirt.'

'Look, can I come in or not? I just want to plead my case. Give me a chance to explain.'

'Good luck with that. You're either very brave or very stupid. I know which my money's on. She'd like to slice your balls off.' Grav turned and hobbled down the hallway as Emily appeared on the stairs.

Richard followed Grav and looked up at his ex-fiancé, as she descended one slow step at a time. 'Hello, love.'

She glared at him. 'Love? I think that ship well and truly sailed when you screwed those tarts, don't you?'

'Can we talk, please? That's all I'm asking.'

She blew the air from her mouth with an audible whistle. 'I think you said enough on the phone for a lifetime, don't you? A sex addicts group? Really? Infidelity's an illness, now, is it? That sounds like a lame excuse to me.'

'I'm trying here, just hear me out, please. That's all I'm asking.'

Grav allowed the wall to support his weight. 'Have you heard enough, Emily? I can kick him out if you want me to. It would be a pleasure.'

She paused. 'No, you're all right, Dad. He's got ten minutes. Do you mind if we use the lounge to talk privately? I don't want him upstairs.'

'No problem, love, as long as you're sure. I'll be outside having a cigar, if you need me. Say the word and he's gone.'

'Thanks, Dad. I know what I'm doing.'

'Let's hope so.'

Richard beamed and knew he was winning. 'Thank you both. It's appreciated. I'll do anything I can to put things right.'

Emily sat back in her armchair, trying to look as relaxed as possible. 'So, come on, what have you got to say for yourself?'

'Any chance of a cup of tea?'

'I don't think it's time to roll out the welcome mat just yet.'

He pressed his lips together, and for a fleeting moment, she thought he might start crying. 'I am so sorry. I've been a total prat. I know that.'

'Yeah, you said that on the phone.'

He opened his hands wide and held her gaze. 'Give me another chance, please. I'm begging you. I've been working on my issues. I'll never let you down again.'

She smirked. 'Issues? You were cheating; that's the word for it, cheating.'

'It was all down to my insecurity and low self-esteem. It was an ego boost, nothing more. I know that now.'

Emily laughed humourlessly. 'Oh, and there was me thinking you're just another disloyal bastard who can't keep his dick in his pants, silly me.'

'Look, I know you're annoyed, but the psychologist who runs the group says my behaviour stemmed from my childhood experiences. You know what my parents are like. I thought it was crap at first, but it made a lot of sense when I thought about it.'

'You hurt me, Richard. I need you to understand that. I'd bought my wedding dress. We'd booked the church, the honeymoon. You broke my heart.'

Richard bowed his head. 'I know. It was unforgivable.'

Emily checked the time, watching the seconds tick by. 'That's just over four minutes gone; you've got six left.'

'I want us to get back together. I'll even move down here, if you want me to. It's up to you, just say the word.'

She crossed her arms. 'Do you really think it's going to be that easy? You shat on me from a great height, and that's not easily forgotten – or forgiven. I love you. I'll always love you; God help me. But I don't know if I can ever trust you again.'

'Give me a chance. I'll prove myself. I don't care how long it takes.'

'You're not the only one the opposite sex finds attractive. I've had my opportunities. Perhaps you should think about that.'

He tensed, no longer on the defensive. 'What's that supposed to mean?'

'My new boss took me out for a meal. He's asked me out again. He's good looking, charming, affluent; a lot more eligible than you are.'

He glared at her. 'And will you be going?'

'It's not a nice feeling, is it, Richard? Perhaps now you've got a hint of how you made me feel. Suck it up.'

'So, what's the answer?'

She checked her watch again. 'I told him I'd think about it.'

'Have you slept with him?'

She paused, making him wait. 'No, not yet.'

'Thank fuck for that.'

'Your ten minutes are up, time to sod off and let me think things through properly. I'll let you know when I've come to a decision.'

He leaned close to kiss her cheek but recoiled when she pulled away.

'Don't push your luck, Richard. You're far from forgiven. I must be bloody mad to even consider it after what you've done.'

'Thanks for agreeing to see me, love. It means a lot.'

She chose to ignore the platitude this time. 'You can take me to the pictures tomorrow night. I'm picking the film, and you're paying. And don't expect to stay the night. It's going to be a while until we're an item again, and that's if it happens at all. I'm not promising anything. It's a date, nothing more.'

Richard smiled warmly as he approached the door. 'Anything you say, Emily. I wonder what your dad's going to say?'

'Believe me; you don't want to know.'

Chapter 24

When Zoe first woke in the passenger seat of Turner's borrowed van, she told herself that her change of circumstances was a good thing. Maybe he'd come to his senses. Perhaps he'd decided not to harm her after all. But as she looked down with bleary eyes, she realised she was wearing clothes and shoes that she hadn't seen before, and that her body smelt strongly of lavender oil. It wasn't good at all.

She turned her woozy head and stared across at Turner in the driving seat. 'Where are you taking me?'

The solicitor kept his eyes ahead as he drove along the dark country road with his headlights on main beam. 'There's a nice, quiet estuary beach about eight miles away, with a castle and rolling hills that kiss the sea. My mother used to take me there for days on the beach before she abandoned me. I still visit sometimes. The place is haunted by her memory and always will be. I'm sure you'll like it as much as I do.'

'Are you going to h-hurt me?'

Turner dipped the headlights and blinked as a car sped past in the opposite direction. 'I think you know the answer to that, but it will all be over soon enough, if you cooperate. The end game never lasts as long as I'd like. We can't have everything in this life.'

Zoe's breathing quickened. 'You're the k-killer who's been in the news. The man who murdered all those other g-girls.'

'Well, ten out of ten. And you're about to become the next one. How does that feel? You craved fame. You consider yourself an artist. Think of this as your fifteen minutes. Are you a Warhol fan?'

'Your mother wouldn't w-want you to kill me. I know that much. She'd never forgive y-you. She'd be ashamed of what you've d-done. She'd hate you.'

Turner laughed and didn't stop for about thirty-seconds. 'You don't get it, do you? You look like my mother, you're dressed like my mother, and you smell like the bitch too. It's my mother I'm killing. I kill her again and again and again. I put my hands around her throat, and I squeeze until the light leaves her eyes. You'll experience it yourself soon enough. It's a form of self-therapy; cathartic's probably the word to describe it.'

Zoe wanted to fight; she was longing to fight. She hated him more than she'd ever thought possible. She lifted her arm with the intention of hitting out, but decided the time wasn't right. 'You raped those girls. Why would you rape your mother? There's something wrong with you. You're twisted, broken, perverted, as sick as they come. She'd detest everything you are, and everything you've done.'

Turner lifted one hand from the steering wheel and slapped her hard in the face with his knuckles. 'Shut your fucking mouth, bitch. I don't want to hear another word.'

Zoe repeated herself, provoking another assault, and moved quickly, lurching forward in her seat, and sinking her teeth deep into his thumb. She worried at it like a dog with a bone as Turner tried to tear his hand free.

He attempted to steer with one hand, swerving from one side of the road to the other, but he lost control of the vehicle completely as she sank her teeth in deeper and made contact with the bone. Turner slammed on the brakes and skidded to a stop, causing Zoe to smash her head and crack the windscreen, but she didn't let go. He yelped and began punching her with his free hand until her head finally slumped on her shoulder, unconscious and bleeding. When he finally prised open her mouth and freed his hand, his thumb was hanging, partially severed. He headbutted the steering wheel and screamed as dark blood dripped from his wound. He looked at Zoe, collapsed in the passenger seat, as the red mist descended, and he lunged at her, sinking his teeth into her neck. You're not the only one with teeth, bitch!

Turner spat out a chunk of Zoe's flesh and bit her again, before throwing his arms high in the air and shouting at the very top of his voice, 'What do you think of that, Mother? Did you like it? Do you like the blood? There's no limit to my powers. Your little boy has become a man.'

Chapter 25

Richard didn't see the van hurtling towards him as he walked from his parked car on the outskirts of the town; he heard it, and he looked round to see it bearing down on him as he was about to cross the first of three lanes. By the time he tried to run, it was already too late. The vehicle hit him full on, sending him spinning onto the nearby pavement where he hit a wall with such force and velocity that his skull shattered like a boiled egg being smashed with a spoon.

Charles Turner slowed momentarily to witness a small group of onlookers crowd around his victim's bloody body and sped off, around a nearby roundabout with the engine screaming, over the river and out of town.

His adrenaline-fuelled high soon paled. He punched the steering wheel hard, as a siren sounded in the distance, but relaxed when it faded to eventual silence. By the time the large green gates of Graham Roberts' shambolic paint shop and repair centre came into view, about thirty minutes later, he was gaining confidence again, feelings of unbridled superiority at the forefront of his mind.

Turner sped into the enclosure, manoeuvred past rows of mangled vehicles on either side, and stopped in front of a large, black, corrugated iron building, which served as an office and workshop, at the far end. He rushed from the vehicle and ran back to close the gates as Roberts appeared.

'What's happening, have you finished with it?'

Turner shoved one gate closed, followed by the second. 'I need these chained up before we talk. Now! Get it done.'

'Okay, keep your hair on, where's the fire?'

Turner threw his arms in the air. 'Just get on with it, man.'

'I'm doing it. I'm fucking doing it.'

'Have you had the police here?'

'Not for weeks. Should I expect them?'

Turner walked towards Roberts. 'If they call, you don't mention me. You're a client, and that's all you are. I've never been to the yard. Remember what I know about you, Graham. I could put you away for a very long time. You say nothing.'

Roberts secured the padlock and returned the key to his pocket. 'I don't know what the fuck this is about, and I don't want to know. If you want to keep the van, you can keep it; if you don't, just say so. There's no need for threats, no need for explanations. I'm no grass. The police are no friends of mine.'

The two men walked towards the van, the solicitor taking the lead. 'I need you to change the plates.'

'What, again?'

Turner closed the distance between them. 'I hope you're not going to say that's a problem. That wouldn't be a good idea.'

'Did I say it was?'

'And what about putting a logo on the sides? Something that stands out; something obvious. Something consistent with whatever plates you use.'

'What sort of thing are you talking about?'

'Anything that changes the damned thing's appearance. Is that too difficult to understand? I would have thought it was obvious. The police are looking for a white van, not a white van with branding. Change the plates, change the way it looks, and I'm good to go.'

Roberts nodded. 'If I do this, we're good, yeah? We're quits, no more favours.'

'How long will it take you?'

Roberts' face dropped. 'Does it have to be tonight? I'm meeting some mates for a few pints and a game of darts.'

Turner reached out and grabbed the front of his overalls. 'Do it while I wait, and we're done. I won't ask you for anything else.'

'Okay, okay, you've got a deal. I can stencil something on. It's not an issue.'

The solicitor's relief was almost tangible. 'How long are we talking?'

'Go into the office, make yourself a cup of tea. Give me an hour, and you can be on your way. It won't be completely dry, but that shouldn't be a problem.'

'And you say nothing to anyone. Not a fucking word.'

'Relax, Mr Turner. My lips are sealed.'

Chapter 26

Emily slammed the front door and stormed into the house to find Grav slumped in an armchair with a bottle of Irish whiskey next to him. 'The bastard stood me up. After everything he said, he stood me up. I was standing outside that cinema, in the cold, like a total frigging plonker. And he's not even answering his phone, the damn thing just rings and rings before going to messages. If he thinks he can soft soap me again after this, he's very sadly mistaken. That is bloody well it. He's had it. I may never trust a man again.'

Grav waited patiently for her to finish her rant before looking up and draining his glass. 'Sit down, love. There's something I need to tell you.'

Emily's eyes narrowed. 'Has the wanker changed his mind about getting back with me? Has he told you? He'd better not have, for his sake.'

Grav shook his head. 'It's nothing like that, love. Come on, sit yourself down, and I'll explain everything.'

Emily stared at her father, acutely aware that something was horribly wrong, and unsure she wanted to find out what. 'Is he ill?'

Grav poured a generous tot of whiskey and handed her the glass. 'No, he's not ill.'

She flopped into an armchair and sipped the malty spirit, wincing as it burned her throat. 'What is it, then? He hasn't had an accident, has he?'

Grav reached out and put a supportive hand on her shoulder. 'Richard's dead, love. He was hit by a van when he was on his way to meet you. I'm so sorry.'

Emily began crying. 'How? What happened?'

Grav poured himself another drink. 'There's no way of making this any easier for you to hear; the driver didn't stop. Hit and run.'

'What are you talking about?'

'Do you want me to spell it out for you?'

Emily thought about it for a few seconds and decided she needed to know everything. 'Yes, I do. I have to know.'

'Richard was hit by a van when he was crossing the road near to the River View roundabout. Witnesses say the driver appeared to speed up, rather than slow down, as he approached him. He never stood a chance. The driver only braked after he'd hit him. By the time the paramedics got there, there was nothing they could do. Richard had a fractured skull; he'd lost a lot of blood. He was already dead.'

'Someone just ran him down in the middle of the street? Why would anyone do that?'

'Beats me, love. The driver was either pissed out of his mind, off his head on drugs, or it was deliberate. Maybe Richard screwed the wrong woman. An ex-army guy, who happened to be walking past at the time, said he was certain Richard was run down intentionally. He didn't have any doubt in his mind.'

'Did he see the driver?'

'He said it was a man driving, but that's it. He only saw him for a fraction of a second in the dark. But we'll get the bastard. You can count on it.'

'Who's in charge of the investigation?'

'One of the uniform lads is heading it up, Raymond Rees, Traffic. I think you met him once at that leaving do you came to.'

'Yeah, I remember. He seemed okay.'

'I had a chat with him on the phone just before you came in. We've got the van's index number. Every available officer is looking for it; it's high priority, no expense spared.'

'Whose van is it?'

'It's registered to a building firm in the Croxteth area of Liverpool. Did Richard have any dealings with anyone in that part of the country?'

'He was in computers, Dad. Why would he have anything to do with a building firm, hundreds of miles away?'

'The local police say the bloke running the company has got a history of dealing various drugs. Was Richard using? Is there any possibility? That may make sense of things.'

Emily shook her head frantically. 'No, no way. He was a fitness freak. You know that as well as I do. He only ever had a beer, maybe two, on special occasions, nothing more.'

'What about steroids? A lot of lads are using that shit these days.'

'Not a chance. One of his mates had a heart attack at twenty-three. He was dead against them. He used to say that steroid users were addicts, like any others.'

'Friends and relatives are sometimes the last to know. Had you noticed aggression, anxiety, mood swings, anything like that?'

Her eyes flared. 'No, Dad, no.'

'Okay, love, I had to ask.'

Emily's face dropped again. 'Oh, God, do his mum and dad know? He's their only son. It'll break their hearts.'

'They've been told. South Wales Police took care of it.'

'We should go and see them. We should pay our respects.'

'Finish your drink, love. I've tried ringing the house; their phone's off the hook. They're probably on their way to identify the body. Let's give them some space and ring them in the morning. That's probably best. They know where we are if they need us.'

Emily pushed her glass aside and held her face in her hands. 'What the hell's going on, Dad? Some maniac's killing young girls – girls like me – and now this. If it wasn't for you and Charles, I don't know what I'd do. I don't know how much more I can take.'

Chapter 27

Grav sat opposite Kesey in the quiet Caerystwyth Rugby Club bar and drained his fourth pint of best bitter. 'That's where things get strange, Laura. The van in question was in a secure compound in Liverpool after a clamping. There's no way it could have been in our part of the world at the time of the incident.'

DS Kesey sipped her shandy and placed the glass back on a sodden beermat. 'Have we definitely got the correct index number?'

'Yeah, one of the witnesses made a note of it as it sped away. Our local van had false plates. There's no doubt: they've been cloned.'

'What the hell's that about?'

Grav stood. 'Beats me, love. I'm guessing Richard was involved in something dodgy we don't know about yet. But that's just a theory. Do you fancy another?'

'I'll have a coffee, please, milk no sugar.'

He approached the bar, ordered, and returned to his seat with a coffee in one hand and another pint in the other. 'There you go, love. And I've ordered us a couple of pasties to be getting on with.'

Kesey stirred her coffee and tasted it. 'How's Emily coping?'

'She's doing all right, all considered. I think she's trying to stay strong for the funeral.'

'Good for her.'

Grav half emptied his glass, head back, Adam's apple protruding slightly in his fleshy throat. 'What about you, how are things? It can't be easy.'

'We've decided to try again. We both want kids, so, why not?'

'That's the spirit, stay positive. What's the alternative?'

Kesey nodded. 'My GP wanted to give me antidepressants, like grieving is some sort of illness.'

'You're not taking them, are you?'

'No, the kick-boxing helps. It takes my mind off everything else for as long as I'm there.'

'Makes sense. I tend to rely on alcohol when I need to take the edge off.'

'Yeah, I noticed.'

Grav smiled, as Liz, the shapely, platinum-blonde, middle-aged barmaid sauntered over with a plate in each hand. 'There you go, two Michelin star meals for my esteemed customers.'

'Thanks, love. Have you got any brown sauce?'

Liz walked away with an exaggerated sway of her hips. 'It's on the bar, Grav, same place as it always is.'

'Chuck it over, love, the old knees are playing up.'

She threw it underarm and grinned as he caught it one-handed. 'You'll be playing full-back for the first team if the coach sees you doing that.'

The two officers were in the process of tucking into their warm and unappetising fare when the phone behind the bar rang. 'It's for you, Grav, a PC Gaynor Evans. She says it's urgent.'

He crossed the room and held the phone to his face. 'What can I do for you, love? I was just about to eat my lunch.'

'Sorry to disturb you, sir. Another body's been found on the beach near Llansteffan.'

'Oh, for fuck's sake, not another one.'

'I'm there now. She's in one hell of a state. What do you want me to do?'

'Where are you, exactly?'

'Scotts Bay, on the beach about a hundred yards to the far side of the house.'

'Which house are you talking about?'

'There's only the one. It's a large detached place, set back from the beach. You can't miss it.'

'Is there anyone else about?'

'No, the place is deserted at this time of year. She could have been here for days before being discovered.'

'All right, love. Stay exactly where you are, the cavalry's on its way. We'll be with you in half an hour maximum.'

Chapter 28

Grav led the way along the narrow seaside path, which ran through the woods below the imposing, early twelfth century, Norman castle, with Laura Kesey in close attendance. As they looked down on Scott's Bay from their elevated position, they could clearly see PC Gaynor Evans standing a few metres from what had to be the corpse, laying on a raised area of rocky ground surrounded by sand.

The constable waved as they descended the steps towards the wide, windswept estuary beach. 'Hello, sir, Laura. She's over here.'

Grav stopped on the bottom step, allowing the stone wall to support his weight. 'Stay where you are, love. We'll come to you. The less we disturb the scene, the better.'

Evans nodded in response as the two detectives scanned the beach with keen eyes, evaluating the scene and picturing events as they unfolded in their minds. There were three sets of footprints in all: PC Evans', which led directly to the body; a second set of larger, deeper prints which followed a similar line; and finally, a third set of large prints, with longer strides, which ran along the top of the beach, then suddenly deviated towards the victim's body at an approximate forty-five-degree angle.

Grav stepped on to the beach, turned to his DS, and pointed towards the larger and significantly deeper prints that began just beyond the steps. 'The bastard must have carried her from here. It's the only viable explanation. Nothing else makes any sense.'

Kesey nodded as they walked towards the waiting constable, careful not to disturb the evidence even slightly. 'Yeah, I was thinking the same thing. Maybe she was already dead when he brought her here.'

'Yeah, or drugged. That wouldn't surprise me. Let's see what the blood tests tell us once Sheila's had a look at her. It shouldn't be more than a couple of days before we get the results back.'

'It's a hell of a long way to carry a dead weight.'

'I'm guessing the location means something to him. It's got some sort of significance; he obviously thought it was worth the effort.'

'He's got to be young and strong.'

'Yeah, it's looking that way. I wouldn't fancy trying it.'

Grav acknowledged the uniformed officer with a flicker of a smile as the two detectives approached the body for the first time. 'All right, love. Let's see her. Thank fuck the tides out.'

Gaynor Evans raised the collar of her coat as the temperature began to bite. 'She's above the tideline, but yeah, I know what you're saying. All it would take is a high wind. I've seen the entire area under water before now.'

'Do you come here often?'

'I do a bit of sailing with my husband and the kids in the summer months when the weather's good.'

Grav took a pair of thin, blue rubber gloves from his coat pocket. 'Who found her?'

'A local lad who's training for the Royal Marines rang it in.'

'What, was he out running or something?'

'Yeah, that's it. He likes to make full use of the wild terrain.'

Grav reached out and pointed. 'So those are his prints?'

'Yeah. He was focused on his running and spotted her when he looked up from the ground. He thought she must have been washed up on the rocks, but that makes no sense, given her position. Someone put her here.'

'Do you know him?'

The constable nodded her confirmation. 'Yeah, he's only a kid, nineteen; I know the family. His mum's a teacher at my daughter's primary school.'

'Any history of violence?'

'No, not at all. They're a nice family, and he's a good lad.'

'Scenes of crime officers are on their way. Give them a ring, Laura, and hurry them up a bit; let's get them down here with a camera before the doctor arrives.'

The DS turned her back to the wind and pressed her phone to her ear as Grav examined the victim. 'Oh, for fuck's sake, look at the state of her.'

PC Evans stood and stared as Grav reached up and moved Zoe's head an inch or two to examine her wounds more closely. 'Do you think a dog's had a go at her, sir? I don't know what else could have caused those injuries.'

Grav took his reading glasses from the inside pocket of his padded coat. 'They're bites all right, but not an animal's. I know human teeth marks when I see them. The bastard's violence is escalating. Half her fucking face is missing.'

Evans gagged. 'And her throat's been crushed. You can see the bruising.'

Grav lowered his arms, stiff and cold, and glad to look away. 'Have you had a look round for any potential evidence?'

'I have, but there's nothing to see other than the footprints.'

'Nothing at all?'

'Not that I could find.'

Grav stretched to relieve his aching lower back, as Kesey ended her call and approached him. 'They're nearly here, boss. Another ten minutes, at most.'

'About bleeding time. It's fucking freezing.'

Kesey nodded. 'Yeah, and I thought the sun always shone in Wales.'

Grav laughed, glad that the mood had been lightened. 'You head off, Gaynor. We'll sort things out from here.'

'Thanks, sir. I could do with warming up.'

'Write a statement as soon as you get back to the station, yeah. Just the basic facts, nothing more. I'll have a look at it in the morning.'

'Will do, sir.'

Kesey rubbed her hands together to warm them. 'Am I right in thinking you can get DNA from saliva? I'm sure I read it somewhere.'

'Yeah, of course you can. There could be sufficient cells in her wounds to produce a viable sample, although the weather's not doing us any favours.'

'Is it worth me putting plastic bags over her head and hands?'

'Yeah, go for it. It's probably too late, but you never know your luck.'

Kesey started with the head, keen to get it over with as soon as possible, while Grav watched her, spitting, 'The man's a fucking animal, worse than an animal. She's just a kid, early twenties at most.'

Kesey moved away from the head and on to the first hand. 'They all were, boss. She meets his victim profile perfectly: same hairstyle, similar shoes, similar dress, and the hint of lavender oil in the air, despite the rain. He must have soaked her in the stuff.'

'Yeah, but his methods have changed. The bastard's losing control, Laura. He's not thinking straight. Posing her on the beach was stupid – there's footprints all over the place. And there's a chance of DNA, however slight. It's not a lot to go on, but it's better than nothing.'

Chapter 29

Charles Turner sat at the back of the packed crematorium as Richard's light-oak coffin made its final journey into the enveloping flames to the vibrating sound of a favourite rock song that the solicitor didn't recognise or appreciate. He rose to his feet as the furnace's door slowly closed and made his way outside to wait for the attendant mourners to say their final goodbyes and join him.

Turner stood below a dark-grey slate roof as it began to rain and watched with increasing impatience until Emily finally made her way outside, arm in arm with her father, a few minutes later.

The solicitor caught her eye as she stood in conversation with a morose, middle-aged couple, who he correctly surmised were the grieving parents. He waved and strode into the insistent drizzle to greet her. 'Lovely service, very moving.'

'Oh, hello, Charles. I didn't know you were coming today.'

He gave a half shrug and moved closer. 'It was the least I could do in the circumstances, such a sad day.'

Emily was surprised to find herself relaxing as he put his arms around her and hugged her to his chest. 'I am so very sorry for your loss.'

She freed herself from his grasp and took a step back. 'Come on, I'll introduce you to Richard's parents. They're lovely people. They'll be glad to meet you.'

'It would be an honour.'

Turner shook hands with Richard's father first, and then his mother, who didn't stop weeping during their brief conversation. 'Emily has told me such nice things about your son. Such a tragic event, I am so sorry, it's just awful. He was taken far too soon.'

Both parents thanked him for his kind words of comfort and moved off to speak to distant relatives they hadn't seen in years.

Turner opened a black umbrella and held it above Emily's head, seemingly prioritising her comfort above his own, as the rain got heavier. 'Have you got any plans for the rest of the day?'

Emily looked daggers at him. 'I can come back to work, if that's what you're hinting at. I do realise I haven't built up sufficient leave to take any more time off. All you have to do is say.'

Turner shook his head and smiled. 'No, it's nothing like that, for goodness sake. You can take off as long as you need. I was just wondering if you'd like to go into Narberth for a quick bite to eat before you head for home. What do you think? It's almost lunchtime.'

Emily was about to say no, but changed her mind. 'Can you drop me off at my father's place once we've eaten?'

'Of course, I can. I've got a new CD I'd like you to listen to.'

'Okay, why not? I'll just tell Dad what's happening. I think he's keen to get back to the station as soon as possible anyway. He'll be glad of the reprieve.'

'I parked on the road, rather than risk getting stuck in the car park. My mother was late for everything, that's not my style; I like to plan ahead.'

Emily felt a sudden pang of doubt, thinking it was a strange thing for him to say, but she pushed it aside as he touched her arm. 'Are you still with me, Emily? You look as if you're in a world of your own.'

'Yeah, sorry, I was just thinking about Richard. He was so full of life, always smiling, always laughing. Everything can change in the blink of an eye.'

'You're so right. Funerals highlight that like nothing else. Don't hold back, make the most of your opportunities while you can. Suck the juice out of life, as I said before, it's the only way to live.'

'Dad told me much the same thing after Mum died. One minute we're here, and the next we're gone.'

Turner opened the passenger door for Emily and shielded her from the rain. 'Do you believe in an afterlife; in heaven and hell, good and evil?'

'I don't know what I believe. Maybe there is, maybe there isn't.'

'Let's talk about it more in the car.'

She looked up at him and smiled. 'No, let's talk about something else entirely, something pleasant, something nice. And we'll raise a glass to Richard. He'd like that.'

Emily wound down the window and waved to Grav as Turner jumped in the driver's seat and started the car's powerful engine. 'And we'll raise a glass to catching the bastard who ran him over and killed him. The sooner he's locked up, the better for everyone.'

Chapter 30

Emily downed her third glass of red wine, as a young French waitress in smart livery delivered her crème brûlée to the table. 'Nothing else for you, sir?'

Charles Turner shook his head and smiled engagingly. 'No, nothing for me thanks, I'll stick to the coffee. What about you, Emily? Do you fancy a brandy to finish?'

'Oh, I don't know.'

'If not today, when?'

She sighed. 'Oh, go on, then. One won't do any harm. It's been a rough day.'

Turner reached out and touched Emily's arm as the waitress walked away. 'I think you coped with the funeral admirably. Richard's death was so unexpected, so sudden. It can't have been easy for you.'

Emily stroked her chin before responding. 'In a way, I'd already mourned his passing when we split up. I don't mean he was dead to me, but our relationship was over; I'd been through the heartache. Does that make any sense to you?'

The waitress reappeared with Emily's brandy, placed it on the table, and left quickly, sensing any further interruption would be unwelcome.

'Of course, it does. It makes perfect sense.'

Emily looked away. 'You don't think it makes me seem callous?'

Turner reached across the table again and held her hand in his. 'No, of *course* not. It's human nature, that's all. Don't beat yourself up. You don't deserve that, not for a second. Life has to go on.'

She met his eyes and smiled without withdrawing her hand. 'Thanks, Charles, that means a lot.'

'Drink your brandy. You look as if you could do with it.'

Emily lifted the glass to her mouth with her free hand and drank a generous measure. 'Yeah, I must be looking a right mess. Crying can do that to a girl.'

Turner smiled warmly and released her hand. He relaxed back in his chair and pictured her gasping for breath. 'You always look beautiful.'

She felt her face redden. 'You say the nicest things.'

'It's all true. I'm so glad I met you.'

Emily tilted her head back and emptied her glass. 'I think it's time we made a move. Funerals can make people do the strangest things.'

Turner stood, helped Emily to her feet and handed her, her coat.

'Thank you, Charles, it's appreciated. You're a true gentleman.'

Turner smiled as they walked to the car park, hand-in-hand. 'Take your time; I think that last drink hit you rather hard. You look a little unsteady on your feet, if you don't mind me saying so.'

Emily turned suddenly and threw her arms around him. 'Thanks for being such a good friend. I really value your support.'

He held her tight and kissed her. Gently at first, and then hard with his wet tongue probing her mouth. 'Some say death is an aphrodisiac.'

She kissed him back, dopamine igniting her senses.

'There's a rather lovely hotel in Saundersfoot, with an uninterrupted view of the harbour and the coast beyond, if I'm not being too presumptuous. What do you think? Am I picking up the right signals, or am I deluding myself, driven insane by passion?'

Emily reached up and kissed him again. More gently this time, but still with fervour. 'Come on, let's go before I change my mind.'

'All right, in you get, out of the rain. I'll put some music on, turn the heating up, and you can tell me how your father's progressing with the investigation as we go... How does that sound?'

'Can I choose the music?'

He imagined her pleading for her life and had never felt more aroused. 'Of *course* you can. Why do you feel the need to ask? I'm at your service. A slave to your wants and desires, whatever they may be. You're in control.'

Chapter 31

DCS Hannah Davies sat at the front of the packed conference room, with Grav and Kesey at either side of her, and waited for the loud chatter and flashing cameras to subside. She watched the seconds tick by on the wall clock to her right, until precisely three thirty p.m., and rose to her feet – resplendent in a navy, two-piece designer suit that was intended to reflect her senior rank. 'If you can all quieten down, we're ready to make a start.'

She waited for a few seconds more, surveying the room, as the attendant journalists, baying for the next big story, finally settled down. 'My name is Detective Chief Superintendent Davies, head of the force's Criminal Investigation Department. Also present is Detective Inspector Gareth Gravel, Senior Investigating Officer on the case, and Detective Sergeant Laura Kesey, his second in command. The purpose of today's press conference is to bring you up to date with developments, as far as we possibly can, within the confines of the investigation. There will be some specific matters that we are unable to discuss for operational reasons, that's unavoidable, but with that said, I'm sure the afternoon will prove productive for all concerned. I would respectfully ask that you keep any questions for the end of the afternoon.'

Davies waited for the inevitable murmurs of discontent to die down and added, 'Detective Inspector Gravel will address you now,' in her piercing, high-pitched South of England tone, clearly enunciating every word.

Grav pulled his polyester Caerystwyth Rugby Club tie loose at the collar and struggled to his feet. 'As most, if not all, of you are aware, five young women have died recently, in the locality, in the most horrendous circumstances. That's five young women murdered at the hands of a killer who is yet to be caught.'

Grav pulled his tie a little looser as his face reddened, multiple beads of sweat appeared on his forehead, and damp patches formed under both arms. 'To date, we've identified three of the victims. The first is Stella Worthington, a twenty-two-year-old girl who grew up in local authority care and was working as a prostitute in the Manchester area to fund a chronic drug habit. The second is Carol Lewis, a twenty-six-year-old, working as a prostitute in Swansea at the time of abduction and murder. The third victim is … The third victim is … The … The …'

Grav coughed as his chest tightened, and the room became an indecipherable blur of tiny stars that made no sense at all. 'The third victim… The …'

Laura Kesey jumped to her feet and reached him just as he began to sway backwards and forwards, fighting to keep his balance and gradually losing the battle. 'Are you all right, boss? I think you need to sit down.'

Grav's face contorted as vicious, stabbing pains exploded in his chest and fired down both arms, into his back, as he fell to the floor with a resounding thud that seemed to reverberate around the room.

'Speak to me, boss. What's happening?'

A crowd of journalists gathered round them as Grav's overburdened heart stopped beating.

Kesey dropped to the carpet and began performing CPR to the insistent, imaginary beat of the Bee Gees disco classic "Stayin' Alive," as DCS Davies took control of the crowd. 'I would ask that you give my officers some space. Back off, DI Gravel needs some air.'

Davies took her mobile from her handbag as the attendant journalists formed an impromptu circle and looked on. 'Ambulance, I need an ambulance to Police Headquarters in Caerystwyth. It's urgent. One of my officers has collapsed.'

'Is the patient breathing?'

'Give me a second.' She called out above the chatter. 'Is he breathing, Laura?'

'He wasn't, but he is now. I don't think he's got a clue what's happening.'

The DCS pressed the phone to her ear. 'Yes, he's breathing, but he's not conscious.'

'That's good to hear. Try and get him into the recovery position, if you can. An ambulance is on its way.'

Chapter 32

DS Kesey sat in the detective chief superintendent's spacious office and waited for her to finish her call. 'Sorry about that, Laura, it was the chief constable. He likes to be kept fully informed.'

Kesey fidgeted with her cuff. 'Of course, ma'am.'

'How about a coffee before we make a start?'

'That would be lovely.'

'The kettle's on the windowsill; my secretary's off again. There's another baby on the way any time now. She's hoping it's a girl.'

Kesey crossed the room and switched on the kettle. 'Do you still take it black, ma'am?'

'Yes, please, and no sugar. I've got another marathon coming up in a couple of months.'

'Rather you than me.'

Davies smiled. 'Each to our own. Are you still doing the kick-boxing?'

Kesey spooned instant coffee granules into two overly fussy porcelain cups, decorated with multicoloured roses, poured in boiling water, and stirred. 'Yeah, I'm running a class at the leisure centre, once a week, work allowing. A friend covers for me when I can't make it. I'm planning on fighting again at the end of June.'

'Competition?'

'British Open.'

Davies accepted her coffee gratefully. 'Take a seat, Laura. Now tell me, how's DI Gravel getting on? I've had a quick word with him on the phone, but I haven't had the chance to visit him as yet. Perhaps later this week.'

Kesey frowned hard. 'I've been trying to call at the hospital most days, even if it's only for a few minutes. There's only me and his daughter. It seems like the right thing to do; I don't think he's over his wife's death.'

'Yes, I think you're probably right… Is he making reasonable progress?'

'He hasn't really told me very much. You know what he's like; always putting on a brave face and hiding his true feelings with a smile and a joke.'

The DCS sipped her coffee. 'He could have died. You saved his life.'

'Yeah, I guess I did. I don't think he realises that. I just hope he makes a full recovery.'

'That's what I wanted to speak to you about.'

'Ma'am?'

'I've spoken to the inspector's consultant. He's a family friend. He's assured me that Grav's not going to be back at work for several weeks, at best, and that's if he makes it back at all. Maybe retirement would be the most sensible option.'

Kesey shook her head. 'That's the last thing he'd want. He loves the job. It's what he lives for.'

'Well, that's something I can discuss with him in due course. There's no need to rush things in that regard, but we need to think about how we manage his cases in the interim. That's why I asked to see you.'

'I'm happy to do all I can to help, ma'am.'

'I'm glad to hear it… Remind me, Laura, how long have you been with us?'

'I transferred from the West Midlands force about two years ago.'

'And you've settled in well enough?'

Kesey forced a smile. 'I like to think so.'

'DI Gravel's evaluations have been extremely positive. He has a very high opinion of you.'

Kesey smiled again, spontaneously this time. 'Really? He hasn't said anything.'

'That's not his style.'

'No, I guess not.'

'How would you feel about covering in his absence? Are you up to being an acting detective inspector? You've got the relevant qualification.'

Kesey brushed non-existent fluff from her sleeve before responding. 'Yeah, I guess so. To be honest, I thought you'd appoint somebody with a bit more experience, or perhaps bring in an existing DI from another division.'

Davies nodded. 'Yes, I did consider both options, but DI Gravel persuaded me otherwise. You come recommended.'

Kesey laughed nervously. 'He's a dark horse.'

'So, what do you say? Do you accept?'

Kesey wondered why her mouth felt so dry. 'Would I be heading up the murder investigation?'

'Yes, but with my direct input; I can't stress that sufficiently. We'd meet regularly, and I'd be available to provide you with support and advice, as required.'

'I'd love to do it, ma'am. Thank you for putting your trust in me.'

Davies smiled without parting her lips. 'This is an opportunity, Laura. Acting up won't guarantee you a future promotion, but, if you perform well, if you impress, it makes progression significantly more likely.'

'I'll do my best, ma'am.'

DCS Davies stood, reached across her desk, and shook the newly appointed acting detective inspector's hand with a surprisingly firm grip. 'Chances like this don't come along all that often in small forces like ours. Make sure you take full advantage.'

'I will, ma'am.'

Davies walked to her office door and held it open. 'I hope so, Inspector. There's a killer out there. If we don't catch him, and quickly, this could come back to haunt the both of us.'

Chapter 33

Emily Gravel looked up from her newspaper and waved as Kesey entered the bijou vegetarian cafe in Merlin's Lane, glad to get out of the rain. 'Sorry I'm late, Emily, work's been hectic.'

Emily smiled. 'It's good of you to come at all. Fancy a coffee?'

Kesey sat herself down on a comfortable black leather settee, and ordered an almond milk latte and a dark chocolate brownie from an attentive waitress, with red and blue hair, who had suddenly appeared. 'It's good to see you, Emily. How's your dad doing?'

'You've seen almost as much of him as I have. The ward sister told me he was lucky to survive. I've got you to thank for that.'

'Oh, I think the paramedics may have had something to do with it. Anyone would have done the same.'

Emily sipped her green tea. 'Not everyone, you're too modest.'

'Well, maybe I did my bit. Thank God I did the first aid course when I had the chance.'

'So, how are you and your husband settling in Wales? It must be a bit of a change after Birmingham.'

Kesey glanced around the room and sighed. 'He's a she.'

'Sorry?'

'Look, I should have said something long before now, but he's a she; my partner's a woman. There's no husband.'

'But my Dad said…'

Kesey held up her hands as if surrendering at gunpoint. 'Yes, I know what I told him. It was stupid. It's just that he seemed so old-school when I first met him. I thought he might react badly if I told him the truth. Not everyone's as accepting as they should be. My own father kicked me out of the house when he found out about my relationship with Janet. He just couldn't handle it. I thought your dad may be the same.'

Emily shook her head. 'Dad's no homophobe; I don't think he's got a prejudiced bone in his body.'

'Yeah, I understand that now. But it just seemed easier to keep up the charade once I'd said it.'

'You're going to have to tell him some time.'

'Yeah, I know.'

'Do you want me to do it for you? I'll be seeing him tonight.'

'No, it's something I need to do myself. He's going to think I'm a right prat.'

'He'll understand.'

The same attractive, if unconventional, waitress delivered her order with a smile. 'Anything else?'

Kesey shook her head. 'That'll do it, thanks.'

'Give me a shout if you change your mind.'

Kesey nibbled the brownie and swirled it around her mouth, savouring the rich flavour before swallowing. 'So, what's this about, Emily? I've been wondering since your call. I hope you didn't feel you had to invite me here because of some misplaced sense of obligation; your dad would have done the same for me, we're a team.'

Emily pushed her newspaper to one side. 'No, it's nothing like that … I need some advice.'

'Okay, I'm no fount of knowledge, but I'll help, if I can.'

Emily sipped her cooling tea and placed her mug back on the table. 'I don't know where to start.'

'How about the beginning? That's always a good place in my experience.'

Emily glanced around the room. 'I haven't been here before. It's nice, I'll come again. There's live music on the last Friday of every month, according to the poster by the door.'

'Are you changing the subject?'

Emily dropped her head, closing her eyes for a second. 'Yeah, I guess I am.'

'So, come on, you've got me here, I'm listening. Tell me what this is about. You obviously want to, or you wouldn't have contacted me in the first place.'

Emily lifted her head and nodded. 'Do you know I'm working at Harrison and Turner, the solicitors in the high street?'

Kesey smiled. 'Yeah, your dad did mention it once or twice. He's very proud of you. He made that obvious to everyone.'

'And do you know Charles Turner? He's one of the partners.'

Kesey couldn't resist another bite of cake before replying and talked with her mouth full. 'I met him just the once when he came to the station to represent a client. He's a bit of a charmer, as I remember, and good looking too. You could do a lot worse. I quite fancied him myself, and that's saying something.'

'We slept together.'

'Oh, really, when?'

'After Richard's funeral.'

Kesey hid her surprise, not wanting to offend. 'You're both consenting adults. I don't think you need to feel guilty about it. You split up with Richard long before he died, from what your dad said.'

Emily focused on the low table in front of her and ran a finger round the rim of her mug. 'That's not it.'

'What, is Turner married? Is that where this is going?'

'No, he's single, just like me. I thought he might even be "the one" before it happened.'

'Before what happened?'

Emily took a deep breath. 'The sex was, well, let's just say, it was different.'

'Different in a good way?'

'No, that's definitely not the word for it.'

'You're going to have to spell it out for me if I'm going to understand. I've heard most things over the years – I'm not easily shocked.'

'He asked me to strangle him. He said it's the one thing that turns him on. He asked me to put my hands around his throat and squeeze hard until he was close to passing out. He wanted me to hurt him – to restrict his breathing.'

'I investigated a rape case involving a gasper a few months back. That's what they're called: gaspers. People who enjoy erotic asphyxiation. I did a bit of research. It's a male thing in the main, not many females are into it. I can't say that surprised me. But, I guess it takes all sorts.'

Emily took a deep breath as the memory stung and festered. 'And then, he asked if he could pretend to strangle me. He told me to lay completely still. Not to move an inch. To play *dead* – he actually used the word. It creeps me out when I think about it. It's just not my thing. I like tender and caring. I was scared he'd go too far and harm me.'

'Oh, I don't like the sound of that.'

'No, I didn't think you would.'

'Did you tell him how you felt?'

'I ran to the bathroom and threw up.'

Kesey laughed, despite, or perhaps due to, the emotive nature of the conversation. 'Well, that should have told him all he needed to know.'

'You'd think so, wouldn't you?'

'How did he react when you returned to the bedroom?'

Emily paused for a second, collecting her thoughts. 'It's hard to explain.'

'Give it a try. I'm in no hurry.'

'I don't know if this is going to make any sense, but it was like he was a different person. He had a strange blank expression on his face, cold, emotionless. And then, he snapped out of it, and he was the Charles I know again – dripping with warmth and seemingly sincere charm. It was as if he's got two completely different and independent personalities, Jekyll and Hyde, Mr Nice and Mr Nasty. I saw the other, darker, side of him. The side he keeps hidden from the world. And I didn't like what I saw.'

The DI hesitated, temporarily lost for words. 'Did he say anything when he saw how upset you were, anything at all?'

'He apologised profusely. Said it was a game he sometimes liked to play, and then, he asked me if I'd ever worn a different perfume, something a little more delicate, something floral. What the hell am I supposed to make of that? It was as if nothing of significance had happened. Not in his eyes, anyway.'

Kesey's face twisted. 'I don't like the sound of it, Emily. I'll be honest with you. I think I'd have slapped him.'

Emily grinned nervously, picturing the scene. 'It would probably have given him a hard on.'

'Yeah, you've got a point there. Maybe a bucket of cold water would have been a better option.'

They laughed together as the tension lifted momentarily.

'So, what do you think? I've got to work with the man. I like him. I still fancy him, God help me. But what does that say about me?'

Kesey linked her fingers together, as if in prayer, and spoke slowly and quietly. 'What do you think your dad would say if you told him?'

'It wouldn't be pretty.'

'No, and he'd be right. If you want my honest opinion, I think you need to avoid being alone with Turner for the foreseeable future. If you want to play sex games, that's entirely up to you. There's no law against it. But you could be putting your life at risk. Maybe cool things off a bit until the killer's arrested.'

Emily's eyes narrowed. 'Oh, come on, that's a tad overdramatic, don't you think? If Charles had a criminal record, he couldn't be a solicitor. That's the way the system works.'

Kesey paused for a beat. 'Look, I'm not saying he's the killer. He's very probably got nothing to do with the murders, but why take the risk? He likes what he likes, and it's all a bit weird. You said as much yourself. Investigations are ongoing and the killer could be almost anybody: the butcher, the baker, the candlestick maker. Why not him?'

Chapter 34

Sandra only had to wait for a few seconds before Laura Kesey picked up her phone in the incident room. 'Acting Detective Inspector Kesey.'

'Hello, Laura, it's Sandra on the front desk. Or should I call you "ma'am" now you've gone up in the world?'

Kesey grinned. 'Laura will do just fine, thank you.'

'I've got a Mr Carl Prichard here with me, who wants to talk to a detective about the murder investigation. He's come in response to the recent press release. There's a reward, apparently.'

'Are any of the interview rooms free?'

'One and three.'

'Put him in room one, keep an eye on him, and I'll be with you in two minutes. Do not let him leave before I get the chance to speak to him. This could be important. God knows we could do with a break.'

'I'll make him a cup of tea. That should keep him happy while he's waiting.'

'Thanks, Sandra, it's appreciated.'

DI Kesey entered interview room one to be met by a pencil-thin, retired headteacher in his early seventies; an inane, face-stretching smile seemingly welded to his face. 'Is something amusing you, Mr Prichard?'

He jumped to his feet, with surprising agility for a man of his advancing years, greeted her with a limp handshake, and suddenly flopped back into his seat as if poleaxed. 'I'm so sorry; it's my nerves. I'm a martyr to them. I just can't stop laughing at times of stress. It drives my wife to distraction. Has done for years.'

Kesey sat opposite him and introduced herself. 'Just try to relax, no pressure. Drink your tea, and we can take this as slowly as you need to. Does that sound okay to you?'

Prichard bit the inside of his right cheek hard, in a desperate attempt to silence another giggle, and thanked her profusely. 'That's very kind, I'm so glad you're understanding. I never know how people are going to react. I think it must be some sort of Tourette's syndrome, but without words – my doctor seems to think so anyway. I've tried counselling, hypnosis, tablets, but nothing seems to help.'

The DI handed him a blank A4 sheet of paper. 'If you can start by writing down your full name, address and contact details, that will save us a bit of time.'

He took a gold-plated fountain pen from the inside pocket of his brown corduroy jacket and did exactly that, glad to cooperate. 'Do you want my mobile number as well as the landline?'

'Please.'

Prichard added the number and handed Kesey the completed page. 'I think that's everything you'll need. I've tried to make the writing as legible as possible.'

Kesey noted the scribbled, barely decipherable handwriting. 'Is that a six?'

He nodded.

'And that's an eight?'

'Yes, I'm sorry it's not clearer.'

'Right… Sandra tells me you have some information to share with us? Something pertinent to the murder investigation?'

Prichard nodded enthusiastically, his facial contours relaxing as he began to feel more comfortable in his new surroundings. 'It's the dresses. I saw the photos in the local paper, and I knew as soon as I saw them.'

Kesey rested her forearms on the table and met his eyes. 'You knew what, exactly?'

'I used to volunteer in a rather popular Oxfam shop in Swansea, three days a week. Mondays, Wednesdays and Saturdays in the main, although I tried to be as flexible as possible. I never missed it. I was there for a little over two years in all. I loved it, but I found it too exhausting in the end. I think it's an age thing. So frustrating. I had so much energy as a young man.'

Kesey took a deep breath. 'You were telling me about the dresses.'

Prichard slurped his sweet tea before responding, seemingly deep in thought and enjoying the attention. 'Yes, I was just coming to that. I'm sure I recognise three of the dresses. I can remember them being brought into the shop and sold some time later. Or at least they were very like them. I can say that with absolute certainty.'

'When was this?'

'Now, that I can tell you with confidence. It was the end of September. My wife and I were going to a concert that night. I showed her the dresses when she called to collect me, but they were too small for her.'

'So, you're saying the dresses in question were brought into the shop in September last year, yes?'

Prichard smiled again, the expression dominating his features. 'That's right, by Elsie, a lovely lady who was one of our regulars. So generous and such classy clothes. I remember her saying she'd owned them since the fifties, but they were immaculate, as if they'd come straight off the catwalk. Buy quality and it lasts a lifetime, that's my advice.'

'Can you remember the exact date?'

He shook his head. 'No, sorry, I can't be that specific.'

'What I'm really interested in is who bought them. I'm hoping you can tell me?'

Prichard beamed, playing to the gallery. 'Well then, you'll be very happy to hear that I can help you in that regard.'

'Okay, I'm listening?'

'The dresses were only in the shop for a week or two once I'd put them on display. It didn't surprise me in the slightest. They were so stylish, so classy, I knew they'd be snapped up almost immediately.'

Kesey counted to three in her head. 'Who bought them, Mr Prichard? Who bought them and when?'

'It would have been sometime in October. I can't recall the specific date.'

'Give me a name, just a name.'

Prichard looked crestfallen, despondent. 'I'm afraid I can't do that. He was a rather charming man I've not met before or since. Quite a looker, like a forties film star on the big screen.'

Kesey opened her pocketbook and poised a biro above the appropriate page. 'That's very helpful, thank you. Now, this is important, I need you to concentrate. Can you describe him for me? Take your time. I need you to be as accurate as possible.'

Prichard closed his eyes for a moment, recalling events and picturing them in his mind's eye. 'He was tall, I remember that much. Six feet two, or three maybe, and he was slim. Not thin, mind, but not overweight either. Athletic, I think that's the best way of putting it. Muscular, but not overly muscular like the bodybuilder types with their popping veins. Twelve and a half, or maybe thirteen stone at most. Yes, I think that's fair to say.'

'About how old was he?'

'I'd say early to mid-thirties, certainly no older than that.'

Kesey nodded. 'What colour was his hair?'

'He was a natural blond. I'd swear to that in any court in the land.'

Kesey felt her pulse quicken. 'And can you tell me the style?'

'Short and well groomed. I'd be willing to bet he uses an expensive conditioner, something from a salon. He was a man who cared about his appearance, that was obvious, and he made quite an impression.'

'What colour were his eyes? Can you remember? If you're not sure, please say so. I wouldn't want you to guess.'

'Blue, sky-blue, piercing and clear. Like the sea, if the sea were perfect.'

Kesey smiled. 'You seem very sure.'

'Oh, yes, that's not something I'd forget. I'm a poet, a wordsmith, an observer of life's rich tapestry. Not much passes me by.'

'That's very helpful; you're doing well. Now, is there anything else you can tell me about him, any distinguishing marks such as scars, birthmarks or tattoos?'

'No, nothing like that, at least not that I could see.'

'What about his clothes? Let's focus on what he was wearing.'

'Very smart, very professional, quite the man about town.'

'Can you expand on that for me? Be as comprehensive as you can. Every detail matters.'

'He was wearing a light-grey summer suit and a pristine white cotton shirt, open at the collar. A three-button jacket, turn-ups on the trousers. Very stylish and perfectly fitted, as if they were made for him. I don't think he buys off the peg.'

Kesey's eyes narrowed. 'That's a very detailed description, given the time that's passed.'

'I've a passion for fashion. I think I'd have been a designer, had I not become an English teacher. It's the sort of thing that fascinates me. I remember it as if it were yesterday.'

'Okay, that's good to hear. Is there anything else?'

Prichard paused before responding. 'This may well sound a little odd, but I can remember thinking he smelt faintly of lavender.'

'Lavender? You said lavender. You're sure it was lavender?'

'Yes, that's right, I recall thinking it was a surprisingly feminine scent for such an overtly masculine man. He was something of an enigma, an original. Not your typical local man.'

'Do you think he was local? Did you recognise the accent?'

'Oh, yes, he was local all right. Educated, sophisticated, debonair, but certainly local, south-west Wales, through and through.'

Kesey was almost afraid to ask her next question. 'Are there any security cameras at the store?'

Prichard began laughing again as his nerves took hold. 'There are, but I'm afraid they're not going to help you a great deal.'

Kesey's frustration was virtually palpable. 'Are you saying the recordings were wiped? I know it's common practice.'

'There was a power cut. The cameras weren't working that day. I had to close the shop early for repairs as soon as the daylight began to fade.'

'Are you sure you've got the right day?'

'Oh, yes, I'm absolutely certain. I can remember him leaving shortly before the electricians arrived.'

'Would they have seen him?'

'No, I don't see how they could have. He'd gone by then.'

'Was there anyone else in the shop? Another member of staff for example.'

'I'm afraid not. I was the only one in that day. The usual manager rang in with a migraine, poor dear. She's a martyr to them.'

Kesey hid her dismay as best she could. 'How did he pay? Please tell me it was by card?'

'Cash. He paid cash. And he made a rather generous donation in addition to the cost of his purchases. Ten pounds, if I recall correctly.'

Kesey looked at his smiling face and sighed. 'Yeah, I had a horrible feeling you were going to say that. Give me a second; I'll just fetch some statement forms. We need to get something down on paper.'

Chapter 35

Laura Kesey sat on the end of Grav's hospital bed and wolfed down one seedless grape after another as he looked on.

'I'm glad you're enjoying them. I wouldn't eat the damn things if they were the last food on earth. It's a matter of principle. Fruit never passes my lips. Never has done and never will.'

She swallowed the remains of the last grape and smiled. 'I can bring you something different next time if you like. How about a book or the local paper?'

Grav adjusted his position and grinned. 'If you could smuggle me in a few cigars and a bottle of twelve-year-old Scotch, I'd be your friend forever.'

'You've got no chance. If you want to indulge your self-destructive habits, you'll just have to get better and get out of here. I'm playing no part in it.'

'Yeah, Emily said much the same thing.'

'Good for her.'

'So, tell me, how's the case going?'

This time, it was Kesey's turn to frown. 'That's the last thing you should be thinking about.'

'I've been thinking about little else.'

She nodded. 'Yeah, I guess I'd be much the same in your place. It's the copper's curse.'

'Who's in charge now I'm out of circulation? It's not that Trevor Simpson, is it? He's next to useless at the best of times.'

Kesey threw the empty plastic container in a nearby bin and grinned. 'I am.'

'Oh, for fuck's sake, the world's gone mad. What total numpty came up with that decision?'

'I'm acting up until you're back in the saddle, Acting Detective Inspector Kesey, the DCS asked me personally. And, before you say anything else, she told me you'd recommended me. *Persuaded her*, were the actual words she used. I've shown a great deal of promise apparently.'

Grav took a sip of water and looked at her with a look of feigned surprise. 'I must have been pissed. Either that, or I'd had a bang on the head. It was definitely one or the other.'

Kesey laughed. 'Yeah, yeah, anything you say. I'm the boss now, so watch your step. I might kick your arse for you.'

'No, seriously, I'm pleased for you, love. You're a good detective. It's an opportunity – I'm not going to be around forever. Don't fuck it up.'

'I'll try not to.'

'Any developments I don't know about?'

'The chief super's rearranged the press conference.'

Grav closed his eyes for a second before speaking again. 'Yeah, I guess that was inevitable. I put on quite a show.'

Kesey checked her watch, as the end of visiting time fast approached. 'You certainly did, anything for a bit of attention.'

'Did the media publicise the photos of the dresses?'

'Yeah, they did. The chief super issued another press release soon after the conference went tits up.'

'And I suppose I've been all over the news?'

Kesey grinned. 'You have, boss, you're quite the celebrity. I can't say you were looking your best for the cameras, but you're famous now. Caerystwyth's answer to Columbo, but not as stylish. They'll be asking you for your autograph when you get out of here.'

'Bloody marvellous.'

'Yeah, it's not exactly the focus we were looking for.'

A young staff nurse in an ill-fitting sky-blue uniform put her head round the door. 'Just five more minutes, please. He needs his rest.'

Kesey nodded and stood to leave.

'So, come on. I know there's something you're not telling me. You can trust your old Uncle Grav.'

She shook her head slowly. 'You'd think you were a detective or something.'

'Spit it out, girl.'

'We didn't have any joy with the DNA results from our last victim. Any saliva was washed away by the rain long before we had the chance to test it.'

'What about the bite marks?'

'The forensic dentist examined them; the killer tore pieces of skin and flesh from the body, rather than leave actual impressions of his teeth that could have been compared with dental records – they're not going to help us.'

A bell rang out to signal the end of visiting time.

'What about the footprints?'

'The ones found on the beach were a size ten. The one I found on the riverbank was an eight.'

'You're sure?'

Kesey nodded. 'Yeah, scenes of crime had a good look at it for me. I asked them to double check. There's no doubt.'

'So, it looks like the print on the riverbank was something and nothing.'

'Yeah, that's the conclusion I came to. There's just the one. It could have been anyone's.'

'Do we know who the latest victim is?'

'Let's just say enquiries are ongoing.'

Grav's brow furrowed. 'Have you got any positives for me before you sod off and leave me to get back to sleep? I could do with a bit of cheering up.'

'We may have a description of the killer.'

'May?'

'Someone bought three dresses like ours. We know that much.'

Grav felt his pulse racing at a dangerous high. 'Where from?'

'A charity shop in Swansea.'

'Who was it?'

'We haven't got a name, but he was a smartly dressed blond guy in his thirties. That's as good as it gets.'

'Nothing on camera?'

'Not in the shop.'

'What about in the surrounding streets? Surely the bastard's got to be on CCTV somewhere?'

'Oh, he is. We've got him entering and leaving the shop as clear as day.'

'So, what's the problem?'

'It was raining. He used an umbrella; we never see his face.'

'Oh, for fuck's sake, either he was lucky, or he's one clever bastard.'

'My money's on the latter. It sometimes feels like he's running rings around us. I'm out of my depth, boss, that's the truth of it.'

'Stay strong, love, we all feel like that sometimes – even me.'

Kesey smiled thinly. 'Thanks, that helps.'

'I can't think of any local villains meeting the description, or at least no one with a relevant history that's worth looking at.'

Kesey shook her head. 'No, me neither. I've got Joe Bromley making enquiries with other forces.'

'Anything else?'

Kesey felt her gut churn and buckle like a washing machine on a spin cycle. 'Emily arranged to see me, we had a coffee together. Turner's been acting strangely. I think she's concerned.'

'Strangely? What the fuck's that supposed to mean?'

'He's a bit too touchy-feely and overly interested in the case.'

'Why the fuck didn't she talk to me?'

'She didn't want to worry you. You know what I'm saying.'

Grav's face twisted as his chest tightened, and the monitor next to his bed began to buzz loudly and insistently. 'He meets the description. Drag the bastard in. Sort out an identity parade. If there's even the slightest chance of him being the killer, I want him—'

Kesey threw open the door and yelled for assistance as two nurses and a white-coated doctor ran down the corridor towards her. 'Quick, I think he's having another heart attack. Please, you've got to help him.'

Chapter 36

Carl Prichard studied the six men lined up behind the glass screen in front of him and began to giggle. 'I'm not sure. I just can't say with any certainty.'

Laura Kesey glowered. 'Take your time, Mr Prichard. Have another look. If the man who bought the dresses from you is in the line-up, I need you to identify him for me. Just tell me his number. This isn't some game; it matters.'

Prichard was close to panic now, feeling the pressure like never before. 'It's just so difficult; the last thing I want to do is mislead you and identify an innocent man. I was so sure of what he looked like before I arrived. It seems my memory's been playing tricks on me.'

'Just have another look, please. Take as long as you need. There's no rush.'

Prichard looked each man up and down, left to right and back again. 'It's either number two or number five, yes, two or five, I can't be any surer than that.'

'Oh, come on, you described the man in such specific detail in your statement. You seemed so sure of his appearance, so certain. What's changed?'

Prichard was sweating profusely now, red in the face and agitated, but still smiling the broad Cheshire Cat smile that seemed to define him. 'I took my glasses off when he came into the shop; I think it makes me look younger. I'm a ridiculous, vain man, but there it is. I've said it.'

'Were they reading glasses or distance?' She was clutching at straws, and she knew it.

'Distance, like the new ones I'm wearing today. I think they suit me rather well, don't you?'

'And what's your sight like without them?'

'Not great, I'm afraid. Everything's somewhat unfocused; blurred is a better way of putting it, to be honest. I can't see a damn thing.'

Kesey held a hand to her face. 'And you didn't think of telling me this before now? You didn't think it was relevant?'

'I'm sorry, but I've done my best. That's all anyone can do.'

'But you can't tell me if the man who bought the dresses is here now?'

Prichard pressed his face against the glass. 'It may be number two or number five. I've already told you that more than once, I don't know why I need to repeat myself.'

Kesey rested her hands on her hips. 'May? You're saying may? That suggests you're far from sure on either count. Two and five don't even look that much alike. There are slight similarities – their hair colour, their general demeanour – I'll give you that much, but that's all there is.'

Prichard burst into another fit of giggles as his face contorted. 'I really am sorry. It's the best I can do, you stressed the need to be honest. Now, can I go, please? My wife will be waiting for me.'

Kesey approached the door and held it open, with a look that left him in no doubt as to her displeasure. 'Okay, we're done. Thank you for your time, Mr Prichard. You can leave whenever you're ready.'

Prichard looked back at her on entering the brightly lit corridor and held her eyes. 'You've got anger issues, young lady. Has anyone ever told you that? It's not very becoming, particularly in a public servant. It might be an idea to remember who's paying your wages.'

Kesey glared at him. 'I've got frustration issues. Five girls are dead, there's a predatory killer hunting for his next victim, and you haven't helped one little bit.'

Prichard burst into peculiarly high-pitched laughter, which bordered on the hysterical, stopping suddenly. 'Oh, there is one more thing I remember from that afternoon. I don't know if it's of any importance.'

'What's that?'

'He was carrying a black umbrella. Yes, that's right. Such a sensible man, we were having autumn showers. It had been raining on and off for most of the day.'

Chapter 37

The detective chief superintendent pushed her paperwork aside and picked up her office phone on the fifth ring. 'DCS Davies.'

'It's Laura Kesey, ma'am. I was hoping you can spare some time to discuss the case.'

'Is it urgent?'

'Yes, ma'am, I think it is.'

Davies glanced at the clock. 'You can come now. And don't bother knocking, I'll be waiting for you.'

'Right, Laura, take a seat and tell me what this is about.'

The acting DI sat down in a seat that was smaller and lower than her boss', who appeared perched on a pedestal by comparison. 'There's been a few developments in the case, ma'am. I wanted to consult you before taking the next step.'

Davies adjusted her spectacles. 'Okay, let's hear it.'

'The description provided by the charity shop volunteer, ma'am, matches a local solicitor: a Mr Charles Turner.'

The DCS smiled, genuinely amused by the observation. 'There's a lot of men with blond hair, Laura. And that witness seems less than reliable, from what I read in the records. I hope you're not wasting my valuable time, I've got a lot to be getting on with.'

'I really think Turner's a credible suspect.'

Davies shook her head. 'Oh, come on, I know Charles personally. He's a charming man. We're going to need a lot more than an elderly witness with poor eyesight and a bad memory before we go down that rocky path. Prichard couldn't even identify him in an identity parade. His evidence, if you can call it evidence, is next to useless.'

Kesey bit the inside of her lower lip, determined to make herself heard. 'I've been making some enquiries, ma'am, background stuff; there's significant factors that make Turner a viable suspect, even allowing for Prichard's failings.'

Davies shook her head dismissively. 'I hope asking you to act up doesn't prove to be an error of judgement on my part. That would not bode well for either of us.'

Kesey adjusted her position in her seat. 'I spoke to Turner's GP. She was surprisingly cooperative when I told her it was a murder enquiry.'

'And what did she tell you?'

'Turner hasn't had a vasectomy, but he caught syphilis in his early twenties. It went untreated for a time before he sought medical help.'

'I can't see the relevance. Syphilis may or may not suggest dubious morals on his part, but it's far from criminal.'

'She told me syphilis can cause infertility in men if not treated promptly. It could explain the absence of sperm in the killer's semen.'

'And did it cause infertility in his case?'

'I don't know the answer to that. He was never tested as far as his doctor's aware.'

The DCS sighed. 'It's all rather tenuous, Laura. Charles has a spotless record and an excellent reputation in this town. He's well liked, respected. I don't think he's ever had so much as a parking ticket, let alone anything that would suggest his involvement in a string of vicious murders. I really think you're barking up the wrong tree on this one.'

'I've been talking to a friend of Grav's, at South Wales Police. A DCI with over twenty years' service. Turner was arrested when he was at Cardiff University – a girlfriend alleged assault. She said he'd grabbed her by the throat, but she dropped the case before it went to court. Turner made a no comment interview. The DCI had the distinct impression he was lucky to get away with it.'

'I know Charles rather well. I've never thought of him as a violent man. Far from it.'

'Emily Gravel spoke to me – Grav's daughter. She works with Turner; he's not all he seems.'

'Oh, God, where's this going?'

'They had sex. He asked her to strangle him. He wanted to do the same to her, and then he asked her to play dead.'

Davies' face paled. 'Are you saying she claims that he asked her to mimic a corpse during sex?'

'Yes, ma'am, that's exactly what I'm saying. "Play dead," he used those words.'

'Didn't Ted Bundy's girlfriend say very similar things after he'd gone on to kill and mutilate God knows how many women?'

'Yeah, she most certainly did, I watched a documentary on Sky.'

'I've had Turner in my house. I've invited him to dinner parties. We've played bridge together!'

'Do you think there's enough for us to formally interview him?'

The DCS spoke out loudly, pronouncing each word as if announcing it to the world. 'I do, Inspector, more than enough. I want him arrested on suspicion of murder, I want him interviewed on tape, and I want it done today. Capeesh?'

Kesey wasn't sure of the exact meaning of "capeesh," but she got the general idea. 'Yes, ma'am. Thank you for your support. I'll get it done.'

'Play on his ego, Laura, that's my advice. He has a very high opinion of himself. Challenge his feelings of superiority and see where it gets you. If sufficiently provoked, he may well reveal his true nature and say something he later regrets.'

Chapter 38

DI Kesey placed individual colour photographs of the five dead girls on the table in front of her and waited for a few seconds before speaking. 'Take a good look, Mr Turner. We have very good reason to believe that you were involved in their murders.'

Turner glanced at the photos appreciatively and shook his head. 'If you think your transparent and painfully predictable shock tactics are going to illicit a spontaneous confession on my part, you're very sadly mistaken. You've got this horribly wrong, Detective. I'm an innocent man.'

'Take a good look at your handy work, or is that too much to bear in the cold light of day?'

Turner looked at each photo in turn, taking his time, licking his lips and lingering when a particular detail caught his eye. 'Do you know who I am? Have you got even the slightest idea how influential I am in this town? I've got contacts. Important contacts. If you're not careful, that ill-advised, temporary promotion you seem so proud of, will come to a sudden and dramatic end. You'll be demoted back to constable and directing traffic faster than you can blink.'

'Are you sure you don't want a solicitor, Mr Turner? We're here to discuss extremely serious matters. I can suspend the interview. It's no problem.'

'If that's your idea of a joke, it's fucking pathetic.'

Kesey smiled humourlessly, holding her nerve. 'You seem to be becoming somewhat irate. Are you sure you don't want to reconsider before we continue?'

Turner took a deep breath and steadied himself. 'I'm fully aware of my rights under the law, thank you. That ridiculous identity parade, which you so insistently arranged, clearly didn't result in the conclusion you were hoping for. If it had, I'd have heard about it long before now. I will not require a solicitor. I am innocent, as I've consistently maintained, and I'm perfectly capable of representing myself. Perhaps it might be an idea to consult your senior colleagues before we continue with this ludicrous charade. I wouldn't want you to make an even bigger fool of yourself than you already have.'

'So, you don't want a lawyer?'

Turner tensed. 'No.'

'If you're sure?'

The bitch, the absolute fucking bitch. 'I couldn't be surer. Ask your ridiculous questions, just get on with it, I've never been surer of anything in my life.'

'Have you ever contracted a sexually transmitted disease, Mr Turner?'

'Pardon?'

'It's a simple enough question.'

Turner thought before replying, contemplating her line of questioning. 'I really can't see the relevance, but, as you asked so nicely, I'm happy to play along with whatever game you're playing.'

'What's your answer?'

'Yes, Inspector, I have. In my early twenties. A girlfriend failed to inform me that she was infected. I didn't use a condom. Let's put it down to the inexperience of youth.'

'And did that make you angry, Charles? You don't mind me calling you Charles, do you?'

His face contorted with suppressed rage. 'I wasn't exactly delighted by her failings, but the infection's treated easily enough with antibiotics. Why do you ask?'

'Are you aware that the failure to treat the condition promptly can lead to infertility?'

Turner sat in silence.

'Nothing to say in response? It's a simple enough observation.'

'No comment. It's of zero relevance. Move on, if you want my continued cooperation.'

'Have you ever been arrested before today?'

His expression hardened. 'Ah, I can see where you're going with this. You're asking questions you already know the answer to. That may catch out some suspects, but not me. Don't underestimate me, Detective, that's never a good idea.'

'Have you been arrested, or not? Are you going to answer, or is there something you're trying to hide? Perhaps you're ashamed of your past. Is that it?'

Turner snorted disdainfully. 'I was arrested while studying for my law degree at Cardiff University, as you know full well. A rather misguided young woman with mental health issues made outlandish and spurious allegations that I'd assaulted her during sex. Her statement was a work of fiction, an utter fabrication, and nothing more. She was fortunate not to be prosecuted for attempting to pervert the course of justice, or wasting police time. Maybe if she had been, we wouldn't be sitting here now. You're as misguided as she was.'

'She said you put your hands around her throat. She said you tried to strangle her, before being disturbed by another student. She was scared for her life. I think you lost control. I think you came close to killing her.'

Turner clenched his jaw and sneered. 'The allegations were spurious. The case was dropped. What part of that don't you understand?'

'The girls in the photographs were strangled. Choked until dead. No one came to save them; they weren't as lucky as your student friend.'

Turner jumped up and leered at the officer with angry eyes, causing her to retreat in her seat and press herself against the backrest. 'The case was dropped by the Crown Prosecution Service. It didn't go to court. Is that too difficult for you to comprehend? Maybe you haven't got the intelligence required for your job. In the eyes of the law, I'm an innocent man.'

Kesey waited for him to return to his seat, fighting to retain her composure, keen to appear unfazed by the intensity of his reaction. 'In the eyes of the law? That's an interesting choice of phrase. It seems like an admission of sorts, a convoluted confession. Or didn't you express yourself clearly? Maybe you're not as clever as you like to think you are.'

Turner smiled, picturing Kesey chained to a radiator in his private hell with his hands around her throat. 'Beyond reasonable doubt. That's all that matters. Your case is full of holes. It might be an idea to release me and get on with trying to catch the man who actually committed these crimes. We're a predatory species; it's only a matter of time until he does it again.'

For a moment, an element of doubt entered her mind, and she stalled, losing track of her train of thought.

Turner rested both hands on the table and looked at her. 'Are you running out of questions, *Acting* Detective Inspector Kesey? You're rather new to this, and I'm afraid it shows. We've been sitting here for over an hour, and you've got nowhere. Is this farce finally nearing its end? I'd like to think it is, more for your sake than mine. Your excruciating performance is hard to watch. It's akin to witnessing a car crash in slow motion. You're an embarrassment to the force. Let's hope no one listens to the tape; it wouldn't do your reputation any good at all.'

'What size shoes do you wear?'

Turner swivelled in his seat, stretched out his right leg, and pointed to a highly polished dark-tan Oxford brogue. 'I'm an eight. I can take them off for you to check, if required. I'm more than happy to cooperate, if it gets me out of here.'

Kesey felt a sinking feeling, deep in the pit of her stomach. 'That won't be necessary.'

Turner stared at her, observing her reactions, studying her closely. 'You look a little disappointed. Is there something wrong, Detective? Wasn't it the answer you were hoping for?'

She checked her notes, buying time.

'Oh, I get it. The fifth victim was found on a local beach. There'd have been footprints, lots of footprints. The killer hasn't got the same size feet as me, that's your problem. Reasonable doubt, Inspector. First the identity parade and now this. There's reasonable doubt right there. Reasonable doubt in spades. That should tell you all you need to know.'

Kesey ground her teeth together and glared at him as he began to laugh. 'I can see right through you, Turner. I know exactly what you are, and it's only a matter of time until I've got sufficient evidence to charge you. You won't be laughing then.'

'Temper, temper, Detective. This is starting to sound like a witch hunt, and that never goes down well in legal circles. It's tantamount to career suicide on your part. You're a laughing stock. A joke.' Turner paused, looked directly at the recording equipment, and continued with a smirk on his face. 'You've wasted your time on a senseless and pointless endeavour. The man you're looking for is still out there somewhere, searching for his next victim. It could be anyone, at any time – today, tomorrow, or the day after that. Best let me go, don't you think? There's every chance that someone else is going to die because of *you*.'

Chapter 39

DI Kesey wasn't usually one to break the rules. She believed in the system; in the need for regulations to complement the laws of the land. But the circumstances were exceptional, and her usual black and white world was tainted by shades of grey. 'Come on, Emily, we can speak privately in here.'

Emily Gravel entered the small second-floor office and took a seat near a window with a partial view of the town. 'It's nice to see you again. I appreciated our heart-to-heart in the café. It helped me make sense of my feelings.'

'How's your dad?'

Emily folded her arms. 'Not bad, all considered. The surgeon told him that they succeeded in increasing blood flow to the heart muscle. I really thought he was a goner.'

'Yeah, he had me worried... What did they do exactly?'

'Something called an angioplasty. Basically, a deflated balloon is threaded up to the coronary arteries, and inflated, before a stent's inserted to prevent any further blockages. It sounds a lot worse than it is, apparently.'

'It's amazing what they can do these days.'

Emily checked her watch. 'Look, Laura, I don't mean to rush you, particularly after all you've done for Dad, but it's my lunch hour. I've only got another half an hour before I need to be back in the office. What's this about? You made it sound so urgent on the phone.'

Kesey pulled up a seat and forced a reassuring smile. 'Yeah, sorry this is all a bit dramatic, but I had to speak to you face-to-face. I couldn't take the risk of anyone overhearing what I have to say.'

Emily looked close to tears. 'What's so important? There isn't something Dad hasn't told me, is there? Please don't say that; losing Mum was bad enough.'

'No, it's nothing like that. I need to talk to you about Turner again. It's got nothing to do with your dad.'

'I've decided to end the relationship.'

Kesey relaxed. 'That's good, I'm glad to hear it, but I need to speak to you anyway.'

'Look, I know he's a bit of a weirdo. I'm going to tell him we're finished – isn't that enough?'

Kesey sighed. 'This isn't something I've ever done before, but your dad would never forgive me if I didn't warn you. I think Turner's dangerous.'

Emily glanced at the clock on the opposite wall. 'Look, I know what I told you, but he didn't actually hurt me. That's what matters, isn't it? If he had, I'd be the first one to press charges. I can promise you that. Pretending isn't the same as doing.'

'Turner was arrested on suspicion of murder. He's been released on police bail pending further enquiries.'

Emily rubbed her brow. 'Surely you're not saying he's a serious suspect? I hope it's not because of what I told you; I really don't think he murdered those girls.'

'I'm telling you this in confidence, for your ears only. Understand?'

'What the hell are you saying?'

'I'm not going to go into specific details, but I think there's a very real chance that Turner's the killer. I can't stress that enough. As soon as I've got sufficient evidence, he'll be rearrested and charged.'

'Really?'

'Oh, yes, there's little doubt in my mind.'

'Have you searched his house? Dad always searches the house.'

Kesey shook her head. 'We haven't got enough to get a warrant.'

Emily unbuttoned the top two buttons of her winter coat. 'Have you got time for a coffee? I can make a quick phone call. I don't think I'm in such a rush to get back to work after all.'

Kesey's mouth fell open as she stood and stared at Emily. 'That necklace, where did you get that necklace?'

'Charles gave it to me. Beautiful, isn't it?'

'One of our victims was wearing one exactly like it: gold, sapphires, a single diamond. It was missing when her body was found. Some killers do that. They take trophies.'

Emily resisted the impulse to vomit as she tore it from her neck with trembling fingers. 'Is this going to be enough to rearrest him?'

'I'll need to confirm it's the victim's, that's crucial. But, yes, I think it very probably is.'

Chapter 40

Turner's two-seater sports car was still parked in his driveway when Kesey and three uniformed officers arrived at his impressive Caerystwyth home. Kesey took the lead, rushing towards the front door, while ordering PC Kieran Harris to run to the back of the house to prevent any attempt of escape through the walled garden.

She hammered the door repeatedly and yelled at the top of her voice, 'Open up, Turner, it's the police. We can break it down if we have to.'

The DI waited and listened, but all was silent. She banged again, even more insistently this time, but still no response. 'Okay, boys, let's break it down. As quickly as you can. I want to get in there.'

A large, rugby-playing officer in his mid-thirties stepped forward with a red, metal battering ram. He lifted it behind him and brought it forward with all the force he could muster. The double-glazed PVC door buckled under the force of the blow, but it stayed shut. The officer repeated the process, using all his weight and power to maximise the impact, and on the third stroke, the door flew open, its locking mechanism mangled and useless.

Kesey rushed into the hallway as the uniformed officer threw the battering ram to the ground and stepped aside to allow her to pass. 'Okay, Mike, you search upstairs. Gary, you can stay down here with me. As of now, we're looking for Turner. If he's here, let's get the bastard arrested. We can search for evidence once that's done.'

Both constables signalled their understanding, and PC Michael Griffiths began to slowly ascend the stairs with his police issue baton gripped tightly in one hand.

Within a few minutes, Kesey had satisfied herself that Charles Turner wasn't hiding anywhere on the ground floor. She was approaching the stairs with the intention of searching the attic when PC Griffiths shouted out, his voice wavering with emotion. 'You need to see this, ma'am. It's horrendous.'

She ran up the staircase, crossed the landing, and stood at the bedroom door, a look of revulsion on her face. It wasn't like anything she'd seen before. She'd heard of such things, read about them, but seeing them with her own eyes was different. The chains, the wall mounted camera, the bloodstained floor, and the ingrained stench of intermingling bodily waste. There they all were in front of her, as clear as day, assaulting her senses. For a time, she was lost for words, silenced by the horror of it all, as she imagined the victims' terror while imprisoned in that awful place. The evil was palpable. It seeped from every brick, every fixture, every fitting. She contemplated humanity's seemingly unlimited capacity for sin, in silence.

PC Griffiths waited for her to say something. To issue orders. But she just stood and stared. 'Are you all right, ma'am?'

Kesey shook herself, suddenly back in the moment. 'Have you been in there?'

'No, no way, I just stood on the landing and called you. I didn't want to disturb things unnecessarily.'

'That's good. Let's keep it that way. The place is going to be dripping with evidence. I'll get the scenes of crime officers here as soon as we've finished searching the rest of the house.'

'Makes sense.'

'Have you searched all the rooms?'

Griffiths looked close to throwing up as he responded. 'Yeah, everywhere. This was the last door I opened.'

'Let's get the attic open. I've got a horrible feeling he's done a runner, but we need to be sure before I put out an alert.'

Within ten minutes, the officers were satisfied that the house was empty. Wherever their suspect was, he wasn't there.

'Okay, boys, we need to search the garden and outbuildings before I call the cavalry. If he has done a runner, the quicker people are looking for him, the better. Let's get on with it.'

Kesey wandered around the first-floor rooms, casting a keen eye over the contents, as the two uniformed constables joined PC Harris outside in the cold. She stopped on entering the master bedroom, with its king-sized bed and floor to ceiling fitted wardrobes. It was obviously his room: the cupboards full of clothes; the book of infamous serial killers, and true crime magazines resting on the bedside table, with a half empty glass of water. It seemed he'd been studying their methods, comparing them to his own. Or maybe he just liked reading the details of the cases and wallowing in the misfortune and misery of their many victims.

Kesey opened a drawer and knew she'd found his trophy cabinet. There were gold rings, bangles, a silver pendant, and various items of women's clothing. Even a frigging tampon.

She opened a second drawer, inch by cautious inch, and was met by the unmistakable scent of lavender oil, as a shout came from the hallway, 'He's not here, ma'am, but he's left his computer. He must have left in a hurry.'

'Just bag it up for the tech people to look at.'

'Will do.'

Kesey dialled the detective chief superintendent's direct office number as she descended the stairs and only had to wait a few seconds before receiving a response. 'DCS Davies.'

'Good morning, ma'am, it's Laura. We're at Turner's house now.'

'Have you got him?'

'His car's here, but there's no sign of him. I'm guessing he knew we were getting closer and left. Leaving his car was a clever move.'

Davies dragged a hand through her hair. 'Has he got a second vehicle?'

'There's nothing on record.'

'And he's definitely not in work?'

'No, I spoke to his secretary. She's been unable to contact him for days, she was keen to tell me.'

'What's the house like?'

Kesey took a deep breath as she pictured the room; that monument to evil she knew she'd never forget. 'The women were here, that's copper-bottomed guaranteed. He kept them chained up in what was a bedroom before he stripped it and fitted chains to the walls. I've never seen anything like it.'

'So, they were imprisoned at the house, for however long, before he killed them.'

'There's a drawer full of trophies – items that belonged to the victims. I recognised some of them from the descriptions we were given. I'm surprised he didn't take them with him. He must think he's coming back.'

There was an air of urgency in DCS Davies' voice when she spoke. 'All right, Laura, I've heard enough. I'm assuming you've arranged for the scenes of crime team to make a thorough examination of the place?'

'That was going to be my next call, ma'am.'

'Okay, understood. I'm going to issue an immediate alert to all UK forces, and to the various ports and airports. If he's on the run, I don't want him leaving the country. That complicates things legally. If we can prevent it, it's to our advantage.'

'Are you going to notify the public? He's a risk; he'll kill again, if given the opportunity. People have the right to know how dangerous he is.'

Davies sighed. 'Yes, Laura, I was coming to that. I'll get something issued. A full description, the reason he's wanted, instructions not to approach him under any circumstances, and to contact the police immediately if seen. The usual in these cases. It's not something I haven't done before.'

'Will you be doing that this morning? As soon as you can?'

The DCS smiled. 'I'm writing it as we speak, Inspector. You can leave it with me.'

'Sorry, ma'am, I didn't mean to imply—'

'I'd stop digging if I were you, Laura. Is there anything else you want to say before we end the call?'

'There is one thing, ma'am.'

Davies placed her pen down on her desk. 'Come on, what is it?'

'I think Grav's daughter may be at risk. Turner's got a thing for her. Can we give her some protection until he's caught?'

Davies thought for a second. 'Has Turner made any specific threats towards her?'

'Well, no, he hasn't, but I still think—'

'Every woman who comes into contact with Turner is in danger. We can't protect all of them. Let's just concentrate on catching him quickly. I'm going to need all our resources at my disposal; officers are the one thing I haven't got to spare.'

'But I really think—'

'My decision's made. Please leave it at that. If you identify anything to suggest Emily's at immediate risk, something specific, tell me about it, and I'll re-evaluate. Is that clear?'

'It is, ma'am.'

'I'm glad to hear it, Laura. And ensure you check the CCTV for the area. If Turner's driving another vehicle, we need to know about it.'

'I'll make sure it's done, ma'am.'

'And knock on neighbours' doors. See what they know.'

'I will, ma'am.'

'Today, Inspector, it can't wait.'

'Yes, ma'am, I'll get on to it.'

'And keep me informed of each development, no surprises.'

'Yes, ma'am. As soon as anything significant happens, you'll be the first to know.'

Chapter 41

Laura Kesey didn't get an answer at the first three doors she knocked on, but she could hear the unmistakable sound of daytime television when she knocked at house number four. She knocked again and waited. Why the delay? She was cold, she was wet through, and she was shivering. Should she walk away and try the next house? No, she had a job to do. It mattered.

Kesey took a deep breath and knocked again, as eighty-three-year-old Myra Nicholl was making her slow and weary way down her hallway. The old lady was reliant on a walking frame and was very much hoping that her visitor was still in situ when she finally reached her front door … thankfully, she was. 'Oh, hello, dear. I wasn't expecting a visitor. What can I do for you?'

Kesey held her warrant card in plain sight. 'I'm with the local police. We're making enquiries in the area and are speaking to all potential witnesses. I'd like to ask you some questions, if that's all right?'

'Why don't you come in for a nice cup of tea in the warm? You look as if you're frozen. I'm glad I'm not out there in the cold.'

The detective smiled, thinking that the woman reminded her of her much-loved paternal grandmother. 'I haven't got time for a cuppa now, sorry, but another time. I want you to tell me if you've ever seen Charles Turner driving anything other than his red sports car, anything at all?'

Myra Nicholl adopted a puzzled expression, searching her mind as the long gone past infringed on recent events and clouded her thinking.

'Think carefully, please. Anything you can tell me may be important.'

'Am I right in thinking that Mr Turner is that rather nice-looking young man, living across the road, the solicitor?'

'Yes, he's the man.'

'Another vehicle? Oh, I don't think so, dear. Are you sure you won't come in for a nice cup of tea and a biscuit? It's no trouble. I've got all the time in the world.'

Kesey made a mental commitment to call again when she had more time. 'I'm sorry, I'd like to, but I've got more houses to call on.'

The old lady looked despondent. 'Oh, all right, dear, but you must visit again when you can. You're always welcome.'

'I will. Goodbye for now.'

'Goodbye, dear, don't forget to call.'

As the detective walked away, pulling her coat around herself against the stinging rain, the old woman called after her, in a sing-song voice that sounded younger than her years. 'Oh, there was one thing, dear, now that I think about it. I did see someone driving an old van into Mr Turner's garage. I thought it was a bit odd at the time. Why would anyone do that?'

Kesey stopped mid-step. 'I think I will have that cup of tea after all.'

'Come on in, dear.'

She followed the old lady as she manoeuvred herself towards the lounge, every item of furniture an obstacle. 'Have a seat on the sofa, and I'll get you that cuppa and a biscuit or two.'

'That would be lovely, thank you.'

'Milk and sugar?'

'Just a drop of milk, please.'

Mrs Nicholl reappeared from the kitchen a few minutes later with a walking stick in one hand and a cup and saucer in the other. 'I'm on my way.'

Kesey rose from her seat and rushed towards her. 'Let me give you a hand.'

The old lady shook her head and smiled. 'I'll manage with this, but if you could fetch your cup and the biscuits from the kitchen, that would be wonderful.'

Kesey did as instructed, keen to expedite matters. 'You were going to tell me about the van?'

Mrs Nicholl sipped her tea. 'Well, I don't know how much more I can tell you.'

'But you're sure you saw a van?'

'Oh, yes, a big white one, covered in rust.'

'When was this?'

She looked downhearted. 'I'm not getting any younger. My memory's not what it was I'm afraid. I couldn't put a date on it.'

'Roughly how long ago are we talking? One week, two weeks, three weeks or more?'

Mrs Nicholl blew the air from her mouth. 'I'm sorry, I'd be guessing. I don't want to mislead you. I can remember looking through the window, and I can remember seeing the van I mentioned, but that's it. I think it stuck in my mind because it seemed so out of place.'

Kesey considered pursuing the matter further, but decided against. The old woman looked close to tears. 'Did you see the driver?'

'Not that I can remember. It was dark and my eyesight's not what it was.'

'But you are certain you saw a van? A van being driven into Turner's garage?'

'Oh, yes, dear, I definitely saw one. I just don't know when it was or who was driving. I hope I haven't wasted your time.'

Kesey dunked a ginger biscuit into her tea. 'You've been very helpful, Mrs Nicholl. It's appreciated.'

'Thank you, dear, I think the police do a marvellous job. I'm glad to be of service.'

Chapter 42

Emily parked her father's aged green Volkswagen hatchback on the driveway and exited the vehicle just as the luminous grey sky dusted the area with a flurry of snowflakes. She had a strangely disconcerting feeling in the pit of her stomach as she approached the house, inserted her key in the lock, and slowly opened the door. She tried to shake off the feeling, as she entered the hallway, but it refused to let go. She hung her coat on the end of the bannister, and told herself that a degree of anxiety was natural and understandable under the circumstances.

Emily entered the lounge and flicked the light switch just inside the door. The bulb burst into seemingly enthusiastic life, and she froze, statue like, staring to her right, where Charles Turner was sitting, cross-legged, in a brown leather armchair next to the gas fire. 'Welcome home, Emily, I hope work wasn't too onerous for you. There's a pot of coffee ready and waiting. I thought I'd surprise you.'

She seriously considered kicking off her heels and bolting for the front door, but decided she was unlikely to make it before he leapt from his seat and grabbed her. 'I didn't recognise you at first.'

'Ah, yes, the hair and glasses. I thought a new look would be to my advantage, given recent events. I'm sure you know what I'm talking about. You're not a complete ignoramus.'

Emily felt her gut cramp and spasm. 'What are you doing here?'

Turner's smile became a sneer. 'I thought you'd be pleased to see me. Don't tell me we're no longer friends – what have I done to deserve that?'

She took a step back as he rose to his feet. 'How did you get in?'

He laughed. 'The kitchen window was open. It wasn't difficult. You really should be more careful. I'm sure your father would tell you the same thing, were he able to, what with him being a police officer and all.'

Emily took another backward step as Turner slowly approached her.

'Why so nervous, Emily? You look pale and lifeless, and it suits you. Maybe the harsh light highlights your impending mortality. Yes, I think that's probably it. The glare of the bulb on your pale, winter skin; the dark makeup around your eyes. You look like a beguiling corpse awaiting burial in an open coffin, and you've never been more attractive. I don't know how I didn't see it before.'

Emily was quivering now, her adrenal glands in full production; fight or flight, or just stand there, open-mouthed and sweating, and attempt to placate him? 'My dad will be home soon. You'd better go before he arrives, he'll arrest you. You're running out of time.'

Turner placed a hand on each of her shoulders. 'Oh, I don't think so. I know all about his health problems. You told me yourself. Remember? We talked about it, I reassured you. Your erstwhile knight in shining armour is somewhat tarnished these days. Is that really the best you've got?'

Emily resisted the impulse to scream and forced a fragile smile that looked far from compelling. 'Yeah, sorry, I'm nervous, that's all. I don't know what's wrong with me. You've been wonderfully supportive; a ray of sunshine in my life at a difficult time. It was just a shock finding you here, sitting in the dark, that's all. Why don't we go out somewhere for a bite to eat and a few drinks? What about that nice Italian restaurant in Merlin's Lane? Or the place we went on that first night, in Laugharne. We had a great time. You liked it there, didn't you?'

Turner pushed her towards the settee. 'Oh, I don't think so, Emily, not tonight, not ever. Things have changed. We're approaching the end game. I think we both know what I'm talking about.'

Emily fell into the seat and pressed her legs together. 'We're good together, aren't we? Me and you. You and me. There's a spark of attraction between us, something special. I know you can feel it. Why spoil that?'

He sat next to her and patted her knee. 'What are you really thinking in that pretty head of yours? What's on your mind? I've heard enough of your crap for one lifetime. Did one of those moronic police officers your father works with tell you about my arrest? Naughty, naughty. They really shouldn't have done that.'

Emily shook her head frantically. 'No, it's nothing like that. I thought you must be unwell when you didn't turn up for work. I was planning to ring you this evening to ask how you were.'

Turner dug his thumbnail hard into the side of her knee and made her wince. 'I know you're lying, Emily. Who told you? Was it that Laura Kesey with her stupid, infuriating Brummie twang? She seems like the sort of fool who'd break the rules of evidence.'

'Nobody said anything.'

'I had to listen to that bitch for almost two hours. She'll pay for the inconvenience she caused me. She'll suffer one day, I can promise you that much.'

Emily cried as a trickle of urine soaked her underclothes. 'She didn't s-say a thing.'

He pressed his forehead against hers. 'Do you really think I'm that stupid?'

She wanted to pull away, she'd never wanted anything more, but she couldn't move. 'No, of *course* not. I can understand you being upset. Anybody would be if wrongly accused of crimes they didn't commit – particularly something as ghastly as the murders.'

Turner whispered into her ear. 'Murders and rapes, don't forget the rapes. Those girls didn't die easy.'

Emily was sobbing now, a stream of salty tears running down her face and smudging her mascara. 'It must have been awful for you.'

'Oh, it would have been, if the plebs had any worthwhile evidence, anything in the slightest that could link me to the crimes in question. The police are such limited creatures. It's laughable, really. If you're expecting the boys and girls in blue to come to your rescue anytime soon, you've lost already. Just give up. It'll be easier that way. Go with the flow.'

Emily swallowed and spoke through her tears. 'Why don't we have some coffee? You said you'd made some.'

Turner averted his gaze to the ceiling and suddenly jumped to his feet in one athletic movement. 'Yes, why not? The time seems right. I wondered if you'd comment on the aroma when you first came in.'

'I'm full of cold… I'm sure it's lovely.'

He picked up the percolator, poured a single cup of strong, black coffee, and handed it to her with a half-smile playing on his lips. 'I want you to drink the whole cup. Every bit. Don't leave a single drop. I made it especially for you. It would not be a good idea to leave any, you may see a side of me you haven't seen before if you do. Believe me, you don't want that.'

'Aren't you going to have some?'

'Just drink your coffee, there's a good girl.' Turner knelt in front of her as she lifted the cup to her mouth.

'Please let me go, Charles. We've had fun, haven't we? Why not continue our relationship? We're good together. I'd like that, wouldn't you?'

'How gullible do you think I am? Just finish your coffee before I pin your head back and pour it down your throat.'

She raised the cup and drank, forcing herself to swallow the bitter liquid as every cell in her body was yelling no.

'Come on, down it goes. Don't make me ask you again.'

'Why does it taste so odd?'

'Just drink the fucking stuff, you don't have to like it.'

Emily took another gulp and cringed.

'I'm losing my patience, bitch. Get it down.'

She recoiled at the use of the B word and drained the cup. 'It's empty.'

'Every drop?'

She looked in the cup and nodded. 'Yes, every drop.'

'That's much better. Top marks. I want you to hand me the cup, lie yourself down on the settee, and try to relax. Do it now, please. Don't keep me waiting.'

Emily was shaking uncontrollably as she followed his instructions.

'That's it, time to rest. It will all be over soon enough.'

'What'll be over? What are you going to do to me?'

'Just lie back, Emily. Lie back and shut your stupid mouth. I think that's best.'

She stared at him with pleading eyes that were slowly closing. 'What are you—'

Within seconds, she had drifted into a deep, dreamless, chemically induced sleep that would last for hours.

Chapter 43

Turner's long-suffering secretary thought long and hard about contacting the police. She'd changed her mind more than once after watching the early evening news, and the decision wasn't getting any easier. She picked up the phone and started dialling the number, but placed it back on the receiver, thinking a glass of wine may help her relax.

Her husband of six months looked at her and smiled encouragingly. 'Are you going to ring, or not? You heard what they said on the news. We're talking murder, not some triviality. Why not get it over with? You'll feel better once you've done it.'

She screwed up her face. 'Yeah, but he's my boss. Actually, ringing is a lot harder than just talking about it. He's been good to me. I like him. I just can't believe he's done the awful things they said. Why don't we have a nice glass of wine and a bite to eat while I think about it? There's a nice bottle of Chardonnay in the fridge.'

'Oh, come on, Helen. He's wanted for murder. It wouldn't have been on the telly if they weren't sure. You said that yourself. Do you want me to dial for you? Would that help?'

She handed him the phone. 'Yeah, go on, then. Will you speak to them for me as well?'

He dialled the number and waited until he heard the female telephonist say, 'West Wales Police. How can I help you?'

'My wife wants to speak to an officer about Charles Turner, the murder case. She thinks she may know where he's gone.'

'What's your name and contact number, please? Just in case you're cut off before I put you through.'

He provided the information as requested.

'Thank you for that. I'll put you through to Detective Inspector Kesey. She's heading up the investigation. I think she's free.'

'Thank you; I'll just pass the phone to my wife.'

Helen glared at him, with a look that said a thousand words, snatched the phone from his hand and put it to her ear, just as the detective said, 'DI Kesey, CID.'

Helen seriously considered putting the phone down but thought better of it. 'It's about the murder case, all those poor girls. I saw the report on the Welsh news.'

Kesey grabbed a pen and poised the tip above her notebook. 'Who am I speaking to?'

'My name's Helen Edwards; I'm Mr Turner's secretary, Charles Turner, the solicitor.'

'Ah, okay, you must know Emily Gravel, then?'

'Yeah, I do, we work together. Lovely girl.'

'What is it you want to talk to me about, Helen?'

She shifted her weight from one stockinged foot to the other, still doubting the wisdom of calling. 'Look, I don't want to waste your time, but I talked it through with my husband, and we decided I should ring.'

Kesey increased her grip on the phone. 'Why don't you tell me what this is all about and let me decide if it's relevant?'

'I think I may know where Mr Turner's gone.'

Kesey sat upright in her seat. 'Where?'

'I don't know with any certainty, mind, I could be completely wrong. It's just something I overheard him telling Emily in the office a few days back. I wasn't eavesdropping. My office is right next to his. You can't help but hear everything if the door's open. He usually shuts it, but—'

Kesey tried not to reveal her impatience, but it was betrayed by her voice. 'What was it he said to her exactly?'

'He asked her if she'd like to go to Devon one weekend, for a break. I think he fancies her. One of his friends has got a cottage somewhere on the coast. He lets Mr Turner stay there when he's not using it himself. Or at least that's what he told Emily.'

'You said Devon. Can you be more specific for me?'

'I know it's in Devon because he mentioned it, as I said, but that's about it. Maybe they've gone together.'

'They?'

'Emily and Mr Turner. She didn't come to work today. I had to cancel all her appointments at the last minute. I've tried to ring her a few times, but her phone's switched off. It's just not like her.'

'Has she ever done anything like that before?'

'Well, she hasn't been with the firm long, but, no, she seems very dedicated and hard-working … I just hope she's okay, that's all. I'm sure Mr Turner wouldn't hurt her, but—'

'I want you to think very carefully. Has either of them ever said where this cottage is? The name of a town or village, perhaps?'

Helen pressed her lips together and shook her head. 'No, not that I heard anyway. I'm only the secretary. They don't talk to me about that sort of thing.'

'And you didn't overhear anything?'

'I only wish I had.'

'Okay, we'll move on… Do you know the name of the friend, the one who owns the cottage? It would be extremely helpful if you do.'

'I haven't got a clue.'

'You're certain, not even a first name?'

'I'm sorry I can't be more helpful.'

Kesey cursed under her breath. 'Not at all, the information you've provided may well prove useful. I'll be sharing it with Devon and Cornwall Police straight after this call. I appreciate you ringing. And maybe there's something else you can help me with.'

'If I can.'

'One of Turner's neighbours said she thought she saw him driving a rusty, old, white van in recent weeks. She couldn't be certain when it was, she's getting on a bit to be honest. Do you know anything about the vehicle?'

Helen laughed, the tension melting away. 'You have got to be kidding. He loves his cars, he's a right petrol head, but they have to be fast, and they have to be expensive. He wouldn't be seen dead in any van, let alone a rusty one. He'd hate it. I don't think I'm speaking out of turn when I say that he's very image-conscious. Vain would be another way to put it. That Carly Simon song always reminds me of him. Do you know the one?'

Kesey smiled. 'Okay, that's helpful. Is there anything else you can tell me, anything at all? Even the most seemingly insignificant information may prove crucial.'

'No, that's it, there's nothing else I can think of.'

'Okay, we're done for now … I'm grateful, Helen, and you know where I am if you need to speak to the police again. Don't hesitate to ring if you think of anything else. If I'm not here, leave a message and I'll get back to you; someone's here twenty-four hours a day, seven days a week.'

'He's a nice man, you know. Pleasant, gentle and helpful. I was saying the same thing to my husband before ringing. I'm sure all this must be a terrible mistake. Maybe it's a case of mistaken identity. Maybe the killer looks like Mr Turner. That could explain it.'

'If you see him, don't approach him. Ring 999 immediately. People can be deceptive. Not everyone's as they seem. He's a very dangerous man.'

Chapter 44

Kesey gave up on the idea of breaking Grav's ground-floor bathroom window with her elbow, after two bruising attempts, and retreated to his garden shed where she found a hammer and screwdriver in a cluttered toolbox that was half hidden behind a pile of paint cans.

She placed the tip of the screwdriver against the bottom right-hand corner of the window, lifted the hammer, and shattered the glass with one powerful, well-aimed blow, causing the inner and outer panes to break into what seemed like a thousand small pieces that sparkled like diamonds in the winter sunshine. She threw the screwdriver aside, but held on to the hammer, thinking it could prove a useful weapon, if required.

Kesey put her head through the gap and listened intently. What sounded like Radio 2 was playing somewhere in the house, but there were no other signs of life. She called out quietly at first, and then louder, at the top of her voice, to be sure of being heard if anyone was there to listen. 'Emily! Are you in there? It's Laura Kesey, police, I'm coming in.'

She tucked the hammer into the rear waistband of her grey trousers, pulled herself onto the windowsill, belly first, and moved forward, one cautious inch at a time, until her weight acted as a fulcrum, and she fell head first, colliding with the white porcelain basin and crashing heavily to the tiled floor.

Kesey swore loudly as she lifted herself to her feet with the aid of a heated towel rail, and took the hammer in hand, clutching its steel shaft tightly and not letting go. She left the bathroom and entered the small, dated kitchen where the radio was playing on a worktop. She switched it off with a gloved hand, just as the DJ was announcing the next track with a degree of enthusiasm that seemed at odds with the solemnity of the situation. She shouted again, calling Emily's name, hoping for a response, but all was silent.

She crossed the tiny, red-tiled hall into the lounge, walked to the centre of the room, and turned slowly, in a circle, listening for the slightest sound. She didn't see the envelope at first, but as she turned a full three hundred and sixty degrees for the second time, there it was, propped up against a percolator on the table.

For a reason she couldn't explain, she knew the letter mattered as soon as she saw it. It was a gut instinct. A message from the heart to brain. She walked slowly towards it and studied the ivory envelope. It was addressed to Grav, formally – using his rank and full name – in flowing script that she guessed was meant to impress. She told herself that it was of no particular consequence, and she tried to push the feeling of foreboding from her mind, but she knew without doubt that things were about to take an unwelcome turn. The faint, but discernible, bloody fingerprint in one corner of the paper and the scent of lavender were a testament to that.

Kesey prised open the envelope as carefully as possible, keen not to compromise any evidence. As she removed the single sheet of writing paper, a bloody fingernail, torn from a victim's hand, fell to the floor. She gagged and picked up the offending item, dropping it into an evidence bag, before running back to the ground floor bathroom where she threw up until there was nothing left but bile.

Kesey took a gulp of water from the cold tap, squirted some fresh mint toothpaste in her mouth, rinsed, and returned to the lounge with a resigned expression on her face. She resisted the impulse to run, picked up the letter and slumped on the settee to read it.

Dear Detective Inspector Gravel,

I hope you like the small gift I left you. As you can see, I'm not a man subject to humanity's usual, self-imposed limitations.

Empathy and virtue mean nothing to me. I enjoy inflicting suffering on others. It excites me. The greater the suffering, the happier and more fulfilled I feel. And so, I feel sure you'll fully appreciate just how much pain and hardship your daughter's going to experience before I finally strangle her.

I may well keep you updated as the process progresses. Maybe another letter, or two, or even a phone call. That seems fair. You're the reason I've allowed her to live for as long as I have, after all. Have you realised that? No? I picture you riddled with angst, paralysed by dread, and it tickles me. I'll drag the whole affair out for as long as feasibly possible, before the irresistible desire to kill brings her miserable existence to an inevitable end. How does that make you feel as her father? The great detective, powerless to help the one person who matters most. Not great, I'd imagine. And that amuses me no end. I'm laughing now as I write these words. Can you hear me, Inspector? Can you magnify it in your mind? I hope the sound resonates and haunts you forever. I hope it destroys whatever little peace of mind you have left. If heaven can be a place on earth, then so can hell.

Anyway, enough of such musings, it's time for me to leave now. I'll kiss Emily goodbye for you when she finally regains consciousness.

Regards,
Charles Turner

Kesey refolded the letter, slotted it back into its matching envelope, and began to weep. She wanted to scream, she wanted to stamp and shout like a petulant toddler, but instead, she calmed her breathing and centred herself.

She rose to her feet and punched the back of the settee with a clenched fist. The Devon and Cornwall force were searching their entire area; maybe Turner's secretary had been right. And there was his distinctive appearance, the van, a female passenger. At least they knew who they were looking for. They weren't completely in the dark, unless they weren't in a van at all … Say a prayer, Laura. Please, God, let us find her. Please let Emily live. Maybe they'd get a break; maybe they'd save her life, and Turner would be locked up forever.

Chapter 45

Turner's journey south, from Caerystwyth to the Ceredigion coast, passed without incident. He was unshaven, dressed casually, and had dyed his hair dark brown, rendering him virtually unrecognisable as the man that the police were looking for.

It took him a little over ninety minutes to drive to Borth – a remote coastal village, bordered by Cardigan Bay, just a few miles from the atmospheric university town of Aberystwyth. He parked the van at the back of the isolated stone cottage, well out of sight of prying eyes, and carried Emily's unconscious body from the vehicle, wrapped in a multicoloured nylon rug that had lain in Grav's lounge.

Turner struggled with Emily's dead weight initially, as he hurried across the overgrown garden towards the front door, but when the familiar feelings of anticipation flooded his system with adrenaline, the task became easier, and he carried her over one shoulder with relative ease.

He closed the front door, locked it, and made his way towards the farmhouse kitchen where a flight of ten worn, wooden steps led down to the cellar. Turner dropped Emily to the slate floor and left her there while he made himself a cup of instant coffee. He sat at the stripped oak table, cradling his mug with both hands, as she moaned incoherently a few feet away.

Turner pondered his new reality and acknowledged that his life had changed for ever. There was no going back. The die was cast. He pushed his empty mug aside, jumped to his feet, and opened the cellar door. He dragged Emily, by her feet, down the steps; her head bouncing from one to the next until they reached the bottom.

Turner took aim and kicked Emily, before stripping her naked and handcuffing her wrists behind her back. He switched off the light and took her clothes upstairs for burning.

Turner closed the cellar door and ambled into the lounge to while away the hours until his captive finally regained consciousness. Perhaps he'd write her moronic father another letter: something dark, something intriguing. Something to make the pleb squirm.

Chapter 46

Laura Kesey sat alone in her parked car, pressed the call button, and waited until she eventually heard her old university friend say, 'Hello,' with a strong Midlands accent that reminded her of home.

'Hi, Ed, how's it hanging?'

'Like you'd be interested.'

Kesey laughed. 'I can't make it this weekend. All leave's been cancelled for the foreseeable future. Mum's gutted. I haven't seen her for ages.'

'Is that down to the murder case?'

'You've heard about it?'

'Who hasn't? It's been all over the news.'

'Yeah, I suppose it has.'

'Well, at least you know who you're looking for, that's a bonus.'

'It would be if we had the slightest idea where the bastard is. He may as well have disappeared off the face of the earth.'

Ed hesitated before changing the subject. 'How are you doing, Laura? Personally, I mean – after the miscarriage.'

'I won't lie, it's been tough.'

'Yeah, for me too.'

'I want to try again, if you're up for it?'

'With me? Are you sure?'

Kesey laughed again, more nervously this time. 'You're the only one who'd be stupid enough to agree to it. Who else am I going to ask?'

'Yeah, you've got a point there. What does Janet think?'

'I wanted to sound you out before talking to her. The miscarriage hit her hard. She wants a baby as much as I do.'

'The two of you will make great mothers.'

'I just hope we get the chance.'

'Of course, you will. The things I go through to keep you happy. I hope you appreciate all the sacrifices I make.'

'I can't remember you complaining at the time. All that grunting was a dead giveaway.'

Ed grinned. 'Okay, guilty as charged. If there's a job to do, I like to do it to the very best of my ability, no half measures.'

'Well, the least said about that the better, particularly if Janet's around. I've convinced her it was all cold, calculated, and business-like. I think it's the only way she can handle it. We need to keep it that way.'

'So, when am I going to see you?'

'I thought I'd come up for a few days as soon as we've caught the bastard. I can't put a date on it, but hopefully, it won't be too far in the future.'

'Sounds good to me. I can be as flexible as you need me to be. It's one of the advantages of being my own boss.'

Kesey started the engine and turned the heating up to maximum. 'Thanks, Ed. Joking aside, I'm really grateful for what you're doing for us. Janet feels the same way. There's not many men who'd help us out the way you are.'

'So, come on, give me the inside story. What's happening with the case? I've always loved those detective shows on the telly.'

'Do you really want to know?'

'I asked, didn't I?'

'We've got various forces checking the camera footage between Wales and the Cornish border. Hopefully, he'll show up somewhere.'

'Sounds promising.'

'There's an awful lot of white vans on the road. It's just a case of ruling out as many as we can, as quickly as we can, focusing on the ones that are left and keeping our fingers crossed.'

'You'll have him locked up before you know it.'

'We're not even sure he's in the van at all. It's fifty-fifty, but it's the best we've got.'

'That's not so bad.'

'He's got a friend of mine with him, my boss' daughter. That's if he hasn't killed her already.'

'Oh, for fuck's sake, that's bad.'

'How the hell am I going to tell him? He's in hospital after a heart attack.'

'What, he doesn't know?'

Kesey shook her head. 'He's going to be wondering why she's not visiting. I can't delay it for much longer.'

'What are you going to do?'

Kesey fastened her seatbelt and prepared to drive off. 'I'm going to have a word with my chief superintendent to see what she thinks. They don't pay me enough for this shit.'

'Take it easy, Laura. Look after yourself.'

'And you, Ed. I'd better make a move. You'll have to come and visit in the spring when the weather's better. There's some beautiful places in this part of the world, I think you'd love it. You could bring the dog.'

'That would be nice.'

'Yes, and thank you. I mean that from the bottom of my heart. You're the best friend a girl could have. I'll visit you as soon as we've got him.'

Chapter 47

Turner looked down at Emily, imprisoned, naked and shivering on the basement floor, and smiled contentedly. 'What do you think of your new home? I like to think you're impressed. I was beginning to wonder if you'd wake up at all.'

She squinted up at him in the glare of the single bulb that seemed focused only on her. 'I've been in the dark until now.'

'Ah, yes, quite so. I thought you'd find the absence of light relaxing. You were sleeping so peacefully, it seemed a shame to disturb you.'

Emily attempted to raise a hand to massage her aching head, but her wrist jarred against the cuffs. 'Where are we?'

'Where do you think?'

She looked down and juddered as the anaesthetic effects of the drug began wearing off. 'Are we at your friend's place in the West Country?'

'Smoke and mirrors, Emily. We're on the Ceredigion coast, about six miles from Aberystwyth. The cottage belongs to an elderly client of mine who has dementia. There's no friends to speak of and no surviving relatives. The place has been empty for years. It seemed impolite not to make use of it.'

'Have you ever brought anyone else here?'

Turner shook his head. 'You're the first. I kept it in reserve for these precise circumstances. Aren't you the lucky one?'

'Why, Charles? Why are you doing this to me?'

He shrugged. 'Because I want to; because I can. It's the only justification I need. Right and wrong mean nothing to me. They never have. I find life's a lot more enjoyable that way. I've learnt to fully embrace my dark side.'

'We're good together, aren't we? We could have a future, if you let me live. I have feelings for you, strong feelings. Take the cuffs off, and I'll show you how much I love you.'

Turner reached out and ran the fingers of his uninjured hand through her hair. 'It looks much better that way.'

'What does?'

'Your hair. It's blonde. I dyed it copper-blonde.'

'Why would you do that?'

He studied her closely, looking her up and down as she raised her knees to her chest and pressed herself to the wall. 'You look a lot like my mother did at a similar age. Have I ever told you that? I've got a photograph in my wallet. It's black and white, faded, and somewhat frayed at the edges, but you can still see her features well enough. And her dress and shoes. Much like the ones I've bought for you.'

'I'm sure they're lovely.'

Turner smiled. 'We'll wash you and dress you sometime in the next day or two, when the time's right. That's something to look forward to.'

Emily sucked in the fetid air, forcing herself to appear unfazed by events. 'I'd like to see it sometime – the photo – it obviously means a great deal to you.'

He sat at her feet and placed his face inches from hers; she could feel his warm breath on her face. 'Have you thought about why my mother left me? Perhaps it's a female thing. Are you all unreliable?'

Emily hesitated, choosing her words with care. 'I've been thinking about little else since you first asked me. I can see you need closure. I'm hoping I can help you find it.'

Turner placed one hand around her slender neck and began massaging her windpipe between his thumb and fingers. 'You will, one way or another. Do or die. Survive or perish. It's in your interests to impress. But then, you've already realised that, with your oh so polite conversational skills, and feigned interest in my emotional wellbeing. You're an intelligent young woman.

Infinitely more capable than any of my previous guests. But don't think you can play me, Emily. That wouldn't be a good idea. Underestimate me at your peril. This is your one and only warning. I expect total honesty from here on in.'

Emily choked on her words as her tears began to flow freely. 'I just w-want to h-help, that's all.'

Turner lunged forward and bit her earlobe, making her jerk back and wince as dark blood ran down her neck and settled on her shoulder. 'So, come on. What have you come up with? I'm all ears. All ears! Get it? Just my little joke.'

'I think, for whatever reason, your mother thought you'd be better off without her. She made the ultimate sacrifice and did it with your welfare at the forefront of her mind. I'm certain of it. However ill-judged, she thought she was doing the right thing.'

Turner clapped his hands together. 'Yes, that's a reasonable supposition, but why would any child be better off without its mother? Can you answer that for me?'

Emily could feel her heart pounding in her throat. She could hear it like the beat of a drum. 'Maybe she was seriously ill, or protecting you from a violent man you're unaware of. A man like Spencer, a man she couldn't escape, however hard she tried.'

He touched her ear, raised his bloody finger to his mouth, and licked it clean. 'How's your hand? I meant to ask earlier, but it slipped my mind.'

'It hurts like hell. I'd be grateful for analgesics of some kind… What happened to it?'

Turner laughed, head back, faultless teeth in full view. 'Can you imagine your father's shock when he opened the letter and found your fingernail with its torn fragments of flesh? I'd like to have been a fly on the wall for that one. Maybe he had another heart attack.'

Emily winced, picturing Grav's face, and feeling his distress. 'I don't understand.'

'It's a game I'm playing, cat and mouse. Now do you see? I'm planning on sending a second letter, and a third a day or two after that. I could send another nail, a blood-soaked cloth, or even a finger or two. What do you think? Do you find the concept as amusing as I do?'

Emily dropped her head. 'Please, not that. Not my fingers. Anything but my fingers.'

Turner crossed the floor, switched off the light, and began ascending the stairs to the kitchen. 'Be very careful what you wish for, Emily. There are worse things I could cut off than fingers. And don't be getting your hopes up. I'll post appropriately addressed parcels to a like-minded friend in London, and he'll post them on from there. Genius. That should make the police even more confused than they already are.'

Chapter 48

Sandra smiled warmly and welcomed Kesey with a cheery, 'Good morning,' as she strode into Police Headquarters, glad to escape the cold.

'And a good morning to you too. What are you so happy about? You haven't won the lottery, have you?'

'It's my birthday.'

Kesey sang the first line of "Happy Birthday" and grinned. 'Twenty-one again?'

Sandra waved a brown padded envelope above her head as the DI turned and walked away. 'This one's for you, ma'am, I would have stuck it in the internal mail with the rest, but it's marked urgent and strictly confidential. For your eyes only.'

The detective took it and recognised the handwriting immediately. The flowing script was unmistakable. She held the envelope to her eyes and studied the postmark, before holding it up for Sandra to examine. 'Can you read what that says?'

Sandra perched her reading glasses on the bridge of her nose and focused. 'That looks a bit like an N, but as for the rest of it, it's hard to say. It's smudged all over the place.'

Kesey sighed. 'Yeah, that's what I thought. Maybe I'll try a magnifying glass.'

'Are you going to tell me how Grav's doing? I've been worried sick. The place just isn't the same without him.'

'Yeah, sorry, he's on the mend… I'm in a bit of a rush, Sandra. Is the DCS in?'

'She's got a meeting at Probation HQ at ten, but she hasn't left yet. You'll catch her if you're quick.'

'Thanks, Sandra. We'll have a proper catch up when I've got more time. I may even buy you a cake.'

Kesey brushed non-existent fluff from her shoulders as she knocked on the detective chief superintendent's office door and waited for what seemed like an age before being invited in.

'Take a seat, Laura, I haven't got a lot of time. What's this about?'

'We've received a second package from Turner, ma'am. It arrived in the post this morning.'

Davies' expression hardened. 'Where was it posted?'

'I can't read the postmark. My best guess is London, but I wouldn't put any money on it. I'm far from certain.'

'If it is London, we're looking in the wrong places.'

'We've put out an all forces alert. Maybe we'll get a lucky break. Devon and Cornwall haven't come up with anything.'

The DCS began pacing the floor. 'What was in the package?'

'Another letter marked for Grav's attention and a dishcloth soaked in what looks like congealed blood. It's almost certainly Emily's.'

'Oh, for God's sake. Have you sent it for testing?'

'It's on its way. We'll have the results in a couple of days.'

'You've read the letter presumably?'

Kesey nodded. 'It's much the same as the first one – full of threats and taunts. Most of its directed towards DI Gravel, but with an additional message for me.'

'For you?'

'Yeah, he's driving home what he sees as his superiority.'

'What did he say exactly?'

'Basically, that Emily's abduction and torture are my failures … And he's right, when you think about it. I knew she was in danger. I said as much. I let her down; we both let her down.'

The DCS turned to face Kesey. 'Now you listen to me, and you listen well. You can't let yourself think like that. It's what the bastard wants; he's trying to get inside your head. Don't let him get to you.'

'We should have given her protection when we had the chance. All this could have been avoided.'

'Hindsight's an exact science; things are always clearer after the event.'

'It was clear enough to me.'

Davies glared at her junior colleague. 'That's enough, Laura. Let's just focus on catching Turner, shall we? There'll be plenty of time for recriminations when this is all over with. If Emily's killed, we'll both have questions to answer. I can promise you that much.'

'Sorry, ma'am, I shouldn't have said anything. I was just sounding off; if we're fighting amongst ourselves, Turner's winning.'

Davies returned to her seat. 'Is there anything in the letter that gives us any clue as to their location? Anything at all?'

'Nothing.'

'You're sure?'

'I've been through it, time and time again.'

'What about this van mentioned by the neighbour? Have there been any sightings?'

'I've been in regular contact with the forces between here and Cornwall. There's no shortage of white vans on the roads, but no sign of Turner. Worst case scenario, the witness had it wrong in the first place.'

'Tell me, Laura, have you considered the possibility that Emily's ex was run down and killed by Turner? If he does have access to a van, if the witness *was* correct, why not use it as a weapon? Getting the boyfriend out of the way would make perfect sense when you think about it. We know the plates were false, but we've got the details. Let's see if a van with a matching index number has been seen anywhere on the M4 or the M5 during the relevant period. If I'm right, it could point us in his direction.'

'It's been done, ma'am. I've circulated the number.'

'You have?'

'Yeah, because of what Turner's neighbour said – and the witness thought the driver who hit Richard was male. Turner driving seems a distinct possibility.'

'Right, it's time for me to go. Is there anything else before we bring this meeting to a close?'

'Just one thing, ma'am.'

'Let's hear it.'

'It's DI Gravel, ma'am; he hasn't been notified of his daughter's abduction.'

Davies raised a hand to her face. 'Ah, yes, the same thing occurred to me. If we don't tell him, someone else is going to do it for us: a doctor, a nurse, another patient. Bad news is the last thing he needs, given his health issues, but I don't see we've got any viable alternative. We can't isolate him from the world. He's going to find out one way or another. It's just a matter of when and how.'

'Exactly. There's only one thing to do.'

'I could call on him sometime today, but our relationship's been somewhat fraught over the years. You've got a good rapport with him, perhaps you could tell him; in his best interests, you understand. What do you think?'

Kesey sighed, resigned to the inevitable. 'Okay, I'll visit him this evening. It's got to be done.'

The DCS picked up her leather briefcase. 'Thank you, Laura, it's appreciated. Why not do it now? I'm on my way out. We can walk as far as the car park together.'

Chapter 49

Grav was fast asleep, propped up on three pillows, and snoring at full volume when Kesey entered the busy cardiology ward about half an hour later. She'd rehearsed telling him, time and time again, en route to West Wales Hospital, but it hadn't helped. She was dreading the conversation; the hardest of her life.

The big man snorted loudly and opened one eye as she sat to the right of his bed, but within seconds, he was asleep again. She considered nudging him, but she couldn't bring herself to do it.

Kesey sat there for a full ten minutes, staring at the ceiling, twirling her wristwatch, trying to decide what to say. She knew she was simply delaying the inevitable, so as the wall clock opposite her struck ten, she moved quickly, without giving herself time to change her mind. 'Wake up, boss, it's Laura. We need to talk.'

Grav opened one eye, then the other, stretched expansively, and yawned loudly, casting off the remnants of sleep. 'Oh, hello, love. Is it visiting time already? I must have been asleep for hours.'

Kesey shook her head. 'No, it's still morning. The ward sister gave me permission to see you.'

He lifted himself up stiffly and rearranged his pillows before slumping back on the bed with a sigh. 'Do you need to talk about the case? I'm here to help if I can, you know that.'

Kesey looked away, avoiding his gaze. 'I'm not here for advice.'

Grav's expression hardened. 'What's this about? What the fuck's happened? There's obviously something.'

'I've got some bad news, boss. There's no easy way to tell you—'

He pulled himself upright again, grimacing.

'It's Emily, boss. Turner's got her.'

Grav gripped the sheet tightly with both hands. 'Got her? What the fuck's that supposed to mean?'

'Are you all right, boss? Do you want me to call a nurse?'

'Just answer the fucking question.'

'Turner was arrested and released on police bail. There wasn't enough to charge him.'

His eyes narrowed. 'What the fuck's that got to do with Emily?'

'Turner's left the area. He's taken Emily with him.'

Grav sat on the edge of the bed. 'Oh, for fuck's sake! When did this happen?'

'It's been three days since either of them were seen.'

He tried to stand, but fell back on the bed when his legs couldn't support his weight. 'Three fucking days? And you didn't think of telling me before now?'

Kesey placed a hand on his broad shoulder, but withdrew it when he pulled away. 'I'm sorry, boss, but you're in here. You've had two heart attacks. It's up to me now; there's nothing you can do.'

'Like fuck, there isn't; I'm discharging myself.'

'I'm calling a nurse.'

'Call who the fuck you want. I'm out of here.'

She pressed the red button and tried to hold him as he struggled to free himself. 'You're not up to it, boss. What good will you be to Emily if you collapse and die?'

'Out of my fucking way.'

'We can talk about the case. You can give me pointers, directions, I'll tell you everything. You can manage the investigation from your hospital bed, if that keeps you here.'

He relaxed slightly as a young staff nurse approached them with a concerned look on her face. 'Is everything all right, Mr Gravel? You rang your buzzer.'

'A glass of water would be appreciated.'

'There's a full jug next to your bed.'

'Oh, sorry to bother you, love. I just need some time to talk to my sergeant.'

The nurse smiled thinly. 'Not too long now, you need your rest.'

Grav lifted a hand to his head and saluted theatrically. 'Anything you say, ma'am.'

The nurse laughed and walked away.

'Right, Laura, you'd better mean what you said; I want every detail. You leave nothing out, however distressing. I need your word on that.'

'You've got it.'

'Start at the beginning, and we'll progress from there. Let's get the bastard caught before he hurts her.'

Kesey had already decided that some details weren't for sharing.

Chapter 50

Emily closed her eyes against the glare of the bulb as Charles Turner flicked the switch for the first time that day. 'Good afternoon. I'm sorry to have left you in the dark again. I don't like to make excessive use of the electricity.'

'I'm hungry.'

'It's day four, Emily. You're doing rather well. Not many of my guests last nearly as long. You're to be congratulated.'

'I'd like something to eat, please. I'm wasting away.'

Turner looked down at her and shook his head. 'Have you thought any more about my mother? You made some interesting observations when we last spoke. I'd like to hear more.'

'I've had plenty of time to consider things, but I need something to eat. I need to drink. I can't think clearly without nourishment.'

He hurried back up the cellar steps without comment and returned a minute later with a loaf of sliced bread in one hand and a glass of tap water in the other.

'Take the handcuffs off. Please, Charles, take them off.'

Turner placed the items on the floor, dragged Emily into a sitting position, and knelt in front of her. 'Don't push your luck. That wouldn't be a good idea.'

'I can't eat with my hands behind my back.'

He tore the packaging with his teeth, removed two slices of white bread and forced them into Emily's mouth, as she choked and attempted to turn her head. 'Eat the fucking stuff, bitch. You asked for food, so eat it.'

'Water, I n-need water.'

Turner picked up the glass and hurled the contents in her face. 'Is that enough for you?'

Emily closed her eyes and continued chewing until she could swallow. 'I was going to tell you about your mother.'

He sat back on his haunches, suddenly calmer. 'That's good, Emily. I hope you've come up with something worth hearing.'

'I don't think she left you at all.'

Turner's eyes lit up, more from intrigue than anger. 'What are you trying to say?'

'You were an intelligent child, a handsome child, a credit to any mother. Why would she give you up?'

'That's the question I've been attempting to answer.'

'The social workers lied to you; your foster parents lied to you; everybody lied to you. She didn't leave. She didn't abandon you. Either she died, or something happened to her – something terrible. An accident that left her without memory. A blow to her head that wiped her mind clean. Something along those lines. It's the only credible explanation. Why would any mother leave the perfect child?'

Turner's frown slowly became a beaming smile that looked strangely devoid of emotion. 'You really could be right.'

'I'm sure of it.'

'I'm going to secure your hands in front of you; as a reward you understand. It'll be more comfortable, less painful, but if you try to escape, I'll kill you. Make no mistake on that count.'

'What happened to your thumb?'

'Best not to know.'

'I love you, Charles. I won't try to escape. Why would I try to escape? I want us to be together forever.'

He took a small key from his trouser pocket, unfastened the cuffs, and secured them again with her hands resting on her bare thighs. 'Right, that should be a little more comfortable for you. Now would be a good time to thank me.'

'Thank you.'

'Again.'

'Thank you.'

'Louder.'

'Thank you.'

'You're doing rather well, Emily. I may allow you to live for a day or two longer.'

Emily resisted the impulse to throw herself at Turner and attack him. 'I want to know more about you; you've opened Pandora's box and allowed me to peer in. You once asked me if I find the extremes of human behaviour as fascinating as you do. And I do, Charles, I do. You've broadened my horizons; introduced me to a world I didn't know existed. It's exciting, intoxicating. I want you to tell me how you became a killer. I want to be a part of it. Perhaps we could hunt and kill together.'

'You really want to know?'

Emily nodded frantically. 'Yes, more than anything.'

'I was planning to send the police another parcel later today. What do you think about that?'

She forced a smile. 'I'll do anything, absolutely anything. Just tell me all about yourself. That's all I ask.'

Turner adjusted his position and made himself as comfortable as possible on the cold, hard floor. 'You really want the details?'

'Yes, a thousand times, yes.'

'You can't unhear something once you've heard it. You do understand that, don't you? You may not like what I've got to say. You can't wipe your mind clean.'

'I want to know it all, I need to know it all. Just tell me, Charles. Please tell me. I want to be like you.'

'I knew I was different from a young age. I didn't empathise the way other people seemed to; I felt my own distress intensely, but nothing for anyone else.'

'I think I know what you're talking about. Can you give me an example, so I can fully understand?'

He looked ahead, deep in thought. 'My first foster parents had another foster child in the house, a five-year-old girl, who seemed to have boundless energy and affection. I loathed everything about her.'

'What happened?'

'She had a severe asthma attack – I'd hidden her inhaler. They fought to save her life, but she died gasping for breath. People seemed concerned that watching her had been a traumatic experience for me. They thought I was in shock, hiding my feelings. And in a way, they were right: I'd loved it. The urgency, the desperation, the girl's mournful whelps as she fought for breath. And then, it all came to a dramatic conclusion. The girl lay in a lifeless heap, my foster mother was wailing like a demented banshee, and I was jumping about, desperate to see it all over again.'

Emily looked away for a beat, then made herself look at him, masking her revulsion surprisingly well. 'Your eyes were opened.'

'Just so.'

'What happened after that?'

'They had a funeral for the girl, with a white coffin, flowers and tears. A spark had been ignited. I'd discovered my passion in life, never to be extinguished. I'll always be grateful to her for that. I think her name was Rosie. Yes, that's it, Rosie. They never did find her inhaler. I made sure of that. I've still got it to this day. It's a treasured possession.'

'How old were you at the time?'

Turner chuckled quietly to himself as Emily looked on. 'Seven or eight.'

'Really, as young as that?'

'Oh, yes. I believe I was born to kill.'

Emily dropped her head and dry gagged as Turner closed his eyes and focused on the past.

'I found the entire process utterly intoxicating. She died because of me. I had the power. I decided if she lived or died, and I chose death. Do you find that shocking?'

Emily shook her head. 'No, not at all. You know how to live life to the full. I respect that. Not many people experience life with such a burning intensity. I've never met anyone like you before.'

'I took every conceivable opportunity to kill animals after that – dogs, cats, the school rabbit – but I soon learnt it was never going to be enough. By the time I went to university at eighteen, I was desperate to kill another human. I don't know how I resisted the temptation for as long as I did. The frustrations were horrendous. At times, I felt ready to explode.'

Emily hid her hands between her thighs as they shook more violently. 'Why didn't you do it?'

'If the opportunity had presented itself, I would have. The possibility of incarceration held me back.'

She nodded. 'You resisted your impulses for fear of arrest and punishment.'

'Precisely.'

'That must have taken some doing.'

'I fantasised about murder almost constantly. It was always the same: the victim was young, female, and looked like my mother in the photograph I mentioned. The more like my mother she looked, the more turned on I'd be. And then, I met a girl, a fellow law student, who was willing to experiment. Willing to dress up. Willing to play dead. We searched for suitable clothing in local charity shops, and we role-played. Societal norms impose such life-limiting restrictions on the majority. I thought she wasn't one of those unfortunate people; my soulmate. But I was wrong. In the end, she let me down.'

'Let you down how?'

'We were playing a sex game. I was strangling her, cutting off her oxygen until I came. Her neck was bruised, she'd passed out, and the next morning, the bitch went to the police and made a statement. I'd gone too far, apparently.'

'Were you arrested?'

'Oh, yes, the pigs came to my student digs, lights flashing, sirens blaring, and dragged me to the police station in cuffs. It shook me – I'm not afraid to admit it. I wanted to be a solicitor: the status, the power, the money. It could have been the end of my career before it had even started.'

Emily adopted a puzzled expression. 'Were you found not guilty when it came to court? You must have got off somehow.'

Turner laughed. 'She dropped the case. I was never prosecuted.'

'What happened next? You were a student at the time of your arrest. You're in your thirties now. A lot of time has passed.'

'There were various women over the years, who were willing to indulge my interests and inclinations to varying degrees, but no one who's fully embraced my dark side. My longings were satisfied to an extent. My desire to kill controlled for the most part, but I knew I'd do it again one day. I'd had the room ready for almost three years before I finally used it.'

'Room? What room?'

'Oh, of course, you have't seen it.'

'No.'

'I converted a bedroom at home into a cell of sorts. Somewhere I could take my time and get to know my guests properly before killing them. You would have experienced it for yourself, had things worked out differently.'

'What changed? When did you finally give in to your urges?'

Turner's eyes lit up, and Emily noticed his erection bulging under his tailored slacks. 'I was in Manchester, visiting a client on remand at the local prison. I stayed the night at a hotel near the city's red-light district. I was walking along the street at about two in the morning, in search of a prostitute who took my interest, when I saw her: a vision; a fantasy brought to life. She had the hair, the dress, the shoes – just like in the photo. It was uncanny, as if my mother had been reincarnated before my eyes. I knew I had to kill her from the second I saw her.'

'She was your second victim?'

'We agreed on a price, I took her back to my hotel room, drugged and raped her, and took her home in the boot of my car in the early hours.' He laughed. 'She'd passed out in a Manchester hotel room and woke up in Wales – with her wrists shackled to the wall. I'd never witnessed such terror. She was like a rabbit caught in the headlights. A trembling creature, desperate to live but devoid of hope. I think she knew it was over for her as soon as she opened her eyes. It was intoxicating, mesmerising, and I loved every single second.'

'And then, you killed her?'

'Two days later. I took her to a local beauty spot, loved by my mother, put my hands around her throat, and squeezed until all signs of life had left her face. It was the greatest moment of my life. Nothing else compared. Nothing even came close. And I had to do it again.'

'And you did.'

'The temptation was just too great to resist, whatever the risk, whatever the price. The longing became utterly irresistible. Killing gives me a sense of accomplishment. It satisfies my soul.'

Emily reached out and rubbed his erect penis with her painted toes. 'I've been thinking about it; I'm willing to play dead. I'll do almost anything. You've found your soulmate this time. We were destined to be together. Take the handcuffs off, take me upstairs to bed, and I'll show you how far I'm willing to go.'

Turner looked at her, weighing up his options, and took the key from his pocket for a second time. 'Hold your hands out.'

Emily's breathing quickened as the hope of freedom leapt and danced in her mind. 'I love you, Charles. I'll never let you down.'

He unfastened the cuffs, dropped them to the floor, and slapped her across the face. 'Lie on your back and stay completely still. Don't move an inch. Do it now. I'm losing patience.'

She took a deep breath as her hopes sank. 'Let's go up to bed. We'd be more comfortable upstairs. I could shower. Clean myself up. Apply some makeup. We could take our time and indulge our carnal desires to the maximum.'

Turner slapped her again, harder this time, and shoved her down on her back, snarling, 'Which part of playing dead don't you understand? Corpses don't talk. Open your legs and shut the fuck up. Maybe then you'll survive the experience.'

Chapter 51

The Right Honourable Sir George Fleming MP, a respected stalwart of the Tory Party for some years, met Detective Chief Inspector Roy Donovan's eyes with a dismissive sneer. 'Just get me the commissioner, man. I'm not used to dealing with the likes of you.'

The detective sat back in his chair, looking significantly more relaxed than he felt. 'The commissioner's fully aware of the circumstances of your arrest, sir. I'm going to be conducting the interview. You're just going to have to get used to it.'

'I want to talk to him now, do you hear me? Now!'

Donovan held his gaze right up to the moment it was no longer comfortable. 'It's not happening. I'm under strict orders to treat you as I would any other suspect.'

Sir George sounded incredulous. 'Did the commissioner tell you that himself? I'm assuming the answer's a resounding no; he's a good friend of mine. Has been since our school days.'

The DCI rested his elbows on the table and nodded. 'Yes, he did. He was crystal clear on the subject. No one's coming to your rescue. There'll be no special favours, no secret handshakes. You're not beyond the law. It's time you learnt that. Now would be a good time to start answering my questions. Unlawful sexual intercourse is a serious offence. In the eyes of the law, she's still a child.'

For the first time, Sir George's confidence began to slip away. '*Alleged* offence, it's an *alleged* offence. You can't prove a damned thing.'

'The girl talked to her social worker. She's made a written statement. There's security cameras in the bar. You went in alone, and you left with her fifteen minutes later. Can you explain that for me?'

'We could simply have been leaving at the same time, rather than together. Have you not considered that possibility?'

'There's a camera, in the street, outside the bar. You got in a black cab together. You were holding her arm. There's more than enough evidence to charge you.'

Sir George held out his hands. 'I thought she was sixteen, for Pete's sake. She looks sixteen. She told me she was sixteen. What more do you need to know? If I'd known she was fourteen, I wouldn't have gone anywhere near her.'

'That's no defence in law. She's under the age of consent, you're culpable. It's that simple.'

Sir George was panicking now, considering the potential damage to his reputation and career. 'Haven't you ever made a mistake, Detective? There but for the grace of God. It could happen to anybody.'

'You're in your forties. She's ten days past her fourteenth birthday. You can't see the problem?'

'I'm a high-profile figure: an ex-cabinet minister. If you charge me, it could cause irrevocable damage to our great country's reputation. These are difficult times. It's not in the public's interest. Surely you can see that?'

'I'm a police officer, not a diplomat. You should have thought about that before offending. I've got a job to do.'

Sir George reared up and snarled, 'She's just a little tart off the fucking streets. What the hell does she matter? She's of no consequence.'

'Sit down, Sir George. I don't think her parents are going to see it that way, do you?'

The MP slumped back in his seat, breathing hard and sweating. 'Parents? She's in the care of the local authority, you fucking halfwit. She lives in a children's home. She's street trash, worthless. The parents won't want to know.'

Donovan drummed on the table. 'I thought you said you knew nothing about her – that she's a stranger to you. It seems you know a lot more than you first let on. Perhaps now would be a good time for some honesty.'

Sir George loosened his silk tie and pushed a white, gold embossed business card across the table. 'I want to consult my lawyer before I say another word. I'm saying nothing more until she's here.'

Sir George was represented by his very capable and experienced solicitor when DCI Donovan restarted the interview about ninety minutes later. She knew more than enough to appreciate the magnitude of the situation.

The detective switched on the recording equipment and settled in his seat. 'I need to remind you that you're still subject to caution, Sir George. Anything you say could be used in evidence.'

The solicitor shuffled some papers as her client looked on in silence. 'I have a pre-prepared statement to make on behalf of my client.'

DCI Donovan moved to the edge of his seat. 'I'm listening.'

'Are you aware of the serial killer case in Wales? There are five dead women and a sixth who's in very grave danger.'

Donovan looked at her and shrugged. 'Yeah, I've seen it on the news. But what the hell's that got to do with this?'

'The Welsh police are looking for a Mr Charles Turner.'

'What's your point?'

'Sir George and Mr Turner originate from the same part of Wales. They know each other personally. They were friends until Turner rather lost his way.'

'What's that got to do with me? I still can't see the relevance.'

'My client has been in recent contact with Mr Turner – he sent a package, and Sir George knows where it was posted. The police are looking in the wrong places. A young woman's life is at risk. In the right circumstances, we may be able to help.'

'Right circumstances? What are you saying exactly?'

The solicitor paused. 'We're looking for a deal. Drop the case against Sir George, and he'll tell you everything you need to know. No deal, no information. Make your choice.'

Donovan switched off the tape. 'I'll have to consult my superintendent. It's not a decision I can make.'

The solicitor smiled. 'We require immunity from prosecution and a guarantee of confidentially. And we want both, in writing, with the commissioner's signature at the bottom of the page. It needs to be a cast-iron guarantee; no ambiguities. Nothing less is acceptable.'

Donovan looked back as he reached the door. 'I'll see what I can do.'

Chapter 52

DI Kesey entered the incident room with a swagger intended to exuded a confidence she didn't feel. She looked around the room, pleased that all assigned officers were ready and waiting. There was an air of excitement, of anticipation. Something significant was about to happen, and these were the days that made police work worthwhile.

The loud chatter stopped abruptly when she stood at the front of the room and raised a hand above her head. 'Good morning, everybody. Thanks for being on time. I know it's early. It's going to be a busy day.'

Kesey waited for a response that didn't materialise. 'As you all know, the search for Charles Turner, and his abductee, Emily Gravel, has been focused outside the force area. That situation's about to change. The Met has provided us with intelligence that strongly suggests they are both somewhere on the Ceredigion coast. Contrary to evidence given by Turner's secretary, it looks as if they never left Wales. Turner may or may not be driving a white van. Keep it in mind.'

A long-serving constable sitting at the back of the room held his hand in the air like a child in a classroom. 'How reliable is the information, ma'am? How the hell would the Met know what's happening in our part of the country?'

'The source of the intelligence has to remain confidential, for operational reasons pertinent to the Met, but I'm assured it's accurate. Turner was in the Aberystwyth area after leaving Caerystwyth. Let's hope he's still there for us to find.'

'Thanks, ma'am, seems reasonable.'

'Local Aberystwyth police have already begun door-to-door enquiries – starting in the town initially, and then moving on to the outlying areas and villages along the coast. We'll be joining them in the search, together with all available officers from other divisions, who will meet at Aberystwyth police station at eight a.m. precisely. You'll then proceed from there under the direct supervision of nominated sergeants, who will notify you of your allocated geographical area. We're talking about a lot of properties, residential and otherwise. We need to be organised, we need to be thorough, and we need to be quick. If Emily Gravel's still alive, and we're going to assume she is until proved otherwise, we need to find her. We're going to look today, and tomorrow, and every day after that, until we achieve our objective. We owe it to Emily, and we owe it to Grav. He's one of our own. Don't forget that … Are there any final questions?'

All was silent.

'Right, the clock's ticking. I'll be available at Aberystwyth Police Station throughout the day. Keep me fully informed of any developments. Follow your supervisor's orders closely, and we should have a successful outcome. On your feet, let's make a move, transport's waiting.'

Chapter 53

Charles Turner pulled up his pants and trousers and smiled. 'Not bad at all, Emily. I barely heard you breathing that time. And you've learnt not to move. Eight out of ten. Perhaps if you'd lost consciousness, it would be a nine.'

Emily raised herself upright and opened her mouth wide, greedily sucking in the pungent air. 'There's going to be a next time?'

'Possibly. I'll give it some thought.'

'Oh, come on, why only possibly? I told you I'm up for almost anything, and I meant it. Why kill me when we can have so much fun together? There's a million girls out there to hunt down and imprison. We could do it together. I could source the clothes and the shoes and help you dye their hair. We were destined to meet. I truly think we're meant to be together. Why bring all that potential to a premature end when you don't have to?'

'I may consider it. On the other hand, I may not.'

'I helped you work out what happened with your mother, didn't I? There's so much more we could explore together, me and you against the world.'

He clutched her hair and forced her head back. 'You sound a little hoarse. I hope the pressure on your throat wasn't too onerous? I thought you'd stopped breathing at one point. I've never been harder.'

'I'm absolutely fine. Why not let me come upstairs? I badly need a shower. I could freshen up, make myself more presentable, and cook you something nice for breakfast. We could eat it together with a cup of coffee. What do you think? You could play me some opera. I'd love to learn more about it. You once said you'd take me to Verona.'

Turner looked at her and shook his head. 'Oh, I don't think so. I'm not ready to trust you just yet. You'll live another day or two. That's a triumph of sorts. I'd be grateful for that, if I were you.'

Emily settled herself on the cold concrete floor, hiding her hands underneath her, and carefully placed her lower leg on top of the handcuffs. 'What was that?'

'What are you talking about?'

'I thought I heard something upstairs. I think someone's there.'

Turner tensed. 'Are you sure?'

'Yes, I could swear I heard something.'

Emily felt a combination of anxiety and hope as he hurried towards the stairs and flicked the light off before ascending. This was her chance, maybe her only chance. If she wanted to see the light of day again, she had to take it.

Chapter 54

Emily lifted herself to her feet in the darkness, placed the palms of her hands against the wall, and moved slowly to her right in a cautious sideways motion until she discovered the light switch. She opened her eyes slowly, taking in the room, as they adjusted to the electric glare. There were no windows, no coal hatches, and only one door at the top of the stairs, but there may be a weapon. She had to find a weapon.

Emily searched every inch of the cellar, taking her time looking in every nook and cranny, but there was nothing, absolutely nothing. When she'd almost given up and was walking towards the stairs, trying to build up the courage to ascend, she saw something glinting on the floor, half hidden by an oil stained tarpaulin.

She rushed across the floor and picked up a rusty replacement blade for a utility knife; discarded or misplaced at some point in the past. She held it in her right hand and ran the still sharp edge over the thumb of her left, causing dark blood to seep from the resulting wound. She clutched it tightly, not letting go, never letting go, and said a silent prayer of thanks to a God whose existence she sometimes doubted.

Emily stood at the bottom of the stairs for five minutes or more before placing her bare foot on the first step, which creaked alarmingly under her weight. She withdrew it quickly and stilled herself, listening for any sign of movement from the ground floor, but all was quiet. She tried again, avoiding the first step this time, and slowly climbed to the top, stepping tentatively, until she reached the door with the comparative relief of a climber conquering the summit of the Eiger.

She took a deep breath in through her nose and out through her mouth, before placing a trembling hand on the door knob. She turned it to the right and pushed the door open, slowly, until the gap was sufficient to place her head through and peer into the farmhouse kitchen.

Emily froze, every cell in her body on full alert and screaming, run, girl, run, but there was nowhere to go. She stood on the top step, staring at her captor with blinking eyes that were filling with tears. There he was, perched on a chair in the centre of the floor, directly opposite the door, with his arms folded in front of him and a cold sneer on his face. 'Well, hello, Emily. I was wondering how long it would take you. It seems I can't trust you after all.'

Emily considered retreating into her cellar home, but instead, she stood her ground. She pushed the door a few more inches and leant forward so her upper body was in the room. 'I wasn't trying to escape. I just wanted a shower. Look at the state I'm in. I just wanted to see you, that's all.'

Turner kicked his chair aside. 'Do you really think I'm that stupid? I told you not to underestimate me, but it seems you've done exactly that. That, my lovely, may well prove to be a fatal mistake.'

Emily took a slow step back as he walked towards her, but then, she moved quickly with agility and grace, taking one stride, and a second, before launching herself in an upward trajectory, smashing into him in mid-air, the blade flailing in every direction but not finding its target.

Turner fell backwards and crashed to the tiled floor. He looked up, dazed and shaken, as Emily sat astride him and repeatedly slashed at his face with the razor-sharp blade. By the time he reacted, his face was a bloody mess, totally unrecognisable as the man she knew. He bucked one way, then the other, attempting to shake her off, but she clung on like a limpet. She slashed again and again, and kept striking, blow after blow, until he used all his remaining strength to knee her hard in the back, causing her to fall off with the blade still clutched in her bloody hand.

Turner moved swiftly this time, faster than his quarry, and kicked her in the face as she raised herself on all fours, attempting to continue the fight. Emily tumbled sideways, hitting her head on a table leg, and she lay there with him looming over her, his blood pouring from his open wounds on to her naked body. He stood there, looking at her semi-conscious form; shocked – as much by the fact she'd dared to do such a thing, as from the searing pain. He lifted his right leg and stamped on her hand, breaking her fingers, before kicking the blade across the floor and well out of reach.

Turner pressed a tea towel to his face with one hand and clutched Emily's hair with the other, dragging her towards the cellar steps with lurching movements that tore sections of skin from her scalp as he adjusted his grip. He stopped when he reached the door, panting hard, and rested for a moment to regain his strength. He dragged Emily upright by her throat, and sent her crashing down towards the cellar floor, where she lay moaning quietly to herself, temporarily oblivious to her reality.

When she finally came around, an hour or so later, she was back in the dark, cold, alone, bruised and battered, waiting for the end. It was the lowest point of her life.

Chapter 55

PC Kieran Harris parked his West Wales Police patrol car on an area of rough ground, about twenty yards from the stone cottage. He turned off the engine just as bright rays of winter sunshine were breaking through the clouds. His first child, of six months, had slept fitfully during the night, waking often, and he was feeling somewhat jaded as he pulled on his cap and walked towards the front door, his shoulders hunched against the cold.

PC Harris knocked, and kept knocking, without response. He peered through the letter box but all he saw was a small hallway and a closed internal door. He was about to head back to the car, on the assumption that the place was deserted, or locked up for the winter, when he noticed tyre tracks leading to the back of the building.

The young constable hurried round the side of the cottage and stopped at first sight of the vehicle. He walked around it and tried the driver's door, then the passenger door, and finally the rear doors, all of which were locked. He peered through the windows but there was nothing of significance to see. PC Harris, yawned, made a note of the number plate, and took out his radio. 'PC 143 to control. Come in, please.'

The response was almost instantaneous. 'Go ahead, Kieran.'

He provided the index number and requested a Police National Computer check.

'Control to PC 143. The vehicle is a white Transit registered to West Wales Plumbing in Ammanford. It is not stolen, and the keeper is not wanted. Repeat, not stolen and no outstanding warrants.'

'Thanks, Control, over and out.' He returned his radio to his tunic pocket, noting the large WWP logo emblazoned on both sides of the van, and relaxed.

PC Harris approached the cottage and knocked on the back door, moving to look through a grubby ground floor window when he didn't receive a response. He couldn't quite believe his eyes when he pressed his nose against the glass. There was a man standing behind a half-open internal door at the far side of the room. A man he didn't recognise. A man whose face looked like a grotesque parody of a Halloween mask, with its patchwork effect of blood and red-raw flesh that was almost beyond comprehension.

PC Harris rapped the glass with his baton, and struggled to hide his revulsion when Turner crossed the room and opened the window with a scowl. 'What the hell do you want?'

The young officer took a step back but didn't look away. 'Sorry to bother you, sir. My name's PC Harris, local police. We're looking for a man in his thirties, with short blond hair, who goes by the name of Charles Turner. He may or may not be accompanied by a young woman. Have you seen anyone meeting that description?'

Turner weighed up his options. 'No, I haven't seen anyone like that. We're a bit off the beaten track here. I haven't seen anyone at all.'

'What does the logo on the van stand for?'

'West Wales Plumbing; we're an Ammanford firm. Why do you ask?'

'You're a fair way off your patch.'

Turner gripped the windowsill with both hands. 'It's my mother's place. I'm doing a bit of work for her – putting in a new bathroom. There's no law against it, is there?'

'Is she in?'

'Who?'

'Your mother.'

'No, it's a holiday place. She only comes in the summer. There's just me.'

'Do you mind if I come in? I'd like to take a quick look inside, if that's all right with you?'

Turner took a deep breath and exhaled slowly. 'Yeah, no problem. Go around to the front. I've lost the key to the back.'

When the solicitor opened the front door, less than a minute later, he was clutching a ten-inch carving knife behind his back. PC Harris stood in front of him, recoiling at his second sight of Turner's face, unable to compute the severity of his injuries. 'Look, I've got to ask. What the hell happened to you?'

Turner tightened his grip on the knife's shaft. 'I was attacked by some madman with a beer glass after a few drinks in Llanelli. I'm lucky to be alive.'

'What, he did all that with a glass?'

'Yeah, he hit me once, and then again when I tried to fight back.'

'Have you reported the assault to the police?'

Turner shook his head and winced as his injuries screamed for attention. 'I haven't had the chance. It only happened last night.'

'What, it happened last night, and now, you're here, fitting a bathroom?'

'That's what I said.'

'Those are serious injuries. We're talking grievous bodily harm, possibly wounding with intent. I'm surprised the hospital didn't contact us. It's usual in this sort of case.'

Turner moved the knife in front of him as he turned and walked across the kitchen, into the lounge, and spoke without looking back. 'I didn't go to a hospital.'

'Who attended to your wounds?'

The solicitor turned and faced the officer, the knife still carefully hidden. 'I did it myself with a needle and fishing gut. Aren't I the clever one.'

There was something about the man's eyes that was familiar, but Kieran Harris couldn't work out what. By the time Emily had dragged her bruised and battered body up the wooden steps, and yelled out for help at the cellar door, it was already too late.

Turner raised the knife high above his head and brought it down with all the force he could summon, plunging the tip of the blade deep into the officer's upper chest and puncturing a lung.

PC Harris was already dying when he moved away, swinging his baton with his last breath, striking Turner a severe blow to his right temple. Both men fell to the floor as if in unison and lay there, unable to move.

Emily listened for any sound of motion, any sign of life, and opened the cellar door with her one good hand, half expecting to see Turner sitting there waiting to pounce. She took one step, then another, creeping into the kitchen and towards freedom. But as she glanced through the open door to the lounge, she saw the young constable, collapsed on the carpet, with blood bubbling from his chest wound and soaking into his uniform. She couldn't remember his name at first, but she recognised his face. Then, it came to her, Kieran, Kieran Harris, as she walked slowly towards him.

Emily crept around her dazed tormentor, every nerve jangling, and she knelt at the officer's side, holding two fingers to his neck to feel for a non-existent heart-beat. Turner moved, not much, and not to any great effect, but she could see his chest rising and falling as he breathed shallowly in his unconscious state.

Emily wanted to run. She was desperate to run. But instead, she took a blue satin cushion from the nearby settee and held it to Turner's face, pressing down with all her weight and strength, cutting off his oxygen until she was sure he posed no further threat.

She struggled to her knees, threw the cushion aside, and looked into Turner's eyes at touching distance. He was staring at her, as he had so many times in life, focused intently on her familiar features, but seeing nothing at all. She lifted her hand to his face and closed his eyes; she had never felt so exhausted. It really was over. The monster had lost his power, and the world was a better place.

Emily struggled to her feet and reached to take Kieran Harris' two-way radio from his pocket. She held it to her mouth and pressed down on the yellow transmission button. 'Hello, hello, is there anybody there?'

'This is control, who's that?'

She smiled thinly, her mind flooded with mixed emotions. 'My name's Emily Gravel; I'm using Kieran's radio, PC 143. Turner killed him.'

'Where's Turner now?'

'He's here, but he's not breathing.'

'He's dead?'

'Yes.'

'Definitely?'

'Yes.'

'Hold on, Emily, the inspector wants to speak to you.'

Emily fetched a single quilt from a first-floor bedroom with a view of the sea, and wrapped it around herself to cover her nakedness. She returned to the lounge and stared at the two bodies just a few feet away from her, half expecting Turner to rise up and drag her back to that awful place she knew would haunt her forever.

'Hello, Emily, are you there? It's Laura. Are you okay?'

'I think so.'

'Oh, thank God, I thought I'd lost you for a minute.'

'No, I'm still here.'

'You said Kieran's dead?'

'Yes, Turner stabbed him. He lost a lot of blood. He's gone.'

'And he's definitely dead, you're certain?'

Emily looked across at him. 'Oh, yes, he's dead all right. Turner's final victim.'

'Where are you?'

'I'm in an old cottage somewhere. It's, um, Turner said it's on the Ceredigion coast. I think that's what he said. Somewhere near Aberystwyth maybe.'

'What can you see when you look out?'

Emily approached the lounge window, with the warm quilt wrapped around her shoulders, and peered out as the rain began to fall. 'There's fields on one side and the sea on the other.'

'Okay, I've got a list of Kieran's allocated addresses. It sounds like one of two.'

'I think my hand's broken. And my head, it's covered in blood. He kept me in the dark. Everything's hurting, and I haven't eaten. I, err, I don't know, I don't know what to do. Please tell me what to do.'

'Help's on the way. We'll be with you as soon as we can. Just hold on.'

'It's over, isn't it?'

'Just hold on, Emily. I'm coming myself. I'll be with you before you know it.'

'Where's my dad? Is he okay?'

'He's still in hospital, but he's doing fine. I'll ring and give him the good news. He'll be doing cartwheels.'

'He is going to get better, isn't he? Please tell me he's going to get better.'

'Yes, he is. He'll be home soon.'

'And you're going to ring him? You're going to tell him I'm alive?'

'Of course, straight away.'

Emily dropped the radio to the floor without another word. She sat on the sofa and began rocking rhythmically in her seat, while humming an operatic aria quietly to herself, as she waited for the emergency services to arrive.

Chapter 56

Grav was sitting at his daughter's bedside when she woke the next morning in a private room at Aberystwyth's Bronglais Hospital. She thought she was dreaming when she first opened her eyes and looked at him, but when he gently squeezed her hand, she knew she was free.

'It's good to have you back, love. You had me seriously worried for a while.'

Emily reached out and hugged him tightly. 'Aren't you supposed to be in hospital?'

'I discharged myself.'

She released her grip and frowned. 'Oh, Dad, what were you thinking?'

'Seeing you safe and well is better medicine than anything the doctors could give me. I'm absolutely fine.'

'Poor Kieran.'

'Yeah, terrible. I'm going to call on his missus when I get back to Caerystwyth. They only recently had their first child.'

'Rather you than me.'

'I can't say I'm looking forward to it.'

'Charles is dead.'

Grav nodded. 'Now that's one thing I'm not unhappy about. Did he…? Did he…? You know what I'm asking.'

'No, he didn't.'

He blew the air from his mouth. 'Oh, thank God.'

'Did the police find the cushion?'

'Cushion? Laura didn't mention anything. Why do you ask?'

'I held it over his face.'

'Turner's?'

'Yes.'

Grav's expression hardened. 'Are you telling me you killed him?'

'I think so…maybe… I think he was still breathing. I had to know he couldn't hurt me again.'

Grav placed a hand on Emily's shoulder and looked into her eyes as he had so many times before. 'Now listen to what I'm saying, Emily, and listen carefully. Fuck Turner. The bastard's ruined enough lives. He's not going to ruin another one.'

'Tell me what to do.'

'Laura's going to take a statement from you as soon as you feel up to it. As a witness, you understand, not a suspect. You won't be subject to caution.'

'What do I tell her?'

'You tell her everything, right up to when you saw Kieran fighting for his life. He smothered Turner, in a desperate attempt to survive, before collapsing himself. You may have thrown the cushion aside at some point, but you can't remember when or why. You weren't thinking straight. And that's it. You say no more. Sometimes our memories are our enemies, rather than our friends. Some things are best forgotten. We're going to put this behind us and get on with our lives.'

'Really, just like that?'

Grav rose to his feet. 'Right, time for a cup of tea. I may even have a fry up. Bacon, eggs, sausages, hash browns, beans, the lot. Do you fancy one? You could do with putting on a few pounds.'

'What was it your GP said? Can you remind me?'

'Porridge or muesli, but what the hell does she know?'

Emily threw back the bedclothes, lifted herself upright, and sat on the edge of the bed with tears running down her face. 'Hang on, I'm coming to the canteen with you. You're going to keep me safe, and I'm going to keep you alive. That's the deal. Your diet starts today.'

Acknowledgements

A big thank you to everyone who's supported my books.

Printed in Great Britain
by Amazon